MIRROR MIRROR

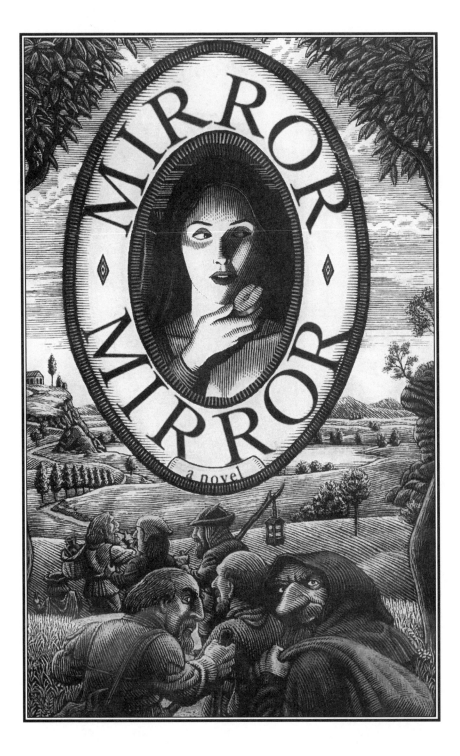

MIRROR MIRROR

Gregory Maguire

ReganBooks
An Imprint of HarperCollins*Publishers*

HarperCollins books may be purchased for educational, business, or sales promotional
use. For information please write: Special Markets Department, HarperCollins Publishers
Inc., 10 East 53rd Street, New York, NY 10222.

FIRST EDITION

Designed by Judith Stagnitto Abbare / Abbare Design

Printed on acid-free paper

Library of Congress Cataloging-in-Publication Data

ISBN 0-06-039384-X

03 04 05 06 07 XX/QW10 9 8 7 6 5 4 3 2 1

For
Jane Langton,
Jill Paton Walsh,
and
John Rowe Townsend

Se non è vero è ben trovato.

Even if it's not true, it's a good invention.

I am a girl who did no wrong

I am a woman who slept with my father the pope

I am a rock whose hands have appetites

I am a hunter who cannot kill

I am a mercenary with the French disease

I am a girl who lived among stones

I am a woman who poisoned my enemies

I am a rock and my brothers are rocks

I am a cleric who trafficked in curses

I am a gooseboy or am I a goose

I am a girl who did little wrong

I am a gooseboy or am I a boy

I am a farmer who stole something sacred

I am a monster who let the child go

I am a dog with an unlikely past

I am a hunter who followed the coffin

I am a girl who did something wrong

I am the other side of snow

I am a mirror a mirror am I

Mirror mirror on the wall
Who is the fairest one of all

Do PEOPLE say that I am both your father and your lover? Let the world, that heap of vermin as ridiculous as they are feeble-minded, believe the most absurd tales about the mighty! You must know that for those destined to dominate others, the ordinary rules of life are turned upside down and duty acquires an entirely new meaning. Good and evil are carried off to a higher, different plane . . .

Remember this. Walk straight ahead. Do only what you like, as long as it is of some use to you. Leave hesitation and scruples to small minds, to plebeians and subordinates. One consideration alone is worthy of you—the elevation of the House of Borgia, the elevation of yourself.

—Alexander VI's speech to Lucrezia Borgia, from Arthur de Gobineau's *Scènes historiques de la Renaissance* (1877), as quoted in *The Borgias* by Ivan Cloulas (1989)

ONE DAY some Lombard masons working near the cloister of Sta. Maria Nuova just off the Via Appia had opened a sarcophagus and found the body of a young Roman woman of about fifteen, so well preserved that it seemed alive. A crowd had gathered around and admired the girl's rosy skin, her half-open lips revealing very white teeth, her ears, her black lashes, dark, wide-open eyes, and beautiful hair, done in a knot . . .

– *The Borgias*

Contents

❧———— 1519 ————☙

MIRROR
MIRROR

·1502·

The Roofs of Montefiore

From the arable river lands to the south, the approach to Montefiore appears a sequence of relaxed hills. In the late spring, when the puckers of red poppy blossom are scattered against the green of the season, it can look like so much washing, like mounds of Persian silk and Florentine brocade lightly tossed in heaps. Each successive rise takes on a new color, indefinably more fervent, an aspect of distance and time stained by the shadows of clouds, or bleached when the sun takes a certain position.

But the traveler on foot or in a hobble-wheeled peasant cart, or even on horseback, learns the truth of the terrain. The ascent is steeper than it looks from below. And the rutted track traverses in long switchbacks to accommodate for the severity of the grade and the crosscutting ravines. So the trip takes many more hours than the view suggests. The red-tiled roofs of Montefiore come into sight, promisingly, and then they disappear again as hills loom up and forests close in.

Often I have traveled the road to Montefiore in memory. Today I travel it in true time, true dust, true air. When the track lends me height enough, I can glimpse the villa's red roofs above the ranks of poplars, across the intervening valleys. But I can't tell if the house is peopled with my friends and my family, or with rogues who have murdered the servants in their beds. I can't tell if the walls below the roofline are scorched with smoke, or if the doors are marked with an ashy cross to suggest that plague has come to gnaw the living into their mortal rest, their last gritty blanket shoveled over their heads.

But I have come out of one death, the one whose walls were glass; I have awakened into a second life dearer for being both un-promised and undeserved. Anyone who walks from her own grave re-lies on the unexpected. Anyone who walks from her own grave knows that death is more patient than Gesù Cristo. Death can afford to wait.

But now the track turns again, and my view momentarily spins back along the slopes I've climbed so far. My eye traces the foothills already gained, considers the alphabet of light that spells its unreadable words on the surface of the river. My eye also moves along the past, to my early misapprehensions committed to memory on this isolated outcropping.

The eye is always caught by light, but shadows have more to say.

Rest. Breathe in, breathe out. No one can harm you further than death could do. When rested, you must go on; you must find out the truth about Montefiore. Granted a second life, you must find in it more meaning than you could ever determine in your first.

The Name of the World

THE WORLD was called Montefiore, as far as she knew, and from her aerie on every side all the world descended.

Like any child, she looked out and across rather than in. She was more familiar with the vistas, the promising valleys with their hidden hamlets, the scope of the future arranged in terms of hills and light.

Once a small dragon had become trapped in the bird-snaring nets slung in the *uccellare*. Bianca watched as the cook's adolescent grandson tried to cut it down and release it. Her eyes were fixed on the creature, the stray impossibility of it, not on the spinney in which it was caught. How it twitched, its webbed claws a pearly chalcedony, its eyes frantic and unblinking. (Despite the boy's efforts, it died, and his grandmother flayed it for skin with which to patch the kitchen bellows.)

Bianca regarded visitors to Montefiore with fierce attention:

emissaries of the world. But the bones of her home—the house it-self—remained as familiar and unregarded as her own fingernails.

Montefiore was larger than a farmer's villa but not so imposing as a castle. Too far from anywhere important to serve as a *casale*—a country house—it crowned an upthrust shoulder of land, so its fortifications were natural. On all sides, the steepness of the slope was a deterrent to invaders, and anyway, Montefiore wasn't large enough to interest the *condottieri* who led their small armies along the riverbank on one campaign or another.

Had Bianca an adult eye, she might have guessed from its mismatched roofs and inconsistent architectural details that many owners had lived here before her family arrived, shaping the space with a disregard for symmetry or loveliness. When its masters had had money, they'd made attempts to drill a little grandeur into the old stone hull, like crisp starched lace tied under the wet chins of a drooling *nonna*. A recently completed interior courtyard, handsomely done with columns and vaults in the revived archaic style, provided relief from the roaring breeze.

Except for the courtyard, though, most attempts at improvement had been abandoned in mideffort. Some windows were fitted with glass, but in most windows squares of linen had been nailed to the shutter moldings, pale light conferring a sense of height and volume to the dark rooms. Along one retaining wall, a loggia ran unevenly, its walls inset with terrazzo putti whose faces had become bubonic with the remains of insect cocoons. For half a century the chapel had stood with a roof beam and naked struts, the old cladding and tiles having been swept away in an arrogant gale. When the January *tramontana* blustered in, the geese sometimes sheltered there from the wind, though they seldom took communion.

Fortunately too inaccessible to garrison an army, Montefiore was nonetheless valuable as a lookout. From time to time in its history it had been commandeered for its prospects. On a clear day one imagined one could glimpse the sea.

What child does not feel itself perched at the center of creation?

Before catechisms can instill a proper humility, small children know the truth that their own existence has caused the world to bloom into being. The particular geography of home always charms, but the geography of Montefiore was unarguably pastoral. The arrangement of Tuscan and Umbrian vistas, draped from the very threshold of home through diminishing folds to the horizons, taught soft blues and browns to Bianca de Nevada. That was what they were there for: this brown, that blue: this here, that there.

These moments, more or less, had their flashing existence, circa 1500 anno Domini, though the name of a year means little to one who doesn't yet know the name of corruption.

Lago Verde

THERE WERE the grapes to harvest, the sweeter first olives and the richer late ones, and the second cutting of hay to manage before an early frost sapped it of life. But the weather, this year, was benign, and the agricultural operations around Montefiore were conducted without delay, each in its time. Therefore, the cook's augury of chicken livers predicting success, Vicente de Nevada organized a corpus of laborers to continue work on ditch digging at the far end of the green lake.

Still considered an unacceptable landlord—for the Spanish slant to his otherwise serviceable Italian—de Nevada was tolerated but not admired. Well, he was new in the district still, only these few years, having arrived from the suspicious unknown with a motherless child and a writ of occupancy sealed in a plum-colored wax. He was a quiet man and a gentle one, and his passions, as far as the locals observed, didn't show in a manly, obvious way upon his face; so he wasn't admired. Who could take the time to study a man whose face was the same in winter or summer, in prayer or labor, on feastday or, presumably, at an auto-da-fé in his homeland, Spain? No, Vicente wasn't admired, but he was tolerated: he saw to it that the sick were tended, the dead blessed by the priest attached to Montefiore, and the wheat shared out, and the apples in their time, and the joiner paid for his labors when a coffin had to be built.

Vicente de Nevada loved his small holding, and since the weather was cooperating and the work crew needed encouragement, he pulled off his shirt and got hip deep in the swampy water at the lake's draining edge. He helped to unsettle boulders that had rolled into the mud back in the time of Potiphar.

"Go on, assist the good man, you lazy cleric," said Primavera Vecchia, the cook.

"It wouldn't be seemly," said Fra Ludovico calmly. "If you think he needs help, do it yourself."

"I'm watching the child."

"Leave her in my watch."

"What a mistake that would be. She'd wander up to her nose in the green water and drown before your eyes, while you tiptoed around squealing for an angel to come to her aide. I'd no more leave her in your care than I would my own soul."

"Hmmmph," said Fra Ludovico. "I've never been persuaded you had much of a soul. More like a little damp anchovy stuck between your breasts, trying to breathe. That's what you smell like, anyway."

The small girl balanced on the margin of the moment, toes in the water and heels in the mud. She was thinking that from the house, the small lake did look green, because regular flooding made the poplars stand knee-deep in water. But from here, on site, with the sun sliding westward, the water looked silvered, and there were flicking scales of skyblue and white as well as poplar green and an uncertain black.

The reflections speckled her pale skin. She stopped to ruck her tunic a few inches higher. It was tied in a knot in back, with a vague hope of keeping it dry, but its hem was dripping.

Bianca was interested in everyone's splashing. She had listened carefully about the plan to irrigate a field farther along the slope by draining this wetland above. Her father grunted, holding the small of his back, sweating between the shoulderblades. In formal and courteous words he encouraged the workers. They grunted in mockery, equal parts affection and brave disrespect.

He was the world to her, more than the house was, even.

He felt her looking, and with his unvarying expression he turned and waved. It was that, and that alone, that kept the workers at their task. They would have preferred him on the bank, supervising, upbraiding them. But a man who would pause to wave at his daughter, even if his face didn't change—well, that was a gesture they could read. All together now, and *lift. Lift.*

What did they know of how he cuddled her and protected her, of how he sat by her cot at night so she could sleep, of how quickly he started when a bad dream woke her? What did they know of the disagreements he had had with Primavera, who wanted to take the child to her pallet in the kitchen? They knew nothing of any of this.

She wanted to walk across the water to him, to run on its mosaic of reflections, for even across this glassy space she missed him. She cried out, selfish thing—don't disturb the man while he tries to shrink a lake—but her voice came out as a laugh across the water, no more precise than the call of a bird. He waved again.

"Come here, *bambina*, your behind is mucky," said Primavera, pulling herself off the rotting log on which she had sat.

"You've left a dent in this log," observed Fra Ludovico kindly.

Bianca skipped on along the lake edge, making the old cook cross, and, with pins in her shins, she hobbled after.

"*Papà, Papà,*" babbled Bianca.

"Don't come down this way," said her father. "We don't know which is the keystone boulder. When we've shifted the right one, the rest will give way, and the force of the water might be strong. Primavera, aren't you minding her?"

"I am, but she must mind me first," said the cook.

Fra Ludovico snapped out of the attitude of prayer he'd been affecting and strode forward. He passed the cook, kicking up a spray of dirt with his sandal, smirked, and swooped Bianca up out of harm's way.

"Leave her be, I'm capable," snorted Primavera.

"And lift," said Vicente, *"and lift,"* and the crucial boulder behaved. There was a suck of stone from mud, a small cataract. The men fell back, laughing, to see a waterworks succeed, at least for the moment. The pull wasn't strong enough to endanger anyone, but Primavera, heading for Bianca, trod on an apron of sand as it shifted, and she sat down suddenly, up to her apron strings in water. The laborers jeered and with her deft tongue she cursed them imaginatively. Fra Ludovico all but pranced past, holding Bianca like a boon.

The priest set her down and she ran to her father, across a shallow puddle left by the lake as it receded. She skidded and fell forward onto her hands and knees, as wet as Primavera, and laughing.

Vicente de Nevada swept forward and slipped his hands under his daughter's armpits. "You're a mucky mess, and will sleep in the barn with the pigs," he said. "What's this, though?"

He handed Bianca back to the priest and said, "Now stay out of the water, Bianca, it's unhealthy."

Then he felt the puddle with his palms, and then his fingertips. He pried a slightly bowled edge of puddle up into the air. Or that's what it looked like.

Water ran off it.

"You've unearthed a shard of the pagan past," said Fra Ludovico. "A Roman shield?"

"I've unlaked it, not unearthed it," said Vicente.

"The lid of a large cauldron," said Primavera, huffing.

The workers drew near, but in a huddle. They wanted to see and they didn't want to see.

"It's a mirror," said de Nevada wonderingly.

He took it back to Montefiore and had it cleaned, and a beautiful frame carved for it.

But what was it doing in *Lago Verde*? That was the question on everyone's mind, then, and for many years after.

"I'd guess that someone smuggled it out of Florence, to rescue it from the bonfires of Savonarola," said Fra Ludovico. "Maybe then he suffered fiery hemorrhoids, thought better of his vanity, and pitched it in the lake as he passed. We ought to have left it there."

"Have I admitted aloud to you something I have long suspected?" said Primavera. "You're a *fool*. No one passes this lake but to approach or leave Montefiore, and I've lived here since before mirrors were invented. I'd have known if this thing had a human owner. No, it's a creation of the water nymphs. I don't like it one bit. We ought to put it back."

"I'm not a fool," said the priest, "but though it pains me to say it, for once I agree with you. We ought to toss it back in the deep."

"It's just a mirror," said Don Vicente de Nevada to his little girl, holding her in his arms high enough so she could see herself, and she could see him too, loving her. "Can you see yourself? What do you see?"

"I see Bianca," she said, "and I see *Papà*."

He smiled.

"Where is Mamma?" she said, and craned her head this way and that, as if to peer beyond the mirror's ornate frame, around the frame's edges, into the watery recesses just out of view.

Vicente de Nevada neither scowled nor winced. Evenly he answered her, as he always had. "You can't see your mother; she is dead. This isn't a window to heaven. This is just a mirror."

He didn't look for his wife there, nor was he the type of man to look at himself. Happiness now sometimes meant turning away from what one remembered of earlier, better happiness. When he did look, he saw the view reflected from the mirror, the view out the *salone*'s windows, of Toscana and Umbria in fallow beauty, seductively ready for the next invading army.

But Bianca always thought of it as a curved sheaf of lake, pleasingly cut from water and hung on the wall.

What they told her, what she saw

PRIMAVERA VECCHIA had once had sex with a squid. On washdays in high summer you could still see the marks like a row of puckered bumps that the squid's passionate hold had left on her skin. They began beneath her right breast, circled around her ample hip, and closed in on her cloistered area.

"What were you doing with a squid?" asked Bianca.

"Everything a squid could manage to do," said the cook. "Once you lose your husband to the wars, let me tell you, you become a fish-wife in more ways than one."

"What wars?"

"One or the other of them, I forget. I'm too old to remember what my feet look like, how can I remember my husband? Eat up your supper."

Primavera was older than Gesù, or so she said. She knew how the world worked. She said: You, my child, were conceived in a snowy dale. The forests had lost their leaves, and the trunks of the trees has gone black with the wet of snow. I know this because of how white-and-black you are, that skin, that hair. Eat up that bread, haven't I told you already, before the mice get it.

"What does *conceived* mean?"

Fra Ludovico wandered into the kitchen just then, sniffing for a shingle of ham. Primavera said, "It means thought up."

"Are you corrupting the child?" asked the priest.

"I'm telling her of her origins."

Fra Ludovico sat down at the table as if a symposium on the subject had been called. He said: In the year of Our Lord 1495, on a bright autumn afternoon of stubborn winds and warm rain that smelled unpleasantly of salted cod and violets, the dark-tressed María Inés, originally of Navarre, gave you life. After her difficult miscarriages, you were her first child to come to term, and your mother lived long enough to name you Bianca and seal her devotion with a kiss on your bloodied hairless scalp.

"Oh, the love she had for you," said Fra Ludovico. "I performed the christening with one hand and annointed the forehead of the corpse with the other. And then your saintly mother flew to heaven and became an angel. Now be a saint like your mother, will you, and fetch me a sip of wine to go with this ham. I've a twinge."

Primavera, when the girl had gone: "You simple oaf, don't lie to her."

"Hush, you suppurating old boil of a peasant."

"You weren't present at the mother's death, and you know it. You're a priest, you aren't supposed to lie."

"I'm a priest, I know better than most when a lie is permitted. I would have performed the rites had I happened to be in the vicinity. You know I would."

Bianca returned with the wine. The priest toasted his nemesis. "May you choke on your godless superstitions and spend eternity in coals up to your squid marks. Amen."

"Bianca, the kitchen fire is failing, and I left the kindling on a cloth at the bottom of the steps. Can you bring it to the hearth?" asked Primavera. The girl, biddable enough, went off.

"I know you're an old fool," said the cook, "but really, I'm surprised you would lie to the girl."

"My lie is a slender thing. It serves a purpose. Bianca should see that her birth ushered her mother into heavenly bliss. Isn't it true enough? And isn't it good for her to consider?"

Primavera: For all you know María Inés was a harlot. She may be writhing in hell or removing an ocean with the lid of an acorn in purgatory. How can you promise Bianca her mother is in heaven?

Fra Ludovico: The stories of heaven belong in the heads of children. If, as children grow, the stories evaporate?—oh well. They leave behind a residue of hope that changes how children behave.

Primavera: That stinks more than your chamber pot.

And are you going to heaven or hell, do you think, with your heathen tricks and legerdemain?

I'm not going to die at all, just to spite the architects of the worlds.

Fra Ludovico crossed himself and ate some more ham.

Bianca de Nevada returned with the kindling and helped Primavera stoke the fire. She didn't ask more about her mother: What was there to say? But Fra Ludovico, warmed by the wine and the fire, talked about an arterial system of grace that webbed together human affairs. When he left, Primavera raked the embers again.

"Look, child," she said. "Is this a kitchen fire or is it the fires of hell?"

"There is a pot on a chain for our broad beans," said Bianca. "I don't know if hell has such a pot."

"Is your mother a dead woman or is she a broad bean?"

This was a harder question to answer. Once a mother started being dead, and was planted in the ground, what was to say she didn't emerge, eventually, as a broad bean? "I'm not sure," said Bianca.

Primavera said, "You're young enough to be ignorant, but you are not a fool like some I know. Of course your mother isn't a broad bean."

"They say you are an onion," said Bianca, snuggling toward Primavera's lap.

"That only refers to my distinctive and refreshing odor. Now, listen to me. When your mother died, she died. Maybe the saints came and put her in a sack and took her to visit with Saint Peter. Or maybe the worms broke their Lenten fast to chew on her delicious lips. Nobody knows, but what's done is done, and your job is to be clever and not to listen to nonsense. Do you understand me?"

"How do I know what is nonsense and what isn't?"

"If you're ever in doubt, throw a pepper up in the air. If it fails to come down, you have gone mad, so don't trust in anything."

She made a supper out of peppers and broad beans, illustrating her point obscurely. Bianca ate heartily though wasn't sure she understood the lesson.

She would ask her father, though, when he returned.

When Don Vicente arrived home a few days later, some latest necessary negotiation with the Papal legates having broken off unsatisfactorily, Bianca greeted him with the question. But *Papà, is Mamma an angel or is she a broad bean?*

For once Vicente was in no mood. "Who puts a notion like that in your mind?"

He fired the corrupt old matron, but Primavera refused to leave the kitchen. "It would take me half a day to walk to the village, and you'd just have to send for me again when you changed your mind, and my hips aren't what they were."

"They never were anything much like hips," sniffed Fra Ludovico in passing. But Primavera's point carried the argument, and Vicente relented.

Is Mamma dead? Is she really dead? Or is she an angel, or a bean, or something else?

"I'm surrounded by simpletons," said Vicente.

But he remembered his daughter's birth—in a nook in a tavern on the road from Rome, when María Inés's water broke without warning. The baby came twisted and ought to have died, but the mother died instead. For a payment of florins her corpse was allowed to share a churchyard grave with a local merchant who conveniently had died the same day. (The merchant had been a widower and his dead wife wouldn't know he was buried with another woman until purgatory, when everything was too late to change anyway.)

Whether Vicente began at once to love Bianca in place of her dead mother or whether he had to learn not to despise her for causing his wife to bleed to death, Bianca lived a lifetime without finding out. Fra Ludovico was wrong: Truth is as evanescent as lies, and dissolves in time. But as a father will, Vicente had taken Bianca in his arms, and he continued on the road through Spadina toward Spoleto.

Except for that which pertained to the confusing and contradictory legend of her birth, Bianca de Nevada had been told little about María Inés de Castedo y Nevada. The flattering characteristics that memorialize the person who dies too young aren't altogether convincing. María Inés had been a saint, an angel, a paragon. But Bianca had to wonder. Had her mother never thrown a stone at a cat, or peed in the vegetable garden, or stuck out her tongue at the Archbishop of Pamplona? On these matters neither Primavera nor Fra Ludovico would comment.

So Bianca came to consider her mother something like the stark unsmiling icon of the Virgin that Fra Ludovico kept propped up on a shelf in his cell. In the severe older style, unpopular these days, the piece showed judging black eyes, lips pursed as if reserving a mother's kiss for someone more worthy than Bianca.

"*Papà?*" said Bianca, the question mark carried in the set of her small shoulders. "Where is Mamma now?"

He couldn't answer her inquiry. He held her instead and walked to the steeper side of the mount, where the wind raced up the east face of the slope with such speed that it could carry a piglet from a barnyard below and brain it against one of Montefiore's protruding roof beams.

Vicente regarded his Bianca. Of her beauty there was no doubt, and no description would serve. But the name was correct. *Bianca, a* name referring to the polished whiteness of her skin, almost a marble from the Carrara region; and de *Nevada,* the father's family name, betraying his own humble status in the outlands of Aragon, but pertinent here: *of the snowy slopes.*

And Bianca saw her father too, his wavy chestnut hair standing almost straight up in the wind. She couldn't see her mother in him, but she could see something that she guessed he might have learned from poor dead María Inés: a habit of love. So maybe growling Fra Ludovico was right about the contagious quality of blessings in human affairs.

Don't leave, don't follow

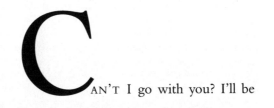C AN'T I go with you? I'll be still and say my prayers.

Her exposure to other girls limited, Bianca nonetheless had learned to sulk prettily enough. It didn't work, though. Her father wouldn't let her off the property. She could go no farther than the orchards and the higher of the hay meadows. Only as far as the bridge, and onto it, but not across it.

"The weather is terrible," he said, and shivered, though it was high summer and the goats sat panting in the shadows, too tired to bleat. "Beyond the bridge a dreadful snow falls. My beard crusts over and in minutes my cloak is stiff as a cuirass. I can't turn at the waist. If you were walking behind me and you fell and called my name, I wouldn't hear you: plugs of ice form in my ears."

"You would always hear me," she said, laughing. "You hear me when I wake up to go in the night, though my water is less than a spoonful."

He tried again. "I tell you, the world is a terrible place to be. I don't want you to come with me until you're older, for if something happened to me, what would become of you?"

"What could happen to you?" she asked.

"Well, a tree might fall on my head and turn my brains into whisked eggs."

His drollery was ineffectual. "*Papà*, really."

"Look," he told her, "here at Montefiore, Fra Ludovico and Primavera Vecchia can keep you safe. But should anything ever happen to me, you are not to come looking."

"I don't understand why." She lowered her chin and looked at him with a severity uncommon in a child.

"Because anything that could happen to me could happen to you. If I was in trouble somehow, it would be a comfort to know you were safe here, and not getting into mischief on my behalf. I lost your mother, through no fault of my own." His voice was stern. "I won't lose you too, nor even waste my time worrying about it, providing you obey me."

"You go and come, and go and come, and nothing ever happens to you."

"I go and come, and play my games, and stroke my beard and nod my head and hold my tongue, all to keep us safely overlooked up here. These are boisterous times, and too many men are greedy for everything. You stay here. You give me your word?"

She wouldn't.

"Bianca," he said. "this bridge on which we stand. Up there is Lago Verde, and the stream runs out, beneath this bridge, to water our lower fields, and eventually to join the other rivulets and power the mill at the edge of the village. You can see the noisy stream, the rushes, the wrens at their work, the hills beyond. But what don't you see?"

"I don't see why you have to leave again," she said.

He snapped at her, "You don't see men thieving for riches. You don't see the calvary or the foot soldiers. You don't see"—here he lowered his voice, trying another approach—"you don't see the ornery creatures who live under the bridge."

She looked at him with suspicion and mock contempt, but he could tell he had found his weapon.

"If you come down here alone, a little slip of a thing as you are, one of them will leap from their damp burrow and snatch you away. And then I'll come home, and cry, *Bianca, Bianca!* And you'll be gone, and no one to tell me where you went. But I'll know, Bianca. I'll know. You *disobeyed your father.*"

"What do they look like?" she asked.

"Scarier than Primavera," he said. "I don't want to terrify you so that's all I'll say. Now kiss me, and let me be on my way."

She kissed him, and let him go. And, more or less, she believed him that the weather in the world was brutal. Every time he came home, it took longer and longer for him to shake off the frozen look on his face, and thaw at the sight of her. Then, when summer had passed and the autumn rushed goldenly in, he was gone again, and this time for a long time—more than a week. Long enough for the staff to relax into mild disbehavior.

"The wall by the back stairs wants a coat of lime wash," said one of the maids. Someone had been drawing instructional diagrams for the others and the male figure looked rather too much like a naked Fra Ludovico for anyone's comfort.

"You're lucky the old fool doesn't take this staircase," muttered Primavera. "He'd collapse in mortification and brain himself on the stone landing, and go on to swell the community of souls in heaven and bore them eternally. No, Bianca, you are forbidden to go look. When the time comes to tell you the glorious nonsense of sex, I'll do it with the help of a carrot and a soft loaf of bread folded in two."

"I know about sex," said Bianca. "I've seen the ram and the ewe."

"And what precisely can you see about the romance between the ram and the ewe?"

Very little, as it turned out. But Bianca was crafty enough to disguise her ignorance and wouldn't say.

The girl had all too few amusements, sequestered as she was. The gooseboy was friendly but vague, and preferred the company of geese. The servant girls from the village thought Bianca was too young for her friendship to be worth cultivating. So needling Primavera or Fra Ludovico was one of Bianca's rare entertainments. At lunch:

"I want to see the funny drawings. Why can't I?"

"What funny drawings?" asked Fra Ludovico.

"Someone has sketched schemes of sex between whores and morons," said Primavera.

"Only a moron would have sex with a whore," said Fra Ludovico. "Bianca, I forbid you to examine these diagrams. You would weep with fright and grief."

"I can see her laughing herself sick," said Primavera. "Or getting ideas. Usually, for the sake of honesty, I have to chop the carrot in half so as not to get a young girl's hopes up." A pause. "There's really nothing to compare to a squid."

"I see a horse," cried the gooseboy, who frequently cried what he saw, though most often it was shapes in the clouds. But today he was right, and Don Vicente would arrive himself by nightfall.

Fra Ludovico posted himself in a chamber to pray that Don Vicente might bring good news to their windswept perch, though he would never elaborate the nature of the hopes he had; his was too lofty a station for him to descend to common gossip. "You don't know what you pray about," snorted Primavera, "that's why you won't tell us. You pray for a reason to pray, that's all. And it doesn't come."

"It'll come soon enough," said Fra Ludovico bitterly. "I've been to Rome, after all; I know how quickly peace concludes."

"If I fell asleep into my grave now, I'd have nothing to think about but the children war has taken from me," snapped Primavera. "No one survives in times of war unless they make war their home. How did I get so old and wise, but for welcoming war into my house and making friends with him? Better to befriend the enemy and hang on. Something worse might come along, which might be amusing or might not."

"Something worse always comes along. That's what I'm praying about."

Primavera left to supervise the preparation of the evening meal. Bianca followed her and mooned about the kitchen, getting underfoot and upsetting a pot of broth, till Primavera scolded her and sent her off.

Fra Ludovico, to Bianca's knock, replied yawnily, "I'm deep in prayer, child. Go away."

She threw stones in the well, but the well didn't throw them back, and she went to the top of the back staircase, where the local girls had begun covering the offending images with lime wash.

"What is that supposed to be?" she asked, pointing.

The girls had no use for her. Had she been the sister of one of them, they might have been kind; but they were always serving, and had few advantages, and the pleasure of sisterhood among them was more luxurious than the appeal of being kind to a younger child. And the girls could see that as the lone child of the local landholder, Bianca was far more likely to attract a desirable husband than they, which made them less than sympathetic to her loneliness.

So the drawings they were covering up were especially galling, and they had to choose their strategy of cruelty. In the end the puddle of soapy water on the top step did their work for them. Down she went, three steps at a time, while the girls laughed.

"Nobody pushed her," they agreed, affronted, when Primavera arrived.

Bianca bled a little and cried, but she cried less than she bled, and then she stopped bleeding, and went to wait for her father in the apple orchard.

The orchard was gently terraced into four broad earthwork steps, each one lined with a double row of trees. The time of apples was nearly here; the first windfalls were jeweling the ground with carmine and green. Bianca knew her father, who was kind to his animals, would bring his mare here, once she'd been unsaddled and watered. He would let her take advantage of a few apples.

Bianca didn't fret but sat quietly in the verdant shade of the top level. She couldn't see through the descending boughs, but she would hear the mare nicker and stamp, and she would run down with arms outstretched, gaining speed on each of the four slopes.

It was closing on evening by the time he arrived. She ran to him. "*Papà*," she cried, for more-than-a-week had seemed to her little-less-than-a-year. She didn't mean to complain of her fall, only to show him who she was, in case he'd forgotten.

But he turned and saw her, and shrugged away the mare's nuzzling head. He didn't notice his daughter's bruise or the scab. Which seemed odd. He said, merely, "What a fledge of your mother you are, and ever more so," and he took her hand in his as he hurried her toward the house. He didn't ask her about what had happened while he was gone. He had something on his mind.

The sun was a stout ball of glowing blood in the haze of thin clouds, and then broke through. The stones of Montefiore were copper butter. The windows that had glass winked blindingly back at the sun. Everything in the world had an eye, and could watch. From beyond, the hoofs of another horse rang out.

She shuddered with a child's pleasurable shiver of fear. She wanted her father to stop, hold her, attend to her. "Something is watching us," she murmured. He thought she meant the moon, rising over the house on the other side, a silver sentinel, and she did. But she meant something dark as well as bright, and in that she was correct.

A pack of dirty thieves

is what they called us. They had no better words for it, not knowing whether we were beasts or men. We knew no better than they did what we were, for we had little language of our own—no names, back then, few habits of civilized living. But we didn't steal. Dirty vagabonds, the lot of us, back then, but not thieves.

Back then, I say, meaning a past moment I can postulate must have existed, but can't in truth remember for itself.

We might have become more human—sooner than we did, if indeed we ever have—did we move according to the rhythms of human beings.

We hear the bells of the chapel on the blossom-scented winds of May, and we realize it's time to pray. If we are to be human we must pray as humans do. So we put down our tools and scour the muck from our nails, for we have learned you must not come to chapel smelling of corpses and shit and gold and blood and the juice of whores. We scrub and arrange what passes for our clothes, and mat down our manes to look more like human hair, and we tuck our cloven feet into sacks of soft leather called boots, and we traipse to the chapel to pray.

And when we arrive the candles are dark, the doors are closed and bolted, the crowds of faithful are snoring their lusty dreams under every swaybacked rooftop in the village. We think, oh, so this isn't the time to pray, then. And we go home, trying not to laugh at the dreams of humans, which are draped like tattered clouds above their homes until the sunlight bleaches them invisible. As we trudge home, the snow crunches under our feet, the icicles dangle like white marble fringe on the pines. Time moves differently for us.

This happens again and again. After some decades I think—I think it was I who thought this, though the notion of an *I* is still a confusing one—I think this: When humans hear the bells of faith, they are there at once. When dwarves hear it, they arrive too late.

Bur our lives are longer than human lives. Just yesterday Primavera Vecchia was slipping off the lap of her grandmother and landing in the basket of onions and pissing on them. They made a better soup for it, those onions. Today Primavera is hairy of chin and tomorrow no one will remember who she was.

Our lives are more secret too. Humans shorten their lives by gossip, and dwarves can barely talk. Speaking uses us up, speeds us up. Without prayer, that act of confession for merely existing, one might live forever and not know it.

I was in the shadows on the night of the copper moon. I had been following her father to lay a bargain at his door, to spend my words in the hope of an exchange, to negotiate for the return of what we'd lost. But he was frightened of the coming dark and spurred his tired horse up the last slope before I could trudge into his path and confront him.

So I followed behind, and heard what I saw, and saw what I heard. As he and the girl-thing came down from the orchards, the moon and sun both witnessing, a horseman arrived on a stallion, caparisoned in black and red, and said, "Have you readied the house? He's here."

Trouble and his sister

I N THE shadows, I watched Don Vicente de Nevada hand his daughter to the housemistress and begin to shout orders. Some associate was on the road, following along behind with an entourage that included a noblewoman. They were making their way up the slopes at a slower pace, but would arrive in an hour or so.

If the bedding was rank with disuse, it must be aired at once. Mulberry twigs scattered under the bedsteads, to draw the fleas from the mattresses. Flowers gathered for the tables, floors swept, pastries prepared, wine decanted. Everyone at Montefiore must come at once to receive instructions. Is there asparagus in the ground, or has it gone by?

They ran to their work, as humans will, with vigorous shortsightedness. As if the presence of a fresh pastry can change how the world works. As if flowers might interrupt the flow of slow ire, or a better bottle of wine halt in its path the progress of verdigris upon a bronze statue of a horse and rider in some town square.

But I sat in the shrubs, chewing the haunch of some boar that had crossed my path and biding my time. I enjoy the spasmodic tics of human endeavor, the aimless urgency, the pride of it. The *superbia*. Hurrying feet, muttered curses, cross remarks sent winging about the estate. The child fled to keep out of the way, and hunched on the bottom step of the outer staircase, hugging her knees to herself.

I could make out the very lashes on her inky eyes, you see, I could smell her very purity.

Vicente was tersely chiding a maid about the unsavory state his better attire seemed to be in. From the kitchen, Primavera's voice rang with impatience. Fra Ludovico kept himself safely out of the way, polishing the ornamental candlesticks to be used at Mass. So Bianca happened to be alone when the entourage rounded the last steep curve in the road and drew abreast along the stone wall that shored up the gardens hanging above. The urchin stood there with her chin dropped, studying the roof of the palanquin, until the mounted soldier said, "Run and tell the lord of the house we have arrived."

"Who is it in there?" said Bianca, a reasonable enough question, as the man was only one, and *we* implied a pair at least.

"The Duc de Valentinois and his sister."

A pale hand appeared in a seam of velvet drapes, as if considering whether or not to open them to the light. My eye fell on the jewel, an irregularly faceted ruby of uncertain clarity but with striking purple depths.

"Oh," said Bianca, "a friend to play with."

Then the hand disappeared—perhaps the sister had caught a glimpse of Bianca, or had realized that a voice so youthful wasn't worth the effort of attending. The brother apparently knew his sister well, and waved the bearers on. Sweating and grunting, the attendants pressed forward until the equipage had been lifted up the last rise to the villa's front door, and set down on a length of tapestry laid out for the purpose.

"De Nevada. You rascal, we're here," shouted the man. "You'll leave us languishing like a fishmonger and his prize salmon out here?"

The attendants stood back. As Vicente rushed out, in a robe of charcoal blue, the curtains in the palanquin parted and the sister emerged, blinking as if she'd just woken from a sleep.

Bianca moved forward from the shadows to see.

I am a girl
who did no wrong

I am a girl who did no wrong.
I walked this side of Gesù when I could.
I kept an angel in my apron pocket.
I do not think it did me any good.

Cesare

THE MAN was a young brute, one of those handsome men who knock mountains to one side in order to clear his view. Primavera was both smitten and on her guard. She saw how his feet gripped the ground as he dismounted, as if his boots were filled with bronze feet, as if he were in the act of being cast already as his own statue. His dark eyes were tigers, prowling to strike at threats.

"Vicente," he said, "a basin of water for the face, a basin of wine. There are plans to arrange tonight, and little enough time."

"That man has a storm of beauty in his face," said Primavera, backstairs. "He looks as if he could easily wrestle any squid out of the water."

"He is a monster sinner," said Fra Ludovico, fussing at his vestments. "Don't you know who it is? It's Cesare Borgia, the son of the Spanish pope. To plot a vendetta, no doubt, to lay waste to more of our homeland. Is he requisitioning troops again?"

"His campaigns cost me the lives of both my sons," said Primavera. "They were fools to allow themselves to be conscripted, but they were my fools. I hope Don Vicente is cannier than they were, rest their souls."

"He's a guest of our master," said Fra Ludovico. "Don't get any ideas about dishing up vengeance or anything foolish like that, or we'll all be slaughtered in our beds before morning."

"I like a man who wears his implement so prominently," said one of the maids. "It makes my work easier." She rubbed her bosom as if polishing a knob of furniture.

"I like a man who needs forgiveness so obviously," said Fra Ludovico primly. "It makes my work clearer."

"He's a young one, to have taken so many lives in war," said Primavera. "Lives of his soldiers, lives of his enemies. Now, what cruel nonsense does his handsome head plot with our good master? Bianca, take this salver of cheese and fruit upstairs. Bianca! Where is the child?"

Lucrezia

I NEEDED the air, I needed freshness on my skin. I needed to see what was to be seen. I didn't wait for the hand of my brother to prompt me from the carriage. I, the daughter of a pope, I, who had been the *governatrice* of Spoleto at the age of nineteen, I never waited for prompting.

"Vicente. The comfort of reacquaintance." I used our common Iberian tongue, toying with his Christian name as a courtesan teases a drunken courtier, with malice and pleasure at once. "Vicente, before you are seduced into intrigues of state by my brother, be so good as to favor me with your welcome."

I awaited a kiss but accepted his hand. It's best to acquiesce to custom, at least when one is in the country. Avoiding his eyes, I trained my attention on the child instead, feigning an interest I didn't possess.

"Who are you, who looks on a Borgia with impunity?" I said, though the child had hidden her eyes behind her father's legs. I could examine Vicente's form while pretending to play find-the-child. A tiresome pretense, but even a young Borgia had to observe some protocol, as scurrilous spies are always lurking about to report on our deeds and misdeeds.

"Bianca," murmured her father, "surely you remember my Bianca?"

"I haven't taken her measure before," I answered. "She was a shit-smeared froglet the last time I was by. Why, she's turning into a person."

"They do, you know," said Vicente.

"Let me see the *cherubina,* then," I said. "Come to Lucrezia, child."

The child was wary. She didn't obey me until her father nudged her forward.

And we looked at each other, that girl and I. She out of childish curiosity and caution, I out of the need to have something to talk to her father about. I had no native interest in this child. I attest to that now. I would have been happy never to see her again. She was no more than a saucer of spoiled milk to me.

Though she had her beauty, I'll grant you that. She curved, rush-like, against her father's well-turned calf. She had the face of a new blossom, a freshness and paleness one could imagine some sorcerer growing in a moonlit garden. Her hair was pinned up in a womanly fashion, despite her youth, and its blackness, under a net of simple un-ornamented cord, had a steepness to it, a depth. Odd how such things strike one. Her eyes were hidden from me; she wouldn't look up. Her skin was white as snow.

I am a woman who slept with my father the pope

I am a woman who slept with my father the Pope.

They say I did, at least, and so does he.

And who am I to make of the Pope a liar,

And who is he to make a liar of me?

What I saw then

SOME OF us are born many times. Some are born only once. Primavera says that some are born dead and live their whole lives without knowing it.

I can't say much about earlier childhood memories. One knows things with a complicated and unreliable conviction. The sky-blue sky is as blue as the sky. White beans in a brown pot are more delicious than milk. The purr of cats and the claws of cats are not the same thing. One can't remember how one learned to breathe, at least the first time.

But then one is born anew, usually at the moment that the breath begins again after it has been held.

I released the air of my lungs, and breathed again, and looked at my father's visitor. And I remember her with a vividness that strikes me, to this day, as preternatural. But surely this is true of all children?—that one day they come upon an awareness of themselves, of their own knowing, and in that moment they shuck their animal natures off and begin to hoard the treasury of knowledge that will make them capable of grief and remorse as well as pity and love?

In looking at Lucrezia Borgia, I was aware of myself looking: I was aware of myself. I was a dark twist of child hiding behind my father, and she was a coil of effervescent flame in the reception yard before the safehold of Montefiore.

She peered at me (I know to say this now) with the eyes of a child. For all her grandeur and hauteur she wasn't as grown up as she thought. She had other things on her mind, and she wasn't good at disguising her boredom. So I had an uninterrupted access to her, and saw the woman called the flower of her time, the Roman lily.

Lucrezia bit her lower lip, pretending to play with me, though I knew she was playing at something else. She tucked her small chin into her embroidered collar, then cocked her head and looked at me slantwise. She was displaying all her best angles—to her brother, to my father, to slack-jawed Fra Ludovico in the background for all I knew. She had the smooth forehead of a pale squash, and her hair spilled out of her bindings with liberty and energy. It was as yellow and crimped as dried tendrils of runner bean at the end of season. She loved herself, that much was sure. I didn't have a vocabulary for beauty at the time. But she was bewitching: and I knew it right then, that moment too. In knowing that much, I began to grow up.

I am a rock whose hands have appetites

I am a rock whose hands have appetites.
I am a rock whose appetites have hands.
I am a thing unresolved into courteous shapeliness.
I am a creature excluded from limbo and hell,
A thing of which heaven prefers to stay well unaware.
Neither pet, nor beast of the fields, or beast of the woods,
Nor idiot kept, more or less, in the warmth of the hearth
For the sometime amusement of humans and sarcastic angels.
Nothing exists but it rests on me, at the start,
At the end; but I keep to myself, as no one will have me.

A moment ago

I WATCH the affairs of men from the penumbral sanctuary.

It is 1502. Vicente, the widower, tries to keep a low profile in his aerie. Lucrezia Borgia, with her hair newly dyed, is on her way from Rome to Ferrara. At twenty-one she is married for the third time, to Alfonso D'Este. Her father, wicked Pope Alexander VI, has only a year to live. Machiavelli won't publish *The Prince* for a decade yet, but he is busy scrutinizing the life and pursuits of that splendid soldier, Lucrezia's brother, Cesare Borgia. The discovery of Española by some adventurer put out from the court of Their Catholic Majesties, Isabella and Ferdinand, means that the whole planet goes into a fierce wobble: tides sweep up into the front doors of St. Mark's in Venice, earthquakes rock the Levant, pyramids are lost again in sandstorms, as every chin in Europe turns away from Byzantium and toward Lisboa and Castile. The East is about to sink into the dust of mystery—

again—as the light of reason blinds the west. "The world is coming to its senses, as if awakening out of a deep sleep," says Erasmus. And Bianca de Nevada, seven years old, aware of none of it, equally un-aware of me, watches and listens to the people standing on the grass before her.

A stroll in the country

TRUNKS, PROVISIONS, caskets were unloaded, and Don Vicente kept trying to urge the guests in the door, but Cesare was too jittery to be housed, and he walked up and down in the forecourt, talking his political predictions aloud.

"It's been a few years now since that viper, Savonarola, was put to death, and Florence regains her strength and vanity by the minute. He burned the vanities, but he couldn't burn out the high regard they have for themselves. And for that he was immolated. What a pure, savage end for him."

Don Vicente, who had known something of roasting of *converses* by Torquemada in Spain, flinched at the flippancy. But he stood like a Roman legionnaire, his fine shoulders thrown back. "We can discuss things over a libation," he said soothingly. "Welcome, my lord. " His grip on Cesare's forearm strengthened—in this case the handshake betraying its Roman origins: to assess whether a man might have a knife hidden beneath the sleeve of his tunic.

"There are strategies to consider," said Cesare, confirming Vicente's worries, but the famous sister yawned ostentatiously and pulled at her brother's tunic.

"Later for all that, later," she said. "I've spent a good part of these hours behind curtained views. We've been on the road from Rome three days already. I need to stretch and to see something. Don Vicente, let me ask for your arm. I'm faint as a dowager who has taken Madeira at noon." She looked about as faint as a lightning bolt. "Conduct a tour for me; show me some rural interest. Take me for a stroll. Show me something, anything. The views. The geese. Yes, show me the geese."

"I can loan you the arm of Fra Ludovico," said Vicente. Fra Ludovico looked terrified and began to busy himself with his sleeves.

"My father is the pope of the universal Church," said Lucrezia. "I have more spiritual companionship than I can bear. Leave Fra Ludovico to his hours. My brother can spare you for a while, Don Vicente. I insist, Cesare, I will have my exercise."

"Very well; I'll stay and pose questions of state to the de Nevada daughter," said Cesare, pointing at Bianca and making her nervous.

Vicente had no choice but to be courteous. "A stroll, then," he said to la Borgia, and to his daughter, "but you, come with me. The Duc de Valentinois has no interest in talking to an infant. He is only being kind."

Bianca fled to her father's side. "Oh, we are to be a walking nursery?" said Lucrezia. "Very well then. I ought have brought my own babe, Rodrigo. He is four. Beware the cliff edge, my babe; a childish foot can make a misstep and the rocks below—you see them?—look sharp and unwelcoming."

Bianca ran ahead of her father and the noblewoman. She was glad to be out of harm's way, since harm seemed coiled in the military man left behind in the courtyard of Montefiore.

The path, this side of the bluff, sloped down in a gentle zigzag to some outbuildings: a croft, a lean-to for the shepherds; the diminished

Lago Verde beside a vigorous and well-pruned olive orchard. The walls were littered with the leavings of goats, who liked to leap over any obstacle. And below, the bridge that Bianca was forbidden to cross.

Though she was prohibited from the world beyond the farm, she loved to hear the noise of village life scraping beyond her confines. As she fell asleep, on nights when the wind was still, she could sometimes hear tenants singing, joking, building their cooking fires and banking their sleeping fires, leaping up at threats real or imagined. They were safety to her, the vinemaster, the gooseboy, the shepherd, the ostler, the hunter, the smith, the girls who did floor washing and laundry, and the lads who organized the haying and cured the hams and pressed the olives and then cleaned the stones and pressed the grapes when they were ripe. Life on a farm was a universe in itself, but, since the cows had long since been moved out of the bier in the ground floor of Montefiore, Bianca felt she had only a distant relationship with the *contadini* who came and went to work, and who thrived on the farm's yield.

"The news from Rome," said Vicente, after a time, to avert attention from the expressive pressure of la Borgia's arm upon his.

"Oh, Rome," said Lucrezia, "my brother will call it a circus of toadies, my father a nest of vipers. To a noblewoman it's all private chambers. We women work by gossip and innuendo. A man is a cock in armor, a ridiculous proposition; a woman is a hen in veils. Less vivid to see but no less ridiculous to consider. But indulge my appetite for a view, Don Vicente. That long line of hills there—is that Cortona?"

"Nothing like Cortona," said Vicente. "Nowhere near it."

"Understanding how the land chooses to spread itself about isn't my strength. What I long for is the sea. Can we glimpse it from here?'

"We can't. We're as inland as we can be, between the Adriatic and the Tyrrhenian Sea."

Above a crumbling bank by the side of the path Lucrezia found an old stone sill that had been set upon an ancient protruding root. It would make a good seat. She tried to lever herself up but her gown kept catching on the fringe of smaller exposed roots. She pouted meaningfully, and Vicente, who didn't care to touch her, obligingly came forward. He gripped her by the waist as if she were hardly lighter than his daughter, and he set her down. His hands stayed on her waist to secure her there.

"I can see everything," said his guest. "Goats and geese, hills and meadows, vines and laborers, the gooseboy and the gamekeeper. It does my heart good." She sighed, and Vicente, who found her canny and alarming, relaxed a little. Though so often after an effect—and who wasn't?—she had a reservoir of genuine feeling, it seemed.

"Cesare would give you the news from Rome in one manner," she said, continuing the conversation from before, "and I another. You know his motto—*Aut Caesar, aut nihil*—either Caesar or nothing. Well, I tire of it. He has his game to run, and I mine. The old pepper can't keep on forever, you know, and when he goes, the fight to succeed him will be intense."

Vicente raised an eyebrow.

"My father," she said curtly. "My dear father. The most roundly defamed Bishop of Rome in the history of our holy Church. You know what lies the Orsini spread about him? The *infessura*. It's no secret that people credit the so-called *infans Romanus* as being the fruit of a monstrous union between my father and me. And the august Bishop of Rome allows such nonsense to circulate. He believes it unnerves his enemies to think him capable of such wickedness. He doesn't think of the cost to my reputation."

"I can have no opinion about such matters; I'm a country farmer—"

"The things they report. Simony and nepotism the least of it. They whisper about whores taken on the floors of the ducal apartments. Whores stripped of their clothes and required to pick up chestnuts with their nether lips, while bishops make ready the available crozier for penetration."

"My child is present," said Vicente desperately. "She is a young girl, and even more innocent than most."

Lucrezia breathed in and out in sudden anger, and muttered, almost under her breath, "They weren't chestnuts, anyway, they were jewels." But it wasn't clear to Vicente whether she was jesting or not.

"The truth," she went on, "the truth, dear sir, is that I'm a young woman, and these times frighten me. Do you remember a few years back, when a monster was dug up from the mud of the banks of the Tiber? It was huge and deformed; it had the head of a woman and its behind was bearded. The peasants of Rome went mad for fear that God was signaling the end of civilization. At the close of the third set of five hundred years since Gesù's birth. But I think civilization isn't ending, just changing. And the power to change it belongs in the hands of the mighty."

She held out her hand, a pretty delicate thing, pale as pounded leather.

"I don't know why you are speaking to me of this," said Vicente.

"I like to speak in the language of my father," she said simply. "Cesare prefers the Italian tongue as spoken in Rome, and I hear more of sacred Latin than my ears can bear. At home we sang to ourselves as we spoke, in that tone of Spanish that evokes blood oranges and tenor lutes. You give me a greater pleasure than you realize. You provide for me a comprehending ear for this secret familiar tongue we share."

Vicente nodded, indicating he saw it as a duty and an honor both.

After a long pause, she said, "He will not be the lord of all Italy if he does not concentrate his attentions. He must dismiss the distractions from his mind. You will have to help him in that. It is what I ask on his behalf, before he asks it."

"I am happy to provide the succor of my home for a rest and a respite, a distraction from the campaigns," he said.

She studied the workings of the farm before her. "How are the geese?" she asked. "I trust the boy saves them from the foxes in the hills?"

"The boy does well enough," said Vicente. "A goose does not ask much of life, after all."

"No," she admitted. "Those who ask much are more likely disappointed. We should all be as simple as the goose."

"Well, the boy is good to them," said Vicente softly.

"There's merit in that, I suppose," she replied.

Under the twists of thornbank

WHERE I took my rest, I heard them speak. The coquettish wife and the widower. I heard them go on, about the puling exercises of the Holy Father, the gonfalonier of Florence, the vengeful evicted Medicis, the breakaway state of Pisa, the interest of Spain and France in the Kingdom of Naples, the security of Venice, Il Moro of Milan. They talked in large concentric circles, as if any of it mattered: as if Cesare Borgia, Duc de Valentinois, has the power to sink roots in Romagna. Like other mortals, he'll die before Romagna knows he has been born.

I was more interested in the beast pulled from the mud of the Tiber. How had the Tiber conspired to lose her grip on one of its own sinews? What keeps a river in its banks but the spirits of the drowned, the titans and Nereids, whose time has passed, and who in shame and righteous humility cover themselves with their watery blanket?

What did it say about the movement of time, about what was about to happen, that I could understand the hummingbird spin of human voices?

I might have gone back to my brothers then and there. But I left them where they were, and waited to learn what next I could learn. I followed the distinguished woman and the hilltop farmer when they left the spectacle of geese and pond and millworks. I emerged, more a shadow of a rock than a rock itself, and accompanied them unawares. I was there when Donna Borgia saw the looking glass for the first time.

The thing about a mirror is this: The one who stares into it is condemned to consider the world from her own perspective. Even a bowed mirror works primarily by engaging the eyes, and she who centers herself in its surface is unlikely to notice anyone in the background who lacks a certain status, distinction. Or height. Like a dwarf, for instance. Or a young child.

What lies in the mirror

Thit is a lovely looking glass," I
said to Don Vicente. "It's only as lovely as what it reflects," he answered, though his courtliness was studied and heavy.

With more care to amuse, he continued, "We found it in a shallow end of the lake you pass on your way up the hill. How it got there
is a mystery, but it can't have been there long; there is nothing warped
or rotted about it."

"Clearly it must be a mirror from the workshop of the devil," I
said. "Does it have a message for us?"

"Fra Ludovico won't even come in this room," said Don Vicente.
"He is even more superstitious than his old crony and foe, the cook."

"Looking glass, what do you see?" I murmured. My neck was as
white as the swans of Castelfiore and I breathed deeply, to cause the
exposed area of my clavicle to lift and promote my breasts. "Do you see
the corrupted heart of a sinner or the soul of a saint in the making?"

"I suppose it only sees what you show it," said Don Vicente.

"Shall I show it more?"

He didn't look at me. He looked in the mirror instead. "Who is the fairest of all?" he whispered. Did he mean to compare the pair of us, the Lucrezia who stood in the mirror and the Lucrezia who stood before it? A mirrored image has no cologne to seduce; is purer for that. While I had dabbed myself with attar of Persian roses.

He drew in his breath, and I knew that the work I had managed poorly in the farmyard was conducted better before a looking glass.

"My sister," said Cesare, at the door, in admiration. "Will you never learn to govern your clothing?"

Prince Dschem's secret

SUPPER WAS put out by Primavera and her helpers, and the better of the wine casks tapped, and tapers lit. Fra Ludovico was requested first to pray and then to sing, and then to shut up and go away.

At length, Primavera and the staff were excused too. When they tarried in the antechamber giggling and picking over scraps, Cesare took it upon himself to yell them down the stairs. He waited until he heard the door slam shut. "Go bolt it," he said to his host. When that was done, Cesare refilled his goblet with wine and said, "We're here on a mission. Let my sister explain the matter while I dine. Then I'll make a proposal."

Lucrezia made a face and pretended to yawn, though Vicente could see she was crucially involved. "Do I talk, dear brother, about the peninsular wars? About your ambitions for a duchy in Italy? About what you've done right, and what you've failed to manage yet?"

"Don't fiddle with me. You know your task. Talk about the Turk, Lucrezia."

I will offer succor, thought Vicente. This is my table, my food, my wine. This is what is wanted, the distraction. I'll listen as a host ought.

La Borgia took a sip of her watered wine. "I don't know what you follow of the workings of the world," she said to Vicente. "You're a farmer; you're occupied with your own *patria,* your house of Montefiore. How much do you notice of the *condottieri* that pass within your sight? You're no fool, and the view from Montefiore is generous. But your concerns are of the farm, not of the state."

"That's true enough," he said, "a farm is all I can manage."

"It takes a strong man to deal with the scheming Sforzas of Milan, the Medici struggling for Florence, the Doge of the Serene Republic of Venice, the Orsini and the Colonna and the d'Este clans, to say nothing of us blameless Borgias." She laughed; she liked the game of chess as played by principalities. "While you've been breeding your pigs and clearing your land, we've struggled with the ambitious French King as he headed to annex the Kingdom of Naples. Oh, Don Vicente, the alliances shift by the week. The murders are epidemic. Mercy, the men who are declared dead before they have been diagnosed with illness! The reputations we lose between lunch and dinner."

"How attractive to see a woman pursue ladylike pleasures," said Cesare, over a hank of pork. "Get to the Turk."

"We're a practical family when we're in public," said Lucrezia. "We're known for our sensible alliances and our deft way with poison. Is it a reputation we don't deserve? No one takes the time to refute it. Gossip serves its own purposes."

"Beyond our shores on many sides lives the Moor, as you may know. And the Caliphs to the east are the wisest and shrewdest among them. There is a king, the son of Mahomet II, named Bayezid. Do you know of him?"

Vicente shook his head. Lucrezia was correct in her assessment of his concerns. After his evacuation from Spain and his wanderings, his had learned to be a local heart.

"When Mahomet II died, Bayezid succeeded to the throne. Bayezid had a younger brother named Dschem, who even as a lad without whiskers cut a fine figure. Prince Dschem possessed his own appetite for power. He objected to his brother's rule and was duly crushed, but he escaped to Rhodes. There, the canny Governor-Knight handed him over to my father's predecessor in the Holy See, and when my father was elevated to the Papacy he took charge of the Prince."

"As a prisoner of war?" asked Vicente.

"As a prominent houseguest who was too amusing to be allowed to return home," interpolated Cesare.

"The Sultan Bayezid wanted his brother barred from Constantinople," said Lucrezia. "Sensibly enough. If the brother remained in Rome as a hostage of sorts, the Sultan could be expected to postpone mounting an attack against the West—after all, his brother might be endangered. And the Sultan even sent Innocent II the spear of the centurion Longinus—the very spear that pierced the body of Gesù Cristo—as a gesture of homage regarding Rome's power and beliefs."

"This was all to prevent the West from mounting another crusade for the reconquering of Jerusalem," said Cesare. "But you drag it out so, Lucrezia."

"You've given me my task; I'll tell it as I like. Anyway, make your dinner last, it's better for your bowels," she said. "Seven years back—1495, it was, I think—Charles VIII of France came into Rome on his way to Naples and then, it was said, on to the Holy Land. My father tried to hold him back, but Rome is ungovernable at the best of times, and the Pope and Cesare were forced to retreat to the Castel Sant'Angelo."

"Rape and plunder and extortion, murder and mayhem," said Cesare. "Quite a party. It was fun."

"But a section of the wall of the castle collapsed, and Alexander VI had to negotiate his way to safety—and to restore the Papacy of course too."

"He sold me to Charles, that devil," said Cesare through a mouthful of goose breast. He spoke without irritation, indeed with some respect.

"Charles had the upper hand," said Lucrezia soothingly. "That day anyway. He left Rome with Cesare as a hostage and with Prince Dschem. The Prince would serve to protect Charles—what Ottoman army would attack Charles if he had the Sultan's own brother in custody?"

"You said the sultan didn't care for his brother."

"Dschem was worth more alive than dead; he helped neutralize the warmongers. It was a convenient equation for everyone. At any rate, Charles's army passed unimpeded through the Papal States, as agreed. There were nineteen carts lugging trunks of treasures, and a retinue of Turkish onlookers, and Cesare."

Cesare began to snort through his nose with laughter, remembering.

Lucrezia explained. "Oh, the King of France was bested, though. All it took was a bribe, not even a large one; and two of the carts were allowed to disappear and return to Rome, and only later was it discovered that the seventeen remaining carts were heaped with nothing but mud and stone."

"I escaped a few days later," said Cesare. He belched with gusto and held his side. "I had a good laugh with His Holiness when I got back to Rome."

"What matters is Prince Dschem," said Lucrezia. "He knew that the prison of my father's household had been a protection for him, and life would become rough for him now. Maybe some Turkish seer told him how little time he had left."

"I've finished what I want," said Cesare, dashing the plate to the floor in impatience. "All the trekking about, it's a bore. Lucrezia, there's only one thing on my mind: if you won't get to it I will."

Lucrezia looked intently at her brother but her hand, hidden out of his sight on one side of her chair, gestured to Vicente: *Listen to this.*

Cesare's voice became hushed and hurried. He leaned forward in a conspiratorial manner. "Prince Dschem knew that from a position of weakness our father nonetheless had made the better bargain. The

Prince knew the Borgias would always be stronger and smarter than our enemies. Dschem bartered for his life. While we were hostages, he knew I would try to escape, and he begged me to free him when I did. He paid me in advance for his rescue."

"What could he pay with?" said Vicente, another coin of homage spent as courteous interest.

"Ah, the meat of it," said Cesare. "Bayezid had been paying forty thousand ducats annually to Rome to keep Prince Dschem safe, healthy, and far away from the Sultan's court. But the funds were paid directly to my father, and to Innocent II before him. Dschem had nothing with which to bargain except a story, and that he paid me in full."

"The story," said Lucrezia, "of the holy fruit of wisdom."

Vicente picked up a pear on a silver plate and offered it to her.

Her girlish ebullience was cloaked, though as a strategy or a cue to deep feeling, Vicente couldn't tell. He tried to assemble an expression of similar mystery, protecting himself against a danger he couldn't yet identify.

"I can't make merry on this subject," Lucrezia said. "Too much hangs in the balance for us. For us all. Listen well."

"We told you that Bayezid had recovered the spear of Longinus, one of the most holy relics in Christendom," said Cesare. His voice had lost its rasp and become silken with well-harnessed energy. "But Prince Dschem offered news of something older. Something more perfect. So desirable that its very existence had been kept hidden for centuries. A sprig of the Tree of Knowledge, out of the very orchard of Eden from which our kind has sprung."

Vicente said, "You're talking of an emblem . . . "

"*A living sprig,*" said Cesare. "Do you understand what this means?"

Vicente leaned forward and clasped his hands together, thinking of what to say. "I'm not gifted with faith as rich as yours. I struggle to comprehend. How do you know Prince Dschem wasn't just inventing a fancy with which to turn your head, to cause you to help him escape?"

"My brother has a receptive mind," said Lucrezia dryly. "One wouldn't think the mightiest soldier in central Italy would be taken by tales of magic, but that is one of the secrets of his strength. He listens to everything."

"I'm not a fool," said Cesare. "I'd known Prince Dschem for a good deal of my life. He understood that as a prisoner of Charles VIII, his life was at grave risk, and he was ready to spend the most valuable asset he possessed. He told me that the scion of the ancient tree, since the holy times, has been covered with beaten silver. But it still bears three fruits. And they are living. They are perfect. They are Apples with an aspect of the eternal about them. They don't decay. They have never decayed in a thousand years."

"Where is this treasure?" said Vicente.

"Prince Dschem told me," said Cesare. "And then I left. Without him."

"He died a month later, in Naples," said Lucrezia flatly. "Our detractors in Rome say he was poisoned with a particular slow-acting powder that only we Borgias know how to produce."

"I see," said Vicente.

"Our father tried to sell his body back to his brother," said Lucrezia. "One can always use a little extra money in the Vatican coffers."

"And now we come to the reason for our visit," said Cesare. "I want you to go collect the sacred fruit of Eden and bring it to me."

Vicente shot a look at Lucrezia and gave a soft laugh. "Oh, you credit me with more bravery than I deserve. And more naïveté. I have no interests in traveling abroad, nor in leaving my motherless child here. I have a farm to oversee, my friends. Even if I believed the story of Prince Dschem, and I knew there was a branch of the Tree of Knowledge still flourishing—and in this dark life I fear there isn't—I possess too little faith to be entrusted with such a magnificent quest." He wagged his head with an acknowledgment of their confidence in him, though when he refilled their glasses the stream of wine wavered as his hand trembled.

"I have been making my way about the country this season," said

Cesare conversationally. "You know I have been busy removing from power the various arrogant lords of Romagna. I'm looking to consolidate my power before my father dies. I'm building a temporal base for the sacred power of Rome. Therefore, I'm conscripting the heads of households for my army. You would be useless in an army, but I would take you if I had to."

"It would leave my household undefended, and my daughter—" said Vicente. "I'm a countryman, Don Cesare."

The use of a common title with the Duc de Valentinois was a bold move. Overly familiar. The room grew uncomfortably still.

"Were you to undertake the task I set out for you," said Cesare, "I would put a protective restriction upon your property for however long your journey might take, be it months or years. If you refuse my petition, I'll have you anyway for my army, and leave your house to fall down the hill with disuse. Either way, you leave tomorrow morning."

Vicente looked from one Borgia to the other. "Is this the price you exact for my hospitality?" he sputtered. "I've given you my loyalty time and again. I've opened my doors to you and killed the fatted calf."

"Always kill the fatted calf, lest it grow to become a cow, and produce in its time a bull who will gore you," said Cesare. "What will it be?"

Lucrezia had turned her face to the wall at this point.

"I am being cut out of my own life," said Vicente despondently.

"The Prince had his supporters in Constantinople," continued Cesare, as if Vicente had just acceded to his request. "They knew that centuries ago the Apples had been removed from a garden in Babylon. They had been hidden in a treasury near the Agia Sophia. From abroad, Prince Dschem organized a theft, and he had proof that the theft was successful. But the Apples were apprehended by pirates off the Levant, and they fetched up on the shores of Agion Oros, the Holy Mountain, that spit of land in the Aegean east of Thessaly. There the relic is hidden in one of the ancient monasteries. It's said no females can go on to the Holy Mountain; the governors of Agion Oros allow only male students. Idiorrhythmic monks or cenobites."

Vicente made a desperate face. "Hermits, on their own in the wilderness, and cloistered brothers in community," explained Cesare. "They don't answer to Rome, nor to the Eastern patriarch. They live in their own holy time, fools for God. It's likely they don't even know what they have, but they treasure it for its beauty."

"I speak no Greek," said Vicente. "I can't chant to adore an Eastern Christ."

"They are waiting for you," said Cesare. "The Apples are waiting."

"I can't go overseas."

"Go over land, through the Venetian marches, through Illyria, through Thessaly," said Cesare. "I'll secure you passage, funds, horses, and translators."

"How am I to manage wrestling a relic from a horde of rabid monks?"

"You'll make a most graceful thief." Cesare began to yawn. "If not, you'll make a clumsy conscript and find yourself positioned in the front rank. Now I've concluded my request. I'm turning to my bed." He stood and left the room without thanks, without permission, without waiting to hear which of his offers would be accepted.

Vicente turned to Lucrezia. "You asked me to hear him out, to pay some attention. And you reward me with this sentence of exile from my home? Who will protect my daughter?"

"Oh, that," said Lucrezia Borgia. "Don't worry about that. I shall look in on her from time to time. Montefiore is about halfway between Rome and Ferrara. You know I like to stop here. So I'll take her under my wing. I'll treat her as if she were my very own."

"Lucrezia," said Vicente. He had only one strategy. He stood and went to her and knelt before her. She was a woman of appetites and she had dallied with him by the thornbank. He held his hands out shoulder height, palm out, leaving himself defenseless, opening himself to her.

She didn't buckle. She said with the crispness of a prelate issuing a penance, "His mind is too full of fancy, Vicente. It was always like that. He is more devout and superstitious than your cook and your cleric taken together. He won't succeed in his military campaigns if he continues to moon on about this relic. He needs to discharge an agent to accomplish his goal so he can turn his attention to the truly pressing matters. You are the necessary distraction; now he can consolidate his campaign in the Romagna and build up the Borgias to be the kings of Italy."

Then she got up and left the room too, and Vicente was left alone, all alone, but for the dread about how his life was to change, and for the dwarf who sat hunched and more or less invisible in a shadowy corner of the piano nobile. The dwarf had tried to speak about recovering what had been lost, but Vicente's attention had been diverted. Though the dwarf knew little about time, he was learning about timing, and he'd missed his chance. Not today. Maybe next day.

The three eyes of God

AN HOUR before sunrise Fra Ludovico lighted the torches in the stable yard. He yawned, for he'd been awake all night, praying out of a nameless sense of dread. He wouldn't put it beyond Cesare Borgia to conscript a priest if his numbers were low. And Fra Ludovico deplored visitors of stature anyway. They always expected to make their morning devotions before it was properly morning.

In vestments that could have done with an airing he readied the roofless chapel at Montefiore for the celebration of the Eucharist. With a large flat leaf from a patch of marrows, he picked up the most obvious of the goat droppings. Then he dragged some benches onto the grass and, for the Duke, a prie-dieu.

Cesare and two bodyguards appeared first. The Duc de Valentinois sank to his knees and groaned, in piety or excitement or to deliver himself of gas. At a dirty look from the priest the bodyguards left their halberds leaning against a pillar, just out of reach. "Even the doves in the barn rafters don't wake up for morning Mass," Fra Ludovico muttered, "why should these assassins bother?"

Because they need the grace the more, he knew. That was why.

As he set out the implements for the sacrament, he studied the Borgia. A man in his pinkest health, halfway through his twenties or so, the priest guessed. The rugged appeal of a knight-at-arms. In his bed Cesare could have any guest he wanted, Fra Ludovico surmised; and rumor had it that he was generous in his affections and catholic in his tastes. Fra Ludovico, who found that sharing his cell with the Holy Spirit was a bit too close for comfort sometimes, was surprised to notice that his wariness of the Duke was coupled with curiosity. A rogue with a passion for prayer. See how he furrowed his brow in devotion, how the sweat drew hot lines down his forehead. Fra Ludovico had to look away in order to concentrate on his sacred business.

Rumor backstairs had it that Cesare was continuing to drum up an army for more Romagnese operations, or perhaps an invasion of Florence. The strategies of a Borgia were hard to guess. The Duke had many intentions, some of which contradicted the others. It was none of Fra Ludovico's concern—so he believed, and so he prayed fervently it would remain.

His routines at the altar had grown casual, and he found reason—liturgical or otherwise—to keep turning his eye to the small and dangerous congregation. He was intoning the introit in his ragged Latin when Lucrezia appeared. As was befitting for a woman at prayer, she'd covered her face in a fine veil that looked to be of Flanders lace. The stories he'd heard tell, of Lucrezia and a girlfriend hiding in the pulpit at the Basilica of Saint Peter's in Rome, and making catcalls at Pope Alexander while he elevated the monstrance. And the sycophants and toadies and bum lickers grinning at the girl's libertine ways in Christendom's second holiest site. Though she had the appearance of glory too; he had to admit it. Even behind that veil, he could see evidence of the hair that Primavera swore was stained blonde with the juice of lemons. The scandal. Beautiful, though.

She had her own road to travel. But Lucrezia had come just this far with her brother, and from here she would continue north without him. She was married, after all! And on her way to Ferrara. Her slender form showed little evidence of the childbearing she'd done—there was Rodrigo, somewhere, and then rumors of an *infans Romanus*—the child of the Pope and his daughter—who had been spirited away in obscurity.

A hussy, though a highborn one. She wore her traveling gown so tight, so fitting on her well-sprung form; it could scarcely be comfortable. She'd continue north through the Papal States to Bologna, and travel then by canal to the Castello Estense in the duchy of Ferrara, there to join her husband, Alfonso d'Este. May she go in safety, thought Fra Ludovico. May her brother go in safety. May they go soon.

Vicente de Nevada appeared then, and Primavera with a peasant look of vengeance, scowling openly at the noble guests. She led young Bianca by the hand. Fra Ludovico straightened his spine and raised his voice. He began the reading of the Acts of the Apostles—chapter 5. "If this counsel or this work be of men, it will come to nought: But if it be of God, ye can't overthrow it."

Fra Ludovico was a simple man, a devout one, and he took his vocation seriously. He liked the message of the reading and said those verses again, this time in Italian, to make sure that the Borgias took note of what God was saying to them today.

He addressed the crucifix behind the altar, and when he turned around toward the penitents again, he saw the stolid Vicente weeping openly, and Bianca struggling out of Primavera's arms to go to him. "Shhh," scolded Primavera, casting Fra Ludovico an apologetic glance. But Bianca wouldn't be consoled. She wrestled free. She pitched herself against the master of Montefiore and stroked his black beard. "*Papà,*" she murmured, as if she knew what must lie ahead for them. "*Papà,* don't leave me. *Papà,* don't."

"Get her out of here," roared Cesare, "I'm trying to pray, damn it."

"I'll take her," said Lucrezia. She hadn't bothered to open her gradual anyway. "Come to me, *cherubina.*"

"Don't bother yourself," huffed Primavera, but she could get off the bench only with difficulty, as her arthritis was worst in the morning. By the time she struggled to her feet, Lucrezia Borgia had whipped Bianca into her arms and was hurrying up the nave with her.

"Stop, I'll manage her." Primavera's voice was like a bellows in a foundry, thunder trying to whisper.

"Silence," roared Cesare.

"I'll read from the Gospel of the Evangelist Saint Mark," said Fra Ludovico. "Everyone listen." But no one did. Bodyguards, nursemaid, Borgias, and the master of the house had all left the chapel mostly in fits of weeping and shouting. Fra Ludovico paused to try to collect some semblance of religious calm. But he found himself shouting out the open doors at them all:

"If this work be of men, it will come to nought."

The dispersals were brief. Up on his stallion leaped the Duc de Valentinois, Cesare Borgia, devotions behind him and the rapture of conquest ahead. Let Lucrezia to her marriage and her affairs, let Vicente to his mission, to achieve the mightiest token of God left in the world or to fail. It was in their hands now. For Cesare, back to his friend Niccolò Machiavelli, back to the summoning of armies and the conquest of states, back to the pleasures of Rome rotting in the summer sun. In the balance of his thighs against the horse, in the heft of his strong backside in the saddle, his eyes sweeping over the hills in the vaporish dawn, he felt himself imperious, invincible. Despite the cold, his cock poked inside his garments. Morning Mass always did this to him, and it was a good way to start a day of bloody bullying.

He left without good-byes to his sister or his host, his thoughts on the road ahead.

"He has provided you a purse for your needs," said Lucrezia to Vicente.

"He said a guard, a translator. The protection of my household," said Vicente. "That was his promise. You heard it."

"Would your daughter not be safer in a convent?" said Lucrezia.

"A child should have a parent and a home," said Vicente.

"I had a pope and a palace," Lucrezia countered. "I had no mother to speak of; the sisters of some tired order or other could do good work to care for your child."

"Cesare may break his promises," said Vicente coldly, "but I will hold you to yours, Lucrezia Borgia. You are no goose. You know I mean it."

He had her. She said, "I will keep my word, then. I will see that your household is maintained and your child protected."

"You take a good deal on yourself for your brother," said Vicente, trying to disguise his contempt.

Lucrezia drew herself up, unsure whether this was a compliment or not. "Don't double back in a week and hope to escape Cesare's notice. He'd only hack your daughter to pieces and send you on your way again."

"I'm on a fool's errand," said Vicente, "which will cost me my life."

"Look," said Lucrezia. She unlatched her gradual and beckoned Bianca forward to see. The illuminated pages fell open and the sudden sun made of the vellum a blinding platter. But even in all that shining, as if the very words of God were singing in light, there was a sequence of brighter shapes, like three drops of fire.

Vicente had to shade his eyes to see. He could barely tolerate the glare. They were ovate in shape, like the slits of skin that pucker about our eyes, and they seemed to blink like eyes too.

"They are three silver leaves from the branch of the Tree of Knowledge," said Lucrezia. "They were sent to Prince Dschem as proof that his campaign had worked, at least at first. They will have to serve as whatever proof you need, Vicente de Nevada."

"You don't believe there is a Tree of Knowledge," said Vicente, "and I don't either."

"I believe you have to go looking," she said. "Maybe you'll grow faith enough to find what the world has kept hidden all these centuries. Now, keep the memory of these in your heart and you won't fail for courage. Go on your way, and come back to us soon, and change the course of history."

"They look like small silver mirrors," said Bianca.

"That's all they look like," said Vicente. "The half-folded leaves of an olive tree in winter are as silver as this, and more useful."

Inside the chapel, struck by a resonant glory, Fra Ludovico began to sing the Credo in unum Deo.

"Take her away; I can't bear this," said Vicente. He wrapped himself in his cloak. While Primavera and Lucrezia Borgia snatched at Bianca's limbs, and she twisted and almost escaped, her father tucked the page of scribbled notes into his sleeve and mounted his steed. He turned the mare's head away from the chapel doors, and toward the smoky blue horizon of the north. He was halfway down the road at a clip, scattering the gossiping geese on their way to the millpond and giving the gooseboy a morning's labor to collect them, when Bianca broke free and began to follow.

The mare kicked up dust, and green growth cloaked the road as it turned into the woods. Her father had crossed the bridge. He was hidden from her, as he left her in her childhood forever, and disappeared into a quest. She followed him as far as the bridge—right to the middle of it—the very middle. And went no farther.

The vision in San Francesco

IN THE absence of his beloved María Inés—an absence whose pang changed in character but grew no weaker as the years passed—Vicente de Nevada found himself ever more readily spooning his daughter up to his breastplate with a seemly devotion.

His taking leave of her, therefore, cut him as deeply as it did her. He had the more capable constitution, and he could make of his backbone a ridge of steel, and manage not to turn around, nor to turn back, though her sobs echoed behind him. He breathed through his mouth to keep from crying out in reply. His nostrils clogged effeminately.

His hard-earned house, his precarious foothold, Montefiore, hovered in his thoughts. He didn't swing his shoulders to watch its roofs become lost in the green tide of uprushing foliage. Through all of Cesare Borgia's cutthroat campaigns to subdue the petty dukes of the

Papal States, Vicente de Nevada had managed to stay out of it. He hadn't ducked from commitment to a cause, but he had learned by virtue of his foreigner status that it was sensible to keep one's mouth shut when opinions were being catapulted about in a drunken rage.

Therefore he suffered gall of a bitter sort, to be wrestled at last from his home for a different kind of campaign.

I'm not religious enough to believe in the assistance of angels, he thought, using the edge of a sleeve to catch the runoff from his sinuses. Were angels available to come to my aid, I'd scarcely recognize them. They'd be smart to move on to campaigns where their assistance might be put to better use.

I'm not overly religious, but perhaps the Duc de Valentinois, a master in so many things, has selected his agent wisely. For if I can't be easily comforted by the notion of celestial helpers, nor can I read dark meanings into the writhings of coincidence. I can't turn back merely because my spirits are low. Human spirits sink, that is what they do. I must just press on and go where I'm told, and do what I can, and expect nothing, neither help nor praise.

And to protect my child, my Bianca, my dove with the cautious eyes, I must leave her to the whims of the world. There is no hope for her if I refuse; there is no trickery I could effect that Cesare and Lucrezia between them couldn't undo, or work against my favor.

What Cesare was capable of! His brutality was legendary, but legend is often just bombast, intended for effect. In Rome he had impressed his lovers of both sexes as a *torero,* bringing the enraged bull to a bloody end. In Florence the Borgias were pilloried, and Montefiore was near enough to Florence—on the border of the Toscana vineyards and olive groves—to pick up echoes of the latest rank opinions of Cesare. But in the long diagonal swath of duchies and strongholds that made up the Papal States, from Rome to the southwest up to northeasterly Rimini on the coast of the purple Adriatic, and then inland to Bologna, the roar of Cesare the Bull was fearfully deafening.

Eschewing the golden raiment of some princes, he entered his conquered cities dressed in black, escorted by a retinue of a hundred black-clad soldiers. A Gonfalonier and Captain-General of the Church, a murderous hot-blooded assassin, a vigilant general able to endure the merciless tides of fate, what wouldn't he do if he discovered Vicente had betrayed him? Cesare would murder his own mother if it might secure for him a better cut of meat at dinner.

No, there was nothing for Vicente to do but swing his steps toward the north and pretend at hope. And perhaps his sacrifice would convince the Fates or the saints or Fortuna or whoever held sway over human affairs to tender some mercy in his direction, and deliver to him the impossible hidden branch from the Tree of Knowledge.

He would go north. He would. Just not immediately.

That he was a skeptic in matters of faith didn't mean he was a fool. The irreverence and the upset in Fra Ludovico's chapel had unnerved Vicente, and he wouldn't undertake an impossible mission on behalf of his child's welfare without applying for holy protection. One needn't rely on the intercession of the saints, but nor should one appear to be uninterested in their favors, especially in what amounted to a sort of indentured thief's holy pilgrimage.

So Vicente, with heavy heart, took himself to the nearest place for succor and for supplies, the walled city of Arezzo.

He was late in arriving and had to bed with a band of soldiers outside the walls, for the city gates had closed for the night. The food was simple and the wine watered, but he slept without fear of brigands. He had dressed as a peasant, and the purse supplied by Lucrezia was well hidden on his person.

He heard mutterings against Cesare and ignored them; he heard soldiers praying to the spirit of Savonarola, and marveled anew at the belief that Italians sustained in the survival of the spirit after death.

In the morning, when the doors had been opened and the livestock driven out to grazing fields, Vicente joined the throng of peasants doing their common business in the sunny *campi* and the shadowy alleys. He made his way up the sloping city streets to where the city's main churches hunched under their impressive roofs and steeples.

The church of San Francesco seemed the quieter today, and there Vicente took up a post. Uncomfortable with Latin prayers, he petitioned for guidance and expected none. He was a poseur. Do I work with the intrigue of a Borgia, he asked, since I have unwillingly become the sinister arm of Cesare, or do I bring to this task my own cool head and sense of fair play? Do I march into this private battle with my daughter's face stitched in the mind's eye, or to conserve my strength do I retire thoughts of her until I return, if ever I should?

A monk with a rasping cough prostrated himself on the stone floor nearby, and began to moan for release of a sort Vicente guessed might not be entirely pietistic. Vicente moved away, moved forward toward the altar.

Someone was working on the floor of the square sanctuary, refitting pieces of tiling, and several candelabras on their own iron stems were planted like trees of light, to help the mason see. Vicente's eye was drawn to the walls, which had been ornamented with ranks of frescoed paintings. The colors were gaudy and not to Vicente's liking; the images seemed the story of a common people, without the glow of hammered gold to signify the sacred. But he found himself studying the images as if for clues on what to do, how to behave. Perhaps, even, why—why bother to go forward at all, when all he loved was being left behind.

"It's a story of the Church," said the mason after a while, in a rural accent Vicente had to work to understand.

"Everything is a story of the Church," said Vicente cautiously. It didn't do to be rude to anyone, especially in a house of God.

"No, no, you mistake my meaning," said the mason. "I've been here for days and the good brothers have read it to me. The walls are divided into panels, do you see?—and if you follow along, and look from here to here, and then drop your eyes and look again, a story is told, scene by scene. It's the truth about the Cross of Gesù. Can you make it out? There at the top, our father Adam is dying, and the Tree of Life is figured. It's from that tree that the Cross was cut. After the death of Our Lord, the Cross was lost, but then it was found, and some descendant of our brother Lazarus, being dragged along to his grave, was raised from the dead. Raised up."

The mason grinned; what teeth he had were brown. "I love that notion. I would relish the raising of my brother, Severino, so that I could explain the better why I murdered him in the first place, and then do it again."

Vicente said, "Do you believe in such stories?"

The mason said, "I believe in the floor. I put it in place and I walk on it. Faith is a floor. If you don't work at making it for yourself, you have nothing to walk on."

Vicente didn't want to enter a discussion about faith. He looked at the painting of the Tree of Knowledge.

"Even the mighty Valentino, bull of the Borgias, came here to pray," said the mason. "The decorations are not all that old—within my father's lifetime, I think—and they have their own lure. I've heard tell that Cesare prayed here. When the mightiest of Roman families still relies on the floor of faith, what does that tell you?"

"That his father is the Pope," said Vicente noncommittally.

"His father didn't paint this wall of faith, nor pay for it," said the mason. "Take of it what you will. Even the Turkish infidel, friend to the Borgia, gaped at its beauty, they say. Its beauty makes one believe."

What I believe, thought Vicente, is that Cesare Borgia came here, to pray and to plan his campaigns, and that Prince Dschem accompanied him. I believe that the Prince noticed Cesare's interest in the story picture here. I believe he used this story to his own advantage at the very end of his life, to try to secure his own rescue. He invented a fable to appeal to Cesare's superstitious nature, and now I'm chained to it.

But then what of those three silver eyes of God in Lucrezia Borgia's gradual? Very special work by Byzantine craftsmen? Or something more?

I'll take of it what I can, thought Vicente. He looked at a square of wall in which a king was sleeping against soft pillows as an angel descended in rosy light over the undefended shoulders and unwitting expression of guards inadequate to their task. How lucky to have a seraphic assistant. But if I'm to have a vision, I must make it myself. I'm neither a sleeping king nor a working mason, and a farmer has little use of floors.

He looked at the painted scenes some more. He saw a city in terra-cotta here, a prophet there. Three men hoisted the vertical post of the cross, and the forward man put such muscle into the task that his genitals had become loose from their bindings and hung in undignified view. The horses were ready to stamp and snort, and one could almost smell their shit. The lances raised in battle were a thicket of strokes against a defeated sky. Here was an angel in an annunciation— why would no angel ever announce a message to Vicente? Here was a battle in terrible crowded circumstance—a battle as conducted on a loggia!—and here was Lazarus again, looking well rested enough. Here was a dwarf with his hand on his hip. Learning a new stature as he gazed soberly upon the cross.

It's all we can do, thought Vicente, to look, and invent our own stature, and see if we can measure up to it. Faith may cloud our eyes or open them; who can say?—but it's up to us to invent our intentions, and live up to them, or fail at the duty.

I intend to save my daughter, he said to himself. With faith or against it, that is what I intend. I have no papal father, like Cesare, no army behind me, no coffers to plunder. I have only my sense of that family, and the way that they turn, they turn; they always turn. If I'm not back quickly, and successfully, they will turn, against my Bianca if they can't reach me.

What miserable leverage Vicente had over Lucrezia would count for nothing in a contest with her brother. There was no angel available to guard Bianca, and Vicente required protection more rigorous than a groveling priest and a cursing cook could provide. Cesare lived by love and war. Since Vicente couldn't woo the man he'd have to pose a threat. Would that he had access to his own army of conscripts!

Well, who's to say he didn't? He looked at the armies in the painting again, and thought: I'll borrow you, or your kin.

He began to devise a protection, to invent in fiction what his luckless life had never provided him. A family, an army, a threat. Now: out to the *campo,* and surely in one of the narrow *vicoli* he could find a scribe for hire who could loan him a quill and ink, vellum and wax? And see that an epistle be delivered? Vicente would use the best of his coin to ensure the best product, and live on scavengings, and walk instead of ride, and do without lodging at inns. His trip would take longer, but, please God, his daughter would be safer.

Please God, that is, should there be such an Element in the heavens.

He turned toward the task and walked out of the door, alone.

The mason shrugged and went back to his task. He repaired the work of fifteen centuries before him as best he could. A floor of faith wasn't impervious to the effects of age.

The mason might have seen a shadow on the floor, had he had faith of a different sort. Indeed, he rubbed his eyes and decided he was tired, for though the candles in the iron trees seemed to burn as brightly as before, he was no longer as clear-eyed as he had been when he started an hour or two ago. In truth, the dwarf was there, lingering. He could catch up to Vicente in a moment. He wasn't much good as an angel and he didn't know why he was compelled to accompany the man on his quest. But the dwarf planted his feet on the floor of the church and gazed upon Piero della Francesca's painting of a dwarf witnessing a holy moment in the cycle of the True Cross. Scarcely fifteen feet away, a Lazarus was ready to rub his shoulders and work out the kinks in his muscles. The dwarf in the painting was looking at the Cross, but he was also looking across the span of holy painted space at the man raised from the dead.

Dwarves made of rock have no capacity for faith, but that doesn't mean they have no appetite for it. Staring at the dwarf painted into the plaster, the other dwarf, the eighth dwarf, shed a richer shadow, and the mason, cursing mildly at what age was doing to his eyes, went to take his lunch early.

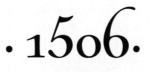

·1506·

Bianca awake

ASTORM had come up from the south, a tarantella of wind and surging smells. Apple trees lost their limbs, and the cow byre its roof, and the cows could be heard singing in plainsong throughout the night. By morning the roads were slick with the fallen fruit of olive trees, and smelled like a fine breakfast.

Fra Ludovico had had a vision in the middle of the night. He had thought it was dyspepsia at first, as he had met with a sausage of suspicious vintage, and his stomach had been shouting at him. But despite bouts of digestive grief Fra Ludovico had kept sinking into a velvety somnolence, pitched between sleep and a wakesome drowsing, and in that state of half-here-half-there, he had seen the girl stepping on clouds of carven ivory, for all the world like Saint Catherine of Siena in her mortal stoles and immortal graces. But she stepped toward a cliffedge, and seemed not to realize it; and though the priest tried to cry out, his voice—with the persistent laryngitis that afflicted him in dreams—was feeble. Too small a thread of warning spun out. She didn't hear. She walked on at her own pace toward a danger.

He stood, relieved his bladder, picked a shred of gristle from his teeth, and noticed, in the yard below, that visitors had arrived under cover of darkness. Sometime between midnight and dawn, during the hours pertinent to the sanguine humor.

The prelate was feeling his age. The years following the departure of his master hadn't been easy. First, Lucrezia Borgia had dismissed the overseer that Don Vicente had assigned to watch after things. Dismissed, or removed from the district, it was unclear which, but in any case the hapless local governor was gone as gone. Fra Ludovico had little practice in standing up to strong beautiful women—not for nothing had he fled into the skirts of the Church instead of the more profane variety—but for all his timidity, his fondness for the true daughter of the house prevailed. He wouldn't leave Bianca alone to suffer at the hands of la Borgia, now the Duchessa de Ferrara. If suffer it would be: and he thought it would.

Well, who could doubt it, really? As far off the public way as Montefiore was, the rumors from Rome arrived, nonetheless. The glamorous Lucrezia, married first to Giovanni Sforza of Milan, didn't demur when her powerful father and brother declared Sforza to be impotent. The courts opined: *virga intacta*. End of marriage—naturally: Sforza had proven too unimportant a match for the Borgias' expanding ambitions. And what about the rumors that Cesare had dared murder a Spaniard whose amorous interest in his sister rivaled his own? Was Perotto Calderon's corpse found bobbing in the Tiber? Well, whose corpse, given enough time, wasn't?

In the way of things, Lucrezia had made a second marriage, to Alfonso of Aragon, Duc de Bisceglie, of the family of the King of Naples. All lutes and sonnets and garlands of posies, right? And Lucrezia was said to care for him, in her limited way, and to care for the notion of living by the sea even more. But a seasoned garrotter broke into the house one night—bad luck, wasn't it?—and Lucrezia once again found herself free to marry to her family's advantage. In his professional capacity Fra Ludovico cherished the sacrament of matrimony as a spiritual union, but he knew that in this time of internecine struggles it wasn't uncommon for a man or a woman to marry several times over. It took a highly cultured woman to manage to marry more advantageously each time her husband, through murder or carelessness or the decisions of the courts, happened to be disposed of.

All powerful families have their detractors. Fra Ludovico had no way of knowing which reports were true and which were slanderous gossip circulated by the competitive Roman families or by the vengeful Sforzas, whose reputation had been besmirched. Over the past few years Fra Ludovico had carefully remade himself from a solemn cleric into a harmless, beneficent idiot. It was a charade of witlessness designed to protect his position. And so carefully conceived. He knew, for instance, that Lucrezia Borgia had a delicate constitution and rank odors offended her. So whenever she was in residence, he would be sure to traipse through the ripest of cow muck and track it in onto Montefiore's clean, strawstrewn floors. He spilt milk on his garments and left it there to sour. When she confronted him in his disgrace, he affected a beatific smile and quoted Scipture in a raggle-taggle Latin. *Omnia alterans,* he would say in response to any criticism. She was educated classically, better than he was, but he needn't worry about getting his references straight. His errors served to illustrate his general befuddlement.

With Primavera aging ever more decrepitly, Fra Ludovico felt he had to take larger responsibility. He liked to think, in his careful campaign, that he was cannier than a Borgia. Helpfully, his strategies also afforded him extra hours of napping and woolgathering, which conserved his strength for what he feared might be mortal combat someday.

Of course, Primavera did most of the work of caring for Bianca. The girl slept on a rush pallet next to Primavera's, and helped with the household chores. The local maids came less often, as there was little entertaining to speak of, and Bianca and Primavera managed what domestic work there was.

As to the farmwork—such was the awe in which the Borgias were held that the *contadini* kept to their schedule of tasks without much supervision. Yearly the olive trees were cut back just far enough to allow a bird to pass through the main branches without its wing tips brushing the leaves. During the spring, the fields were planted on the seventeenth day after the full moon. Now that Lago Verde had a better channel for drainage, worries about *mal aria*—bad air—could be countered by a more conscientious attention to the letting out and the stopping up of the water flow.

Beyond, tenant farmers harvested the apples and grapes and olives, and hayed when haying was on, and slaughtered a spring lamb or two and an autumn hog, and a goose for the Christmas season. One could hardly have imagined a landlord was needed, so practiced were olive trees and ewes and meadows and apple orchards at producing, without instruction, their signature offerings. Or maybe the threat of Lucrezia Borgia's inevitable return bullied the farm into behaving itself: that's what Primavera said.

Bianca lived in her house like a child on an island—not quite alone, but a priest and a cook for company weren't enough, either. She was about eleven years old now. She begrudged the sacrifice she'd been required to make, but she wasn't a fool: she could tell that showing contempt to Primavera or Fra Ludovico would be misdirected. She misbehaved mildly, as was fitting for her age.

She dreamed of leaving, but she had too little exposure to the world to imagine where to go. And her father had made her promise. Would the terms of that promise ever expire? What if she were as old as—oh, a village maiden, or la Borgia, or Primavera even, and her father had never come back? Would she be bound to live and die on the hilltop all because she'd once given her word?

The notion of disobedience occurs, in time, to everyone. One summer day when the sky featured blazing, portent cloudscapes,

Bianca decided she had to leave Montefiore, she had to break her promise and run away. If she could do nothing else, she'd begin a pilgrimage to find out what had happened to her father: to rescue him if she could, to mourn and pray over his grave if she must.

She got as far as the bridge at the bottom of the property, where the cultivation ended and the woods began, on slopes descending too steeply for agriculture.

She paced noisily on the well-worn boards to the middle of the bridge. She would gain the other side today, and her thumping was to drum courage in her.

She stopped, though; the echo of her footsteps seemed a warning. She remembered her father's story about a mudcreature below the bridge. She leaned on the stone railings to look. "Have you something to say to me?" she said. "If you're going to protest, at least do it in person so I can try to argue you down."

The fact that the mudcreature didn't speak didn't mean it wasn't there, of course. Silence can be tactical. Even God used silence as a strategy.

She looked. She peered further, both into the shadows and into the surface of the stream. The water today was high, but running slowly, and the surface reflective, trees and sky and rocks shivered into interlacing tendrils of green and blue and brown. It was so easy to imagine what might lurk beneath the gloss of the reflected world, a gnarled, hairy hand flexing to grab her ankle.

"Gesù," she said, disgusted at herself. She couldn't make herself pass. Not yet. Sometime when the bridge wouldn't thump at her, when the water wouldn't wink at her: then she would cross it. But today—and in several other tries that summer—she failed, and kept failing. Was it her promise to her father that waited under the bridge, with its hairy hand?

A Borgia entourage had arrived in the dark. A small one, only four horses. Lucrezia made her breakfast from the house stores and supplies she carried with her. Currants from Corinth, bread in honey, a glass of wine imported from Crete. She made a lazy inspection of the farm—the accounts, the state of the orchards, the gooseboy and his geese, the buildings and outbuildings, and in the evening she came to a conclusion. She decided that Bianca no longer needed a nurse, and Primavera could be let go.

"Go where?" said the cook, grinning as toothily as her teeth would allow.

"Go. Retire. Haven't you some feeble spawn to take you in? They've foisted you off on us for far too long. Go back to them and require that they obey the Fourth Commandment, and honor you, whether you deserve it or no."

"There's no one," said Primavera.

"No one who will admit to it," murmured Lucrezia. "Who could blame them?"

"I lost both sons to Cesare's wars," said Primavera pointedly. "The ill-fated attack on Forlì wasn't good for our family line. They were stupid and cloddish but they were my sons, and they're gone. My only grandson is a hunter, and seeing what conscription did to his father and uncle, he keeps out of the way of the *condottieri*. He lives by his wits, no place special, and I can't go roost in a tree with him. I haven't got the hips for it. I should mention that he has no interest in displaying his handsome head on a stake on the walls of some castle Cesare wants to occupy, and therefore the lad uses his head, unlike others in his family."

"So he's off and gone," mused Lucrezia, in a pleasant threatening way.

Primavera was on her mettle. "As it happens, he's here today; when I saw that you'd arrived in the nighttime I sent for him, so he could provide us some meat for the table. He's here to protect me should I need it."

"You're not listening," said Lucrezia. "Go throw yourself on the mercies of the almshouse. Throw yourself off the precipice behind the apple orchard. I don't care. Just stuff your personal items in the cleft of your bosom and take yourself elsewhere."

"My knees won't manage the slope anymore," said Primavera. "I have to stay at Montefiore because I can't maneuver myself down the hill."

"Shall I arrange to have you rolled out in a barrel?"

"I'm sure you could," said Primavera. "There are some wine casks in the village large enough. But you'd have to get them up here first. Now, will there be anything else, Donna Lucrezia? I've the girl's supper to get."

"Send her to me," said Lucrezia.

"She has her supper to eat," said Primavera. "I'll send her to you when she's fed."

"You won't correct me, " said Lucrezia. "You won't dare."

"I beg your forgiveness with all my heart, and trust in your legendary mercy," said Primavera dryly. She took herself off to the kitchen, histrionically wheezing on the stairs.

From the piano nobile Lucrezia listened to the sounds of cooking below. Primavera called Bianca to come clean her hands and wipe her face. Then she bellowed for Fra Ludovico to come bless the damned meal before it got cold. When the meal was over Primavera bullied Bianca out of the rags and aprons of her everyday wear, and into better clothes, and rubbed the Sign of the Cross on her forehead and pressed a leaf of basil into her collar. Then Bianca was released to become the audience of the de facto mistress of Montefiore, Lucrezia Borgia, Duchessa de Ferrara.

She held herself to one side of the door before she entered.

She wasn't a saint stepping on ivory clouds, no matter how Fra Ludovico dreamed of her. Nor was she quite the *bambina* that Primavera remembered. She was at that age of halfling, that moment of sheerest youth that drives elders wild. She was Susanna at her ablutions, the more beautiful in her allure because the more innocent of it. Her bosom hadn't swollen yet. She was as sleek as a kouros oiled for the games of wrestling in old Athens or Sparta, which Hellenic sculptors had memorialized in marble to emblemize human potential. One had been dug up in Ravenna recently and Lucrezia had bought it for her palazzo.

"Come in," said Lucrezia Borgia.

Bianca stepped into the room. When her trips between Ferrara and Rome allowed it, Lucrezia Borgia stopped to supervise the development of Bianca's poise and manners. Bianca couldn't quite remember the arrangement by which she'd come to be a ward of the Duchessa, but it had to do with her father's departure, so Bianca had cultivated a habit of caution.

Still, Lucrezia was so glamorous, so civilized, and spoke in such a dulcet hush. Bianca had to lean close to hear, and closer still. "Come in, come in! Forward into the lamplight. The room is gloomy. I take it the old onion has fed you your supper?"

Bianca nodded.

"Turn, so I might look upon you," she said. "And see how God has formed you in these months since my last examination. What sort of vestment is that robe; does the peasant *nonna* think you are a giantess?"

Primavera had wrapped Bianca in a crimson cloak far too large for her.

"This robe belonged to my mother," said Bianca. "That's what my father used to say." Feeling a fool, she shucked off the heavy garment, and laid it in folds carefully over the arm of a chair. Then she turned back to Lucrezia. She held her shoulders high but tucked her chin into the collar of her dress. Her eyes stayed trained upon the patterned carpet of red and blue that Lucrezia preferred to walk upon instead of to hang against the cold stone walls of the house for warmth.

"You chose to wear a green like a Frankish bottle of may wine, and a white cascade of lace through the collar," said Lucrezia.

"Primavera chooses my clothes," murmured Bianca. "I don't care about what I wear."

"Nonetheless, you're well clad. Clever fingers have stitched that bodice to show you off well. But you don't observe the sumptuary laws. You are above your station. And the redness of that huge cloak!

A laugh. Still, you're a pretty enough child, Bianca."

Pretty enough for what, thought Bianca, but she said nothing.

"Attend to me when I speak, my girl," said Lucrezia. "It offends me for you to ignore my remarks."

"I'm here to do your bidding," said Bianca, as evenly as she could given that her knees, as usual, were knocking. "But I don't know what you wish."

"You will be a woman one day," said Lucrezia. "You need guidance in the womanly arts of conversation, negotiation, deception, prayer, and the management of a private purse. Please, take your place in this chair. I will have a few words with you as a mother might do with a daughter."

Bianca sat, and the silence was profound and grew somewhat tense, as if Lucrezia was studying her and finding her wanting. Perhaps she was intended to speak? "I know little about Donna Lucrezia," Bianca said at last. "I don't know if you have a daughter."

"I have you," said Lucrezia, "which is as close as I come. There are other children, boys, here and there; and at a masquerade ball at Lent the sad miscarriage of my new child began. I'm bereft. This causes me to move from place to place."

She looked less bereft than bored. Bianca felt her skin prickle. "The loss of a child must be a pitiful thing," she said guardedly, but with feeling too, as she couldn't help but think about the loss of her father, and how such a condition became constant, like an appendage or a tumor. Hello, this is I, and these my arms and legs, which are useful, and this inconvenient hump is my sorrow, which is less than useful, but I've learned how to hump it about with me, so pay it no mind.

"I should have liked a daughter," said Lucrezia, "but perhaps it's for the best." She turned and gazed at the mirror that hung over the mantel ledge. When she continued, it was in a voice as if she were speaking to herself, to control her passions: the undertones trembled. "When my father died three years ago, and the triple crown of Rome passed first to Pius III, the House of Borgia was protected, and Cesare's career as the temporal arm of the Papal States in Italy seemed secure. But the new prelate saw fit only to live the month, and no amount of judicious payment could effect another election that favored our line, so under the reign of Julius II we have been hounded. Hounded! And much of our family's wealth has been appropriated. They say Cesare has been secreted out of the country, hoping to appeal to the King of France for the rights to the duchy of Valentinois."

Bianca heard the cautionary phrasing. "They say this? Is it true?"

Her question brought Lucrezia sharply back. "You aren't as empty-headed as you appear," she said. "Did I bring myself to murmur in your presence? Oh, I did, but no matter, for you are as bound to this crop of house on this old Etruscan hill as your feeble nursemaid is. Don't look in the corner of the room, my dear, but someone is here, secretly and without defenses."

Despite herself, Bianca's head swiveled, and she saw that a mattress had been set up in the shadows. Coverlets were mounded upon it. A man was just then propping himself up on his elbow, blinking.

For an unholy instant she thought it might be her father, and she started with an expression of joy.

"Such a welcome," said the man—Cesare Borgia, for it was he—and Bianca fell back, chastened. Cesare had seen the involuntary gasp of a smile, the hopeful eyes, and he worked himself out of his stupor and sat up. "Who is this young thing then?"

"I told you. She's the child of Don Vicente de Nevada. She's the only one of the family left behind, now that the mother is dead this past decade, and the father lost on your fool's errand."

Lost? Lost?

"You said she was a child," said Cesare, watching Bianca appreciatively. "You said she was still bound in a baby's apron."

"Well, she's grown then," said Lucrezia crossly. "I forgot that children grow."

"What a natural mother you are." He looked at Bianca with an expression of sweetness. "Come here, then, my dove. Sit beside me."

His sister snapped at him. "We're after something other than succor. Cesare, remember your aims."

"There's more than one way to tease a secret out of a young thing," he said. "A soldier can be hung in a cage in the sun till he confesses, or he can be wooed into submission if he's pretty enough. Come here, come here, my little mouse."

Bianca knew enough not to come forward. "A mouse doesn't accept invitations from a cat," she said politely. "A mouse wouldn't know how to converse with a cat."

"She's got the trim of your sails!" Lucrezia hooted with unprincipled glee.

"I'm not well," said Cesare, "I need some tending. Be a good girl."

Bianca wasn't a reticent child when it came to pirouetting about the farm buildings. She played with the gooseboy and teased her old nursemaid, and endured Fra Ludovico's tender smiles and muttered benisons. But she thought that the man who smiled at her from a half-raised position was less cat than panther. Clearly he wasn't well, and hadn't been for some time. He must have paid for his adventures with a burden of infirmity taxing his soldier's body. The skin fell on his cheeks and his hair had no gloss. But the panther inside Cesare's exhausted form was still healthy and handsome. It was the panther that frightened Bianca. She stayed where she was.

Some small trinket on the desk snapped in Lucrezia's hand—perhaps a comb made of tortoiseshell. She flung its pieces in a glittering handful at the mirror, and the tines clicked like toenails against the glass. "Brother, you're hounded like a fox, and as near to cornered as you have yet been. You're broken down with the ailment that killed our father, or some version of the French disease calculated to rot your nose off your face. You've squandered the strength you commanded. Don't bring this desperate campaign down to a seduction."

"I'll find out what we need to know," he said to his sister. "In my weakened form I can still break your neck, Donna Lucrezia, should I decide."

But Bianca could tell that Lucrezia held sway over her brother. He brought himself up to a sitting position, steadying himself on the cot with both hands like an aged man. The panther in him retreated, though it seemed to Bianca perhaps more dangerous for it to be hidden. She had a sense of being awake to peril in a way she had never known, and only because of how Lucrezia and Cesare spoke with each other. A peril as evident in their courtesy as in their sharpness.

"State your business to her, now that I'm awake enough to listen," he said.

"Very well," Lucrezia answered. "Bianca, will you sit?"

"I'd rather stand," she said. Children didn't regularly sit in the presence of their betters—primarily so that they could get a head start should they have to run for safety.

"Sit," said Cesare. Bianca sat, though on the very edge of the stool he had indicated. Her heels drummed on the floor.

"I've made it my business to oversee affairs at Montefiore," said Lucrezia in a formal tone, as if addressing an assembly of princes of the Church. "I've been tireless in turning over the papers involved in your father's ownership of this establishment. There are tithes to be paid to the Church, there are costs to the guards who patrol the valley below, and keep you safe from invasion and pillage. All this I've done out of love for your father."

I doubt that, Bianca thought. In what ways could you love my father? For one thing, he's been missing for half my life.

"It turns out that some time ago, blithering Fra Ludovico had a letter from Don Vicente. It was secreted into his book of devotions, and when confronted with its presence he didn't seem to know what it meant. The first part was in Italian, and directed the cleric to maintain the letter in a safe place and present it to you when you were older. The letter then continued in Spanish. It was addressed to you. Have you read it?"

"I'm schooled in my letters," Bianca admitted, "but not so that I can read in the language of my grandsires."

"I thought not," said Lucrezia smugly. "Shall I read it to you, translating as I go?"

"If it's a letter from my father to me, perhaps I should wait until I've learned enough Spanish to read it for myself."

"How ungrateful," snapped Lucrezia. "I can understand how Fra Ludovico might have erred, in that he has become a halfwit; but for a young person you seem to have a head on your shoulders. Fra Ludovico understands no more Spanish than you do. Suppose the letter were a request for help? Suppose your father has fallen into the hands of brigands, or is wasting in an Ottoman prison? Suppose he knows a way you could help release him? Would you have him wait another six months until I could find a tutor for you, and then another six months beyond that until you'd learned enough to attempt a translation? Your father's face might have become mantled with mildew by that time."

Bianca flushed, knowing this could be true. Her lungs kicked in her, as if she were underwater; her vision watered and caused the room to stew. "If you must, then."

"I don't offer because I *must*. It's nothing to me," said Lucrezia. "You must petition courteously if you require my services."

"Sister," growled Cesare, but she cocked her wrist at him as if to say *This is my hand to play; let me do it as I like.*

"Please, Donna Borgia," said Bianca then, wringing her hands together. "I most humbly entreat you to read my father's letter aloud."

"Very well," said Lucrezia. "Since you've asked so nicely."

She unfolded an uneven scrap of parchment that had become creased from being stored between the leaves of a breviary. "So it begins, Most beloved Bianca," she said.

"I write in haste to put down a few details of your family of which you, as a child, have not been made aware. My work in the service of Il Valentino takes me far from you, and I must serve my Duke or risk upsetting what remains of our happy life as a traveling family who has found a welcoming home in the hinterlands of central Italy.

"I cannot know what fate will befall me as I march to a most unpredictable goal. However, should I fail to return before you have reached your maturity, I want you to know that there is help for you abroad. If famine or plague or the danger of war threatens your safety at Montefiore, you should make all haste to your mother's family home in Navarre. There a treasury is reserved for our family's use, and petition can be made to draw upon it once you have reached your womanly estate.

"If, however, news should come to the Castedo family of Navarre or to my kin, the de Nevada family in Aragon, that harm has befallen you, don't worry: our cousins will mount an expedition and pitch battle against your enemies. Those countrymen of ours, the Borgias, have talents in intrigue that they didn't invent wholecloth. The de Nevadas and Castedos could match them in cunning and outstrip them in cruelty. So let these words give you some comfort, that though I've become a simple farmer in Italy, there are impressive resources at my call—and at yours. Apply to the reigning Bishop of Navarre for help, and he will not fail you.

"I've arranged passage cross country to Città di Castello, and I start as much before dawn as a crowing cockerel can wake me. I do this with the knowledge that every step advancing me toward my goal is a step I will be eager to retrace to come home to you. Be good, my sweet Bianca, and keep your father in your prayers and in your heart. Be mindful that only love could make me leave you, and if the Love that governs our days is merciful, it will be love that returns us to each other too. If not in these days of our lives, then in the long golden day without sunset, in heaven."

Lucrezia cleared her throat. "How very tender. Your father's humor is melancholic as well as phlegmatic."

Bianca couldn't speak for the tears in her throat. After all these years, to hear her father's words. *Papà!* Though unschooled in treachery, she knew enough to guess that the Borgias wouldn't hesitate to fabricate a letter from her father if they thought they could gain by it. But this was her father's voice, without compromise, without doubt.

The rawness of his grief at parting from her brought her own loneliness back to her, and she wept silently but openly, as if he had only left that morning, and all the intervening years that had passed so far were yet to be endured. And who knew how many were left, before the reunion in heaven or on this wretched earth?

"How recently has this arrived?" asked Bianca. "May I go ask Fra Ludovico?"

"He's dotty as a dormouse," said Lucrezia. "I asked him the same question and he answered, *tomorrow, or the week after, I'm not sure.*"

"But do you have any word from my father?" Suddenly she was emboldened to ask. "On your behalf he left on a campaign: what you have heard?"

"Nothing, but silence means nothing in itself," said Lucrezia, turning a common viperous thought of Bianca's into a posy.

"Do you have knowledge of this Navarrese Bishop?" said Cesare.

"You ask me questions and you don't answer mine," she said.

"Let me suppose you didn't hear what I said. Do you have knowledge of this Navarrese Bishop?"

"I don't know a Tuscan cock from an Umbrian hen," said Bianca desperately.

"What is meant, herein, by 'womanly estate'?" mused Lucrezia.

"He must mean that a dowry, or a debt to be discharged can be effected when Bianca comes to marrying age, of course," said Cesare. "How old are you, little mouse?"

"She is a child still, with the chest of a boy," scoffed Lucrezia.

"You were engaged to be married when you were eleven," Cesare reminded his sister. "That disgusting *cherubino* from Valencia."

"I was the daughter of Cardinal Rodrigo Borgia," she snapped. "I'd have been engaged in utero, had it benefited the family fortunes, as you know very well. Despite Vicente's implication of wealth and connections, the de Nevada family is neither powerful nor clever. This letter may be a ruse to confound us."

"We weren't meant to see it," said Cesare.

"Of course we were. It's written in Spanish. Who else at Montefiore would have been able to read it?"

"It's written in Spanish to keep news of the family wealth away from prying eyes. Else the threat of kidnapping and ransom might apply."

"Let me think. It could be a ploy. On the other hand, the threat of retaliation by loyal cousins . . . I never knew de Nevada well, but he didn't seem the scheming sort. Was he clever enough to plan a strategic defense of his daughter like this?"

"Was he?" Bianca was affronted. "You mean *is* he." She didn't know or care whether her father was clever; she cared that he still *was*.

"The first rule of success, my dear sister, a rule you should have mastered by now, is not to underestimate the deviousness of your enemies."

"Oh, but who is an enemy?" asked Bianca, meaning it rhetorically: Certainly not us: we've given our father's years to some campaign of yours! Some years, but not a life.

"You're not an enemy, you're a bother. We've learned nothing from you. Run on now, and take the ridiculous cloak with you."

"Oh, let the mouse stay," said Cesare.

Shades of rock

THE YEARS peeled slowly off, one by one, or perhaps dozens at a time. Vicente had lost the ability to read time from the spatter of light the high window allowed to trail across the wall of his cell. Some days he couldn't imagine whether it was starlight or sunlight, and other days—or nights—he felt that each individual stone was outlined with a pressure of silver edging, as if its crystals were yearning to make useful luminescence for him.

He knew that some days must be wintry, for a fine snow managed to filter in through the slitted aperture, and failed to melt for hours on end, but lay like the ghost of a carpet for him to regard. His fingers ached and stung, and then lost feeling. Other days he might catch the sharp sweet smell of a newly cut meadow. He was most aware in the spring, for once a year the monks butchered a lamb, likely for the paschal celebration, and in a matter of hours what started as the stench of searing flesh and bubbling blood became the aroma of choicest meat.

Always, there were the sounds of bells, as the monasteries across the rough forested hills of Agion Oros tolled their times to God and signaled news of their continued existence to one another.

Occasionally the sound of winds, or of distant birds of the sea, spiraled down to his celibate ears.

Once he heard a donkey bray, and he laughed for a while, at the gait of its voice picking its ungainly way through the air.

Never, though, did he hear the monks at prayer or at chant. Indeed, he rarely saw more than two of them at a time. Whenever the door of his prison opened, two new monks brought in his food, or clean clothes occasionally, and swapped a fresh empty bucket for the stinking fly-struck bucket of shit he had prepared for them. Maybe the monks were on a rotation, but there were too many of them for Vicente to identify by sight or voice. They all wore black robes, and the black hair on their chins raveled halfway down their chests identically. Every now and then one might smile a bit more kindly than the others, as he delivered bread and vegetables in broth, or a pastry with pistachios and honey, or a flagon of cool welcome water. But Vicente had not learned enough Greek to be able to converse. Besides, the monks were either living under vows of silence or, without a woman leading them in the arts of conversation, they had lost the capacity to chatter.

Whatever the unit of measure, hours or days or years, too many had passed since Vicente had left the high sanctuary of Montefiore in search of the branch from the Tree of Knowledge. The days on the farm in central Italy glowed in his memory with a rosy impossibility: Certainly olive trees could never have held such silvery light in their leaves, of an April morning; sheep had never lowed like lullabies, had they? And there had never been a María Inés, she of the delicate lemon flower scent, the alabaster breasts, the smile that broadened when she threw her head back in laughter. Of the haven she might have provided in the marriage bed, Vicente was certain he was imagining it from delirium born of loneliness. He was no longer convinced that woman couldn't possibly have been created so accessible, so responsive, so convenient: even God couldn't have imagined such a perfection.

Vicente's recollection of his wife's sex was clouded in his eyes, perhaps because his own sex, these years, had no memory of itself; he resentfully carried nothing but a small cold snail between his thighs, useless but for a dribbly piss. He wouldn't be surprised one day to wake up and learn that what had once passed as his genitals had crawled away in the middle of the night to bury themselves in a hole somewhere and rot in peace.

He wished that he and his wife had had children. How much more possible it might be to endure the passage of eternity if he knew that María Inés had born him a son or a daughter, or several. What a refreshing picture, to imagine somewhere in Italy or Spain a crowd of de Nevada children, cavorting in sunlight. But he knew that this couldn't have happened, for the hole in his heart around the notion of children was so severely black that he couldn't even venture to consider the subject directly. He could only deduce a full and permanent loss in this matter.

But perhaps God had selected him for this assignment: to live a half-death in a holy prison on a holy mountain, among masculine people and creatures and flies and rocks. (Where the spring lamb might come from every year, in a population said to be entirely of rams, was a holy mystery.)

Vicente had followed what guidance had been given him, long ago, and he had worked his way through the Papal States, north by Ferrara, up into the Venetian marches, and then by boat across the Adriatic to Dalmatia. For protection from brigands he'd met up with a caravan of merchants, and proceeded to Montenegro, Rumelia.

By quick degrees the world had grown more barbarian in its inhospitable strangeness. When he ventured beyond the reaches of his adopted tongue, he occasionally could find a tradesman or a sailor with enough Spanish to indicate where he was, but once he left the coast and began the overland trek through Macedonia and Thessaly he had little to trust in but his wits. He avoided wolves and thieves in the wilderness; he swam through a flash flood without drowning. Once he considered murder, when he got so hungry he thought his stomach would begin to digest his own heart for nourishment, but God forbade murder. Believing less in God than in God's laws, he went hungry until the hunger was slaked by Fortune, who gave of her excess a handful of nuts or a slow-running chicken.

The landscape became harsher. Deep forests alternated with stony hardscrabble slopes from which the ancient pagan Greeks had harvested their fulsome stories and upon which their descendants seemed to be dying of starvation. By and by, as those weeks of travel passed in the wheeling pinions of categorizable hours—dusk, dawn, and the hundred permutations between, how lovely, how luxurious, how fatally addictive, the passage of daily light—Vicente moved further into the realm of strange myth, away from the cycles of his adopted *patria,* his farm and home, and toward the strained attenuated life of mad monks and wild fire-breathing boars and the goal of the fruit of the Garden of Eden.

And he'd found what he was sent to find, and been discovered in the process, and tossed like a bug into a hole, and he waited to die, and wanted to die, and he didn't die. So was there a God or wasn't there?

He took out his recollections from time to time, revered them as private landscapes to which he could repair. The spread of his holdings at Montefiore, the far more distant Aragon of his childhood, these sites were available at will. How kind, the thought of a slope of pink and white blossoming almond groves in an Aragonese spring! But his memories seemed unpopulated. So he relied for mental exercise and diversion on the recalling of his approach and apprehension at Teophilos.

As Cesare Borgia had said, the long promontory of Agion Oros was almost an island. Using a sack of florins, the value of which Greek peasants easily recognized, Vicente de Nevada had induced a pair of brothers with a fishing boat to set out from Ouranopolis and take him down the west side of the peninsula. For a day they drifted and fished. The brothers cared little for their passenger's intentions—they threw bread at him, and a fleece when a wind came up, but generally they were happy enough to do their work and ignore his presence.

Vicente spent his time making a mental chart of the shoreline. He noted the monasteries that cropped up on the sheer cliffs, like honey-colored hives generated spontaneously out of their stone foundations. He tried to memorize the pattern of mountains that loomed beyond.

When it seemed the brothers had caught enough to merit their efforts, they began to try to turn the vessel about, hauling on ropes to trim the sails. The fishing boat refused to cooperate. By the glowering expressions of the fishermen, Vicente grew alarmed. He could tell they thought the boat was bewitched. The darker it grew, the more resistance the boat developed, until at last the brothers had had enough. They fell upon Vicente and tossed him into the sea.

Though he was surprised, he was hardly disappointed, as he had come this far in order to go farther. So he struck out for land, and with backward glances saw the brothers bringing the boat around without further difficulty.

It hadn't been a difficult swim, even for someone whose experience of water was limited to duck ponds, sluggish rivers, and Lago Verde. The northern Aegean seemed warm to him, though what did he know of the source of its currents? Across its peacock-feather waters and past the islands of the Sporades and the Cyclades, and beyond the hump of Crete with its minotaur's maze, the sands of the Saharas were said to stretch. Perhaps the hot breath of Africa leaned heavily on the water. Or maybe his passage was charmed. In any event, he made it ashore without mishap. There was a landing and a rude dock of sorts, but no soul about.

He couldn't light a fire, having no tinder or spark, so to warm himself he began immediately to find his way up the slopes, through gray scrub, gnarled aromatic stuntpine, grasses with gritted edges that cut and stung. He wasn't long in the wilderness, circling about to get a good look at the nearest monastery, when he came across what must have been a roadside shrine of some sort. Here hung a tin icon of a figure of indeterminate gender, and a clay cup supplied with a lump of wax: a votive. Protected from the weather in a tin box beneath the ledge he found a helpful flint and tinder, and so within a few minutes Vicente had made himself a small fire and driven the worst of the chill from his bones.

He had said a prayer for the safety of someone, but María Inés was already dead, and he couldn't now remember for whom he'd been praying, nor, for that matter, to whom, either.

He learned to his delight that the natural defenses of Agion Oros were so considerable that the monks were casual about barring the monastery gates at night. Furthermore, during the day, the gates stood open and often unguarded, as the monks in silent procession went to their labors in orchards, fields, and pastures. From nooks and hides, Vicente spent several days watching the monks at their work. Once he saw a donkey pestered with horseflies, and knew that if donkeys and horseflies behaved here as elsewhere, rain was coming. They did. A cloudburst sent up a screen, and in slashing rain Vicente gained access to the courtyard through gates no one had stopped to close.

The next day he found a cloak on a peg, set aside for use in inclement weather by whichever monk most needed it. Though his new beard didn't fringe and frazzle in the same way of Byzantine priests and acolytes, he made his cautious explorations. Vicente never heard a human voice raised in anything but apparent prayer until the day an ancient patriarch came across him with his hand on the door of the monastery's treasury. The old man had shrieked like a woman, and monks appeared from nowhere, fierce as crows, to settle down upon Vicente and protect what was inside. Down into the dungeon he had been thrown.

Memories began to drift and become unsettled in his mind. Sometimes he said aloud—"Cesare, Duc de Valentinois, I came so much closer to achieving your quest than you thought I might."

He said it. "Cesare, this hand nearly touched the fruit of the Garden of Eden."

He said, "The stem was warm to the touch, like stone in a sunny garden, though the door was closed and locked and I had to smash the hinge with a boulder. Did I? Didn't I?"

He rolled on his side and groaned. He said, "There are things I've forgotten, and that's a mercy, but nobody remembers them on my behalf." And in a flood of self-pity, he said, "The very stones of the world are as deaf as God, and God is as deaf as His stones. Will no one remember me, since I cannot remember myself?"

The stones must not have been as deaf as he imagined, for they answered, "God keeps His own counsel, but the stone hears you."

He didn't make a further remark, for to converse with the stones of his prison must be a sign of his mental collapse and maybe good Brother Death would show up at last. It was about time.

I am a gooseboy or am *I* a goose

I am a gooseboy or am I a goose
The margin that separates us is loose

Mirrormirror

BIANCA COULDN'T tell what
they wanted, why they were pestering her so with questions. Did they
want there to be a huge dowry available for her in Spain? Was Cesare
after a new fund with which to rebuild an army? Or were they worried that their appropriation of her father's house would bring trouble? Bianca knew little of the Orsini or the Colonna families of
Rome, the Sforzas of Milan or the Medici of Florence. She did know
their names, though, and their enmity toward Cesare Borgia was particular and public. Surely, in hiding from his many Italian enemies, the
last thing he was worried about was a vengeful distant Spanish clan?
Bianca wasn't sure her relatives even existed. She'd never heard of
them before—but then, four years ago, her father would have been
unlikely to discuss matters of family relations with her.

Lucrezia drew a deep breath and leaned forward, and was about
to embark upon a new line of questioning, when a ridiculous gabble

sounded from the barnyard beyond, and the peal of boyish shrieking. Lucrezia's head pivoted.

"Primavera," she bellowed. "What is that bother."

The only sound, at first, was of the nursemaid's uncontrolled laughter.

"Primavera."

Up from below at last came the old woman's reply, clearly uttered with difficulty, as the laughter beneath it threatened to break through. "The geese have cornered the gooseboy in the pig's trough," she said. "Oh, it's too good. He is hopping up and down and they are pecking his legs."

Lucrezia whipped herself from her chair. "Crezia," said Cesare.

"I won't have it," she said, and left the room.

Cesare rolled his eyes heavenward and made a holy gesture. "She is as kind as a saint," he said to Bianca. "Saint Bathsheba, Saint Salome, anyway."

"May I go now?" asked Bianca.

"Oh, stay the while," said Cesare lazily, "the Scourge of the Apennines will take her time to rescue a useless gooseboy, won't she, while her own beloved brother languishes on his rack of torment."

Bianca said, "The gooseboy tends to get himself in a muddle. Perhaps I should go help your sister? Primavera moves too slowly to be of use, and Fra Ludovico is more scared of the geese than the gooseboy is."

"Let her take care of the cretin. You can amuse me. What do you know of the world, little mouse?"

She didn't want to talk to him, but then, what harm could come to her from a man who couldn't get off his pallet? "I've my small view of the world," she told him. "I seldom leave the farm—only once or twice to the village at the ford of the river a few miles on, and then only with my father. Years ago. This is world enough for me, up here. I play with the birds. I climb the apple trees. I used to try to make friends with the servant girls, but since my father left they have gone away too. Primavera feeds me, and when he remembers, Fra Ludovico sees that I keep to my devotions. I've learned a few letters and I can write my name, some modest sentences. I can swim; the gooseboy taught me how. I milk the cows when the farmer is too drunk to come up the hill to do it. I collect the eggs and help pull beans from their runners and tomatoes from their vines. I help Primavera move the potted lemon trees into the *limonaia* for the winter. In the summer I pick oleander, lavender bells, and fennel for the shrine in the chapel wall. I watch the moon in its swelling and its subsiding."

He looked at her as if she were reciting the most intimate of love sonnets. "What a treasure your ignorance is," he said. "Come sit by me."

"I'm shy," she said.

"I'm safe, I'm the brother of your guardian," he said. "Shall I tell you of the world?"

She held her tongue, and pulled her stool forward a few inches, but still kept a distance from where Cesare was leaning his chin in his hand.

"What do you care of my battles, my successful campaigns, my reversals of fortune?" he said. "I'm old enough to be your father. By the time you were even born I was on my way to being ruler of half Italy. And I would have given the Holy Roman Emperor a good thwacking, and I might have taken on the bully king of France, who has no business in Italy. In another few months, had my father not died . . . Well, it might yet happen, my sweet mouse. Wait and see.

"But the world wags on. Had my esteemed father, Alexander VI, not died three years ago, I'd be lying on sheets of gold with docile girls and lusty boys eight times prettier than you are, instead of suffering here with my own unobliging wounds. And sickness I carry with me in my gut. It stings. I need a distraction. Come here."

"Please, Don Borgia. Your sister will have a hard time with the gooseboy. I'm afraid he's little more than a fool, but he likes me and trusts me. Let me go see to him, and release the Duchessa to keep you company. I'm not fit to entertain you. I know so little of the world of which you speak."

"The world grows and shrinks at once," said Cesare. "Is this a function of my being wise beyond my years, or is the age in which we live contorting itself with confounding knowledge? In this year of our Lord 1506, the Genoese navigator Columbus has died. Do you know of him? He was the one who brought back the news of Española, an island of China so far across the cold Atlantic sea it might as well be Dante's Malebolge. The Moor has been driven from Granada, and the Jew from much of Spain, and Their Catholic Majesties Ferdinand and Isabella cast their eyes on their western prospects, and the canny Lisboans too. I'll go back to Navarre and find your dowry and claim it, and if it is enough for a single horse and a suit of mail, or if it helps to raise an army, I will not be stayed from my destiny. Come here, I say."

Rehearsing the future for the world seemed to energize him.

She might never have the chance for such an audience again. Even if she wanted to flee—what might she learn, with care? She drew herself just a few inches forward and said, "Please, I know nothing of the world, except my father is lost in it. Do you know if he is alive? Do you know where he went, or why?"

"I know where, and I know why. To buy me a miracle." He closed his eyes, as if his internal pain was mounting. "I could use a miracle now." He opened his eyes again. They were swimming in tears. "Come, sit by my side, let me tell you what I suspect of your father's whereabouts."

What she might learn, what she might lose. It was another bridge to cross, and she was struck immobile in the middle. "It's time for my prayers," she said at last.

"I'll teach you how to pray for mercy." With a movement more forceful than she thought him capable of, he reached out and grabbed her wrist, and pulled her toward him. Her heart suddenly a blue onion in her chest, cold and layered and stinging in its own juices, she struggled. With one hand he encircled both her small wrists, and clamped them onto his thigh, forcing her to a kneeling position between his knees. She could hear her voice warble, a mockery of a song; she couldn't make it form words, just an obbligato wail like a reed flute on a single high note.

Bianca heard the Duchess of Ferrara at the threshold of her father's *salone,* and a voice like a storm came down between Bianca and Il Valentino. "Cesare, has the French disease made you mad? Release her at once."

"Come and join me in my devotions, dear sister," he growled. Lucrezia Borgia picked up the first thing she could grasp—a piece of faience—and she hurled it. Her aim was wild. The vase struck the mirror over the mantelpiece. The mirror was unharmed, but the vase's earthenware slivers scattered with force. Bianca saw the blood spring like black gum on his forearm. He let her go so he could sweep shards off the top of his thigh, and this cut the side of his hand.

"Will you take a child to marry and bed her without benefit of a dowry?" asked Lucrezia icily. "Are you entirely insane?"

"I'm insane and I'm still a man," he said to her, "and as you know well, my chill and beautiful spouse Charlotte is the sister of the king of Navarre and therefore lives too far away to be of wifely use to me—and has done so for seven years. I'm practically unmarried."

"I won't be bedded or married, either one," said Bianca, but the Borgias had turned their attention and their contempt upon each other, and neither noticed or cared what she'd said.

Cesare's voice was hard as iron. "And have you forgotten your infatuation for your powerful brother now he has lost stature in the eyes of the world? Now that he skulks under cover of darkness plotting useless campaigns of revenge? Allow me some comfort, sweet sister."

"She is too small. You would only bruise her," said Lucrezia.

"I'm talking about my comfort, not hers."

"Get out of here," said Lucrezia to Bianca. "How dare you linger and taunt my brother like that. Have you no shame? I suppose you haven't, without a womanly woman to raise you correctly. The attitudes of a peasant, courtesy of your Primavera. Go."

"How's your gooseboy?" said Cesare tauntingly to his sister. Bianca fled.

She fell on the stairs, not from fear, but because she realized that blood was running off her temple. Shards from the vase must have struck her too. For a moment she couldn't see. As she crouched there, trying to wipe her eyes clear of blood, she heard nothing at all, and then the sound of slippers brushing a few steps across the floor. Was Lucrezia Borgia approaching her brother to slap him or to kiss him, or to whisper something in his ear?

Bianca heard the Duchessa's voice, a few tones lower than that in which she usually spoke. A voice of false solemnity and genuine menace.

"Mirror, mirror on the wall, who among us is fairest of all?" she said.

Bianca straightened up and listened, as if the mirror might answer. If it did, it was in a pitch too cerebral or too hushed for Bianca to hear. In any event, Cesare either mocked his sister or echoed the mirror's answer when he said, "Well, it's not you, sister. It's that little mouse child, the daughter of our agent de Nevada. Doesn't that just make your Borgia blood boil. What'll you do about that?"

Lucrezia laughed, a houndish laugh, almost a baying. "You have so little power over me now, brother duke," she said, and though her words were rough her tone was intimate and cajoling. "The heyday of the Borgias is over almost before it's begun. I'll watch you rot in a grave before the decade is out, I'll wager. But I'll be damned if I see you casting glances at a child young enough to be your daughter."

"You're jealous because she's lovelier than you," he said. "You always were a jealous type. I still adore you, Crezia. Come here. Come to Cesare."

Bianca tumbled down the stairs, blood in her eyes or no.

I am a hunter who cannot kill

I am a hunter who cannot kill.
The yearling unicorn haunts with taunting eyes,
Ready to lay its sacrificial head
Between my quivering thighs,
Asking the clemency of death
So it can yield
The song for which it lived.

But I am a man whose heart is stiff as stone.
Let unicorns and maidens plead for mercy,
For the wisdom death reveals, for a right of passage
Through the gates of horn to the sacred city,
To Gesù on its steps, to incorruptible parents
Restored from the grave and waiting with opened arms.
I will not grant that privilege to any.
I don't possess credentials bright enough
To vouchsafe anyone passage to paradise.

Bring me her heart carved from her chest

THE *salone* was silent. Cesare had summoned Fra Ludovico to help him hobble down the stairs. Looking for the mouse? Looking for confession and penance? Cesare was a man of superstitions—he had believed in Prince Dschem's fairy tale of the Tree of Knowledge, he believed in the mercy of the Church. He lit votives to Gesù and the Madonna, to Pan, to his hero Alexander the Great, and to Fortuna, all on the same altar. He played at prophecy with a volume of Virgil, opening it at random to read aloud the poet's antique opinion on the decision of the moment.

Lucrezia sat and absently covered her lap with the red cloak that Bianca de Nevada had left behind. As she stroked it, and the day's shadows began to gather, she fell into a reverie. Perhaps it was seeded by the afternoon with the little girl. Thoughts of her own girlhood, at that same age—and later—came rising up.

She didn't often revisit her past, for the future offered more succor.

As a child, she'd been as good as orphaned. Well, when your father is the Pope and your mother his mistress, and your nursemaids cardinals wellplaced in the Curia, even small domestic details of your childhood tend to seem freighted with portent.

After her father was elevated to the throne of Peter, the Vatican's apartments and offices were as crowded as alleys on market day. The commodities on sale were pardons, favors, indulgences to shorten purgatorial jail sentences. Who in those crowded bazaars of the faith might have provided the companionship a girl might need? Not even the solemn sisters who oversaw the housecleaning of Christendom's most magnificent palace to Christ.

All this had begun when Lucrezia was the age that Bianca was now—about eleven. The previous pope, Innocent VIII, had taken ill. His doctors had bled three young boys as a propitiatory offering, to no avail. Innocent VIII had died. So had all three boys. On a sacrifice of their blood, her father, Cardinal Rodrigo Borgia, had been elected to the Papal See, and Lucrezia was removed from the care of her mother, Vannozza.

A famous Roman courtesan, Vannozza had spent her years as Cardinal Borgia's mistress established conveniently near to his palace on the Piazza Pizzo de Merlo. She'd conducted her business with equal parts of hauteur and circumspection. She'd protested at the removal from her household of her older son, Cesare, whose career was being thrashed out by his father; she'd wept piteously when deprived of Lucrezia. But what rights are left to any mother when a father has made up his mind?—and since this father was newly elected pope of the Roman church, Vannozza was required to bear her grief in silence as best she could. She didn't refuse the Pope company when he required it, but she bridled—Lucrezia later realized, she must have bridled—that the Pope's newest mistress, the clamorously attractive Giulia Farnese, was given part responsibility for the raising of Vannozza's own Lucrezia.

Lucrezia had taken leave of her mother casually, mockingly. Well, her robust and homely father was in his ascendancy, and court life seemed more alluring than learning the arts of needlework at her mother's elbow. Lucrezia had been fattened on the notion of Borgia supremacy, after all, and her mother wasn't a Borgia—not even by marriage. With difficulty Lucrezia managed to choke back her impulse to correct her mother's comportment— as Lucrezia left to take up her proper place in the Vatican palace, Vannozza's tears and hand-wringing weren't suitable gestures, *at all*—and, besides, the girl didn't envision what a profound change it would be. The distance to Vannozza's door was, mathematically, exactly as far as the distance from it. Surely?

As it turned out, such measurements aren't entirely governed by the laws of mathematics. The laws of politics and one's personal humors alter the equation.

And Lucrezia, impressed with Giulia Farnese's beauty, was cowed by it. Giulia was her own age, nearly, *and her father's lover.* The paradox of that!

Before state affairs and court life began to restrict her liberty, the young Lucrezia haunted the servants' quarters in the Pope's fortress, the Castel Sant'Angelo. She exchanged her silks and furs for her handmaiden's broadcloth tunic and slipped out a window, and played tricks on fishermen struggling to find dinner in the filthy Tiber. To see how it felt, she'd laid down with shepherds in fields striped with the shadows of poplars. She'd wandered incognita—the daughter of a pope—giving free kisses among the tombstones and cypresses on the Capitoline Hill. In matters amorous, Lucrezia was finding herself talented. Too soon, her beauty became unique. Before long she couldn't show her face inside or out of Saint Peter's Basilica without being recognized.

Study came easily to her. She spoke four languages well. Without much effort she could hear in the rhythm of foreign tongues a certain implied meaning, even when vocabulary and the nuances of grammar escaped her. For a child with spotty tutoring, she engaged in her own private trivium: not grammar, dialectic, rhetoric, the traditional roster of subjects, but glamour, intrigue, and power. She followed the affairs of the court of the pope with closer attention than most bishops. Once, when the Pope was indisposed, she even had managed the affairs of the Church for a short while, until she was prohibited by cardinals from signing a papal document with the question "*Ubi est penna vestra?*"—meaning not only *Where is your pen?* but also *Where is your penis?*

But she'd enjoyed governing, when the time arrived to try it. She'd spent those few months in 1498, when she was scarcely eighteen, as *governatrice* of Spoleto. Five long months there, married to one man, Alfonso of Aragon, and in love with another who would no longer have her. She was pregnant with the child who would be named Rodrigo, after her father, and she was saddled with the other one, the mortal mistake in her arms, the one who cried piteously at night, who wouldn't be thrown over the edge of the aqueduct, all because of the meddlesome de Nevada . . .

Adult as she could be by now, at the age of twenty-six, she sat before the mirror and studied her face within it. Had so much happened in such a short time? In seven years? Vicente de Nevada, having learned of her residency there, had made his way to Spoleto, on the Umbrian flank of the Apennines. He had gone to hear Mass at the duomo. He had ventured forward and caught Lucrezia at the conclusions of the Sacrament. She'd been praying in front of Fra Filippo Lippi's fresco, in which the Virgin hovers in robes of white and gold before God the Patriarch, who sets a crown of surpassing glory upon her head. Lucrezia had been jealous, not of the Virgin's beauty, but of her crown.

"I beg to speak with the Donna Borgia," said Vicente, in Spanish, and from her impious thoughts she had been torn, for the consolation of hearing the family tongue.

De Nevada asked for the *governatrice's* intercession with her brother Cesare. De Nevada had a motherless child, and his profession was agriculture; might Cesare, out of feeling for a fellow Iberian, secure the immigrant a position, perhaps even a small landholding?

"Put the child in an orphanage till she's older, and send her to be a nun when she's ready," decreed Lucrezia. "Neither my brother nor I have property we hand out for the asking. If you need work, Cesare is always looking for *condottieri*. A mercenary earns good pay and can usually find a war to fight. Besides, I don't oversee my brothers' rare administrations of mercy."

Something in de Nevada's expression—his refusal to consider farming the child out—made her feel a modest pity, though. She invited him to visit her in the castle. That afternoon, from a rampart, she watched the father and daughter make their way up the slope and be admitted to the interior courtyard.

There, despite a chill in the air, Lucrezia greeted them. She had dismissed her retinue of attendants and chaperones, and her husband was off hunting for the day. To prove her own motherliness, and as a badge of respectability, she kept the Punishment on her hip. He was docile enough until it proved inconvenient—his usual way.

She had arranged a table to be set with Castiliian lace, and platters of fresh fruit and decanters of wine were at the ready. Vicente had the young girl by the hand. The young Bianca.

The child must have been three years old or so. Good-looking in her way, considering how lumpy and irregular children's faces could be. The dark hair, the skin so white. Pale eyes, the color of water, set wide, and cunningly large, the way children's eyes so often seem. The child was preternaturally self-possessed. She didn't join the other urchins playing chase and seek games among the arches. She didn't interrupt her father, pull at his sleeves, nor did she whine or fuss. She stood with both feet planted, her little stomach a smooth shallow bowl beneath the pleats of her green-black tunic. And while she stood and watched, too wellbehaved for belief, Lucrezia's own Punishment thrashed in her arms, threatening to unbalance her onto the cobbles, maybe endanger the child growing within her.

"Let me help you," said Vicente, a capable father. She despised him for having the nerve to assist without leave. But he had a natural touch, and the squirming toddler settled, and she hated Vicente for that talent too.

They exchanged a few remarks about life in Iberia, in Italy, about the weather and the church services in Spoleto. She asked why he had left his homeland in the first place. That might have been all. But Vicente had touched Lucrezia somehow, in some way she didn't know—perhaps as a speaker of Spanish he reminded her of her brother, whose company she missed so? It was hard to say. And, when the weather grew sharply colder, and a sudden squall fell like white nets around them, she found herself extending the hospitality of the castle to this newcomer. Spend a few nights, she had said; make your beds here. Until the snow lets up, at least. Little hope, really, of my finding you a foothold of property, but I can find you a bed and a meal.

That night, before Alfonso had approached her chamber to take his due as a husband, the Punishment squalled worse than ever. The wet nurses couldn't calm him down, and she wouldn't let them take him away for fear they would kill him before she had a chance. She would rather do the job herself so she could insure that blame fell safely elsewhere. She'd thought it through often enough, hadn't she? And here was de Nevada, a man of no apparent connections, presenting himself as a likely candidate. Fortune smiled on her, for once! She could accuse him and imprison him before morning, and no one would come forward to speak on his behalf.

Long after midnight, she wrapped a bunting around the sleeping child's mouth to muffle any sudden cries, and she carried him down the steps of the courtyard, and exited the palace by a side door. (She had seen that the guard would be deeply asleep thanks to a helpful powder in his evening ale.) She made her way across the brow of the mount, to where the bridge, stepping in Gothic arches on top of a Roman aqueduct, began its lofty walk from the castle, across the gorge carved out by the Tessino River, to the monastery on Monte Luco, the far side of the valley.

Even in the scatter of snow, her step was swift but sure, for she had taken the air and the views from the bridge many times before. It was guarded at the far end, she knew. But the near end was desolate. Not even a viper could swarm up the steep legs of the arches.

She went to where she judged the halfway point must be. She lay down the Punishment to unwrap him, to send him naked to his Maker, and good riddance—when, a whisper on snow, she heard a footstep or two coming from the direction of the castle, though no one could have seen her leave.

She turned and peered. A mist had come up on the valley's western slope. If her pursuer was hidden from her, she must also still be hidden from him.

She hadn't bargained at working hastily. Perverse to the last, the child chose this moment to wake. He kept writhing as she leaned against the edge of the rampart and readied herself to pitch the weight mightily, to clear the wide ledge in an arc and insure fatality. She couldn't get a firm enough footing. Damn. He seemed to have an animal's instinct for what was happening.

Perhaps she would have to bash his head in, first, to reduce his form to dead weight. She gasped with the effort and drew her son back, prepared to batter the wall with his skull—and then the sound of nearer footsteps, a whisper becoming a rhythm through the rising mist.

It was Vicente. The one figured to stand as a culprit was interfering instead. He was aghast. He threw himself between her swinging arm and the wall, so the baby thumped hideously, but not damagingly, against his chest. "Are you mad?" hissed Vicente. "My lady Lucrezia."

She slumped against the far wall with the back of her hand against her mouth. "Who are you? Where am I?" she quavered, working for time in which to gather her thoughts.

"You don't know what you are doing," he said. "Come, take my arm, and I'll walk you to safety."

It wasn't hard to appear besotted with sleep, for she was dizzy with fright. If anyone were to learn what she had been about to do . . . Even for a Borgia, the slaughter of a child was extreme. By the time they had reached the castle side of the aqueduct, however, she'd prepared a defense and a strategy.

"I'm slow to wake," she said. "I suffer from fits of sleepwalking. It's all as a dream, a horrid dream. Do me the honor of keeping my fretful condition a matter private between us. How lucky you were to come wake me and avert disaster."

He saw her in the morning. At a table in the solar, he sat down with the young woman and her husband as they broke their fast. His little girl sat on his lap. The Punishment had been sequestered far enough away so his morning screams couldn't be heard.

"I hope you slept well," said Lucrezia's hapless husband.

"Only so-so," answered Vicente, studying the bread in his hands. "I had much on my mind, and kept turning. I'm scarcely sure what I should do next. Donna Borgia," he continued, looking her in the eyes, "I await your advice."

"I've been thinking," said Lucrezia hastily, "about your predicament. I believe with a little attention, Cesare or I may yet be able to find you a small estate, conferrable upon certain conditions."

"I thought you considered that impossible," said Alfonso de Bisceglie, surprised at his wife.

"I couldn't sleep either, and I put my mind to the task." Her answer was brisk and the topic of conversation changed.

Thus had Vicente come into possession of Montefiore, after Lucrezia, privately, had had the previous owner smothered, to ensure the premises were available for new occupants.

Learning from her panic, Lucrezia had dismissed the Punishment from her life as she had been dismissed from her mother's. In due course, she had given birth to Rodrigo, of more honorable lineage, of better disposition and capabilities than the Punishment. To protect him she had him raised far from herself too. There was reason, in his legitimacy, to worry about his prospects, and she wouldn't see him besmirched by too close an association with her.

She looked at the mirror as these days, seven years past, reframed themselves. It was almost as if she could see the hills around Spoleto, dotted with ilex, lulled by the morose remarks of sheep. The palm trees, the threads of waterfall on the far slope of the canyon . . . She had never been able to guess why Vicente de Nevada had been awake and clever or bold enough to follow his royal hostess out of a dark guarded castle and across a mist-shrouded bridge. He had been certain enough of himself to leave his little girl behind, dozing under her blankets. And *she* had not been screaming through the night, with the pains of teething, of colic, of general disapproval of the world.

That same good little girl, now swaying her boyish hips at Cesare.

The Duchessa couldn't bear what she had seen. Cesare was as good as dying—Lucrezia was no fool—and still the lecherous bastard had found the girl child alluring. Her own brother, the tenderest swift soldier ever to enter her bed—groping at a child. In a seizure of ire she gripped her stomacher and tore it. Good that he had bullied the priest off somewhere—probably to a local church with a real roof, so Cesare could take the sacrament in some sort of comfort. He enjoyed the penance almost as much as the sin. It didn't matter where he had gone. He had left her, that much was clear. He was gone for good.

Sweeping up in a tempest of silks and ermine, before she knew what she was about, she pitched herself toward the door.

"Primavera," she commanded. "Where are you? Someone, get that old cow up here. Isn't it true that she has a grandson who is a hunter? Primavera. He will come and have an audience with me, as soon as he can wash the blood off his hands. Primavera. Does no one listen when I call?"

Primavera was out at the well, rinsing Bianca's face. She heard Lucrezia Borgia bellow. Primavera's lips set more firmly together. When, at last, she heeded the summons, and stood to obey, her ankles shook.

Interview with an assassin

You appreciate the reward?"
She looked down at the soft purse of coins in her hands, and shifted it gently back and forth, to make the musical remark of the money within more alluring. He wasn't used to being in the house, at least not farther than the kitchen. He stood as if before a magistrate and looked her in the eye. "Enough to ask about the service required."

"Take the child from the house, deep into the woods, far beyond where anyone might find her."

"There are woods enough to lose a child in."

"I want her more than lost. I want her life."

"The woods will take her life."

"I want you to take her life."

"She has seriously offended."

"It's not your place to ask why. Nor are you to find yourself capable of remembering this interview. You are a hunter. Wait until night has begun to fall, and take her life however you must."

"You trust a lot to a man you don't know."

"You have an aged grandmother in my employ. You will want her to see her final days in comfort, not—otherwise."

"I've no one else but an aged grandmother. My father and his brother were both killed in the bombardment of Forlì, and my mother died of grief soon thereafter."

"What is your name?"

"I'm the hunter."

"What does your grandmother call you?"

"Obedient."

"Fair enough. Do as I say. Bring me her heart carved from her chest."

Ranuccio lifted his bearded chin.

"I don't want her to survive, to call on relatives from across the sea to avenge her abandonment. Make good my request, and you shall have this purse, and your silly grandmother shall sleep on her own straw pallet until the end of her days." She threw the purse on the table. "Her natural days."

He picked up the purse and weighed it in his hands and didn't speak at first. It was as if he'd never come across coin before. They both heard the sound of his *nonna's* voice calling the chickens in. It was an old voice, and the only one left he knew. He said, "I can hope to commit a murder and to eliminate a child. I can decide not to ask questions about your reasons."

"Can you also manage to forget that we have ever discussed any of this?"

"Any of what?" he said, and smiled, for the first time.

A walk in the woods

BIANCA HAD eaten already, but she sat in the kitchen helping Primavera prepare a meal for the Borgias. It felt safe there—well, safer than anywhere else. Primavera was scowling and cursing protectively. "What is that monstrous bitch up to, that your face is covered with blood?" she'd said.

There wasn't anything to say, because Bianca could hardly describe what had happened, or why. "It was an accident," she insisted.

"You were standing like a docile sweet orphan and a vase flew into your head by accident?"

"I'm not an orphan."

"Of course not, and a vase isn't a bird with silver wings either. The blood in your eyes, mercy. I should tell you about blood."

"Please, Primavera, not that again. I know about that."

Upstairs, Lucrezia had picked up a lute, and tuned it. The familiar melody that skittered down the stairwell was lopsided, its syncopation the result, perhaps, of a snapped string not yet replaced. Primavera didn't talk over the sound of the music. She supervised a joint of pork bound in strings, and took from a hook in the chimney stack a parcel of olives she'd been smoking. Sharply, her worry showing, she told Bianca to stir the white beans simmering in a pot suspended from a chain in the kitchen fireplace.

Bianca's eyes were cleared of blood. She was glad to have something common to do—stir the beans—and already she felt better. She was afraid that the presence of blood was going to bring Primavera around to discussing her favorite topic, the imminent arrival of a young woman's menses. Bianca was neither skittish of her female development nor eager for it. But Primavera, sensitive to her own desiccation, found no more enjoyable a topic than the rehearsal of what the monthly complaint was like. The cramps, the mess, the induction into a life of fecundity and danger.

Tonight Primavera restrained herself. She felt the atmosphere curdle and pause. The house had a musty air, as if an atmosphere of grief was leeching through the stones from an underground source. No obvious message in the beans or the clouds. Ranuccio had bought her a chicken and wrung its neck, and after she finished cutting it she'd spill its liver and see what mischief was afoot.

What was the source of the sour miasma? Had a rat died beneath the floor joists, and was it extruding its malodorous juices? Or was the spirit of the house's previous owner making itself felt? When she wasn't being a superstitious seer, Primavera was a realist. Her grasp, increasingly, was on the present. If the ghost of the former landlord was bent on causing their skin to crawl, he was doing it effectively, but he was still no more than a ghost, and in any contest, the quick overcrowded the dead in all geographies but the churchyard and the spiraling corridors of hell.

Or might it be a more recent arrival, the ghost of Vicente de Nevada himself? Perhaps, months ago and far away, he'd met his end and his ghost had taken its time returning to the family home.

Primavera knew it didn't do to turn a blind eye on such things.

She descended to the cold keep below the stairs to get a dip of oil, for intestines spilled in augury should then be cooked and eaten, for the sake of economy as well as spitting at the fates. Below steps, she heard a gasp from the kitchen. It took her a minute to turn—she'd put on a few pounds lately. She needed to step down a level or two and find room to negotiate her bulk on a flat bit of flooring rather than to risk twisting on a stair. By the time she returned to the kitchen, she saw the stool on which Bianca had been sitting, overturned in a clumsy way. The spoon for stirring the beans was on the floor.

Bianca had made no protest when Primavera's grandson entered the kitchen, picked up a heel of bread with one hand and grabbed her own forearm with the other. He shoved the food in his mouth and yanked her from her seat roughly; she was dangling like a newly caught trout. She kicked not out of alarm but with an instinct for balance.

Then Ranuccio barreled out the door, knocking the crown of her skull on the stone doorframe, and she was abstracted with swimming sparks of pain. By the time she could focus her eyes through her distress and register something discernable, she was outside—this is the meadow, now this is the lower meadow, and Montefiore is retreating above me, like a storm cloud in reverse. Its low wings and barns close their arms against the bulk of the main house, its red roofline lowers like a furrowed brow.

The house became richer, more obtuse, a red-brown rose growing in reverse, back toward secret potent bud.

She saw the gooseboy who stood gaping at the side of the road, adrift in his snowy cackling blanket of friends. She tried to utter —a *Help me!* or a *What?* or a *Come now!*—but all she could manage was a strangled sort of duck quack. He waved his hand and smiled at her—they were hardly friends, Bianca and the gooseboy, just people who lived on the same hill, basically—and then he and his downy companions had been swallowed up in the arms of apple trees, which in turn became an apron of apple trees sweeping in a single tide away from her. She was past Lago Verde and up to the bridge her father had forbidden her to cross.

There Ranuccio stopped. Was he going to throw her over the side? Or did he somehow know about her father's prohibition? But no—he was fishing with one hand inside his shirt. He came up with a sack of coins. He tossed them in the water. He was distracting the mudcreature! Must be so. He continued down the other side of the bridge, and she was being hustled away from Montefiore without further assault. As if this assault weren't enough.

Montefiore was becoming the dense irretrievable past, the dead childhood, dead, cold dead on its slab, and no mercy existed in the world or out of it to slap it back to life again.

Ranuccio wasn't a giant, though; not a mudcreature, not an ogre from some comic hearthside tale. He was a strong man and a big one, but he was only a man, and she was after all eleven; she ought to be able to figure this out.

She hadn't seen him often. Occasionally when the weather was harshest he would show up and share some food with his grandmother—either bring her some treat, a brace of pheasants or rabbits, sometimes a haunch of venison or a slithery set of steaks cut from the flanks of a boar. Primavera would prepare the meat; she was no stranger to the benisons of wild garlic, lemon, and black peppercorns from the East. But though Ranuccio and his grandmother shared a grief—the death of the generation between them—they seemed to have no other common language. In the years in which Bianca de Nevada had come to be aware of Ranuccio, his arrivals and disappearances had been conducted in an almost conspiratorial silence.

Thumping against his side—for even as slight as she was, she had some weight, and so in time his muscles ached—she twisted and finally caught enough breath, and enough sense, to begin to complain. She yelped her confusion, at first, and, her breath ignited, she began to wail, and to try to twist her arm free so she could beat against his side. "Where are you taking me?" she said, "where are we going?"

The promontory for which Montefiore was named leaned above them, and the house was lost in its leafy opacity. "Where is my home?" she demanded, more frantically. "Where are we going?"

"A walk in the woods," he said.

"I'm not allowed to go alone into the woods."

"You aren't alone." He set her down and jabbed her playfully in the side with one hand, though with his other he continued to keep her wrist in a circling grip stronger, she imagined, than iron shackles could possibly be.

"The dark is coming on, and Primavera will worry."

"The old smelly goose mother knows what is about. Don't worry about her."

"But she didn't say a word to me. She would have told me—"

"She didn't want to alarm you. She wanted it to be a surprise."

Bianca stood still to consider this. There was so much unclear about how adults behaved, and Primavera, it was sure, was more quixotic and fickle in her behavior than most.

"What is your intention?" said Bianca, as firmly as her quavering voice would allow.

"Let's walk a while together and learn our intentions."

"If you let go of my hand, I can walk more comfortably."

"If I let go of your hand, you will run away."

"I will not run away."

"You will run away. I know children, and when they are scared they are foolish as hens. They bolt at the first chance they get. I tell you, there is little reason to be scared." He picked from a leather pouch slung on a strip of leather around his waist a dagger with a handle of worn antler.

She shrunk from him as best she could, as if she could shed her own hand and leave it there in his grip. Her underskirt had gone damp.

"What use is that knife to you here?"

"To protect us in the woods," he said. "Do you see that it's getting dark?"

"I don't see as much as I would like."

"Because it's getting dark." But the light in the sky was ample enough to shine on the silvered blade, making it stand out against the blue-black undergrowth. They poked deeper into the woods, and the sky darkened now as the canopy of trees closed above them.

"If I let you go, you will run," he said again, many minutes later, when the dark was no longer considering a visit but had moved in for the night. The only light was the luminescence of late summer bugs, the stripe of silver along the blade, and the wet in Ranuccio's eyes. She could smell from her own body a sour moisture, the reek of her body's fear.

"If you let me go," she said, and faltered.

". . . you will run," he said, completing her sentence.

And then she understood him. She stopped and stood still. He let her go. He raised his knife. He held the handle with one hand. With the fingers of his other hand he gripped the point of the very sharp blade, teasingly. A single drop of black blood stood out on his thumb.

She gave a genuflection that she didn't know he could see, and then she turned and walked carefully away, into the dark.

The heart of the woods

R ANUCCIO WAITED until
the sound of the girl's progress had become swallowed up in the back-
and-forth of wind through leaves. Now there was the creak of an oak
limb, now a silence through which a distant stream could be heard to
murmur. Now a rush of wind again—and

and—the world had sealed over, had healed itself of the girl's presence, as if she had never lived. Had even forgotten her absence. Even
he, used to hearing a beetle pause and inspect itself under a fallen log,
was dizzy with the mystery of how fully she had been taken away.

What was her name, even?

He stopped to rest, leaning against a boulder. He hugged himself
for warmth. What was to be done now? For the beautiful Donna Lucrezia had requested the child's heart as proof of her death. Ranuccio didn't understand the root of Lucrezia's malice, but he was clear
on this: she wouldn't rest until she was certain her campaign had

been carried out as requested. So there was the matter of the heart to consider.

Ranuccio's *nonna* was a fabulist, a pagan oracle, equally conversant with the saints and angels as she was with the crooks, shimmies, elves, and frostlings of local renown. Her wisdom hadn't prevented the death of her sons in battle. So to avoid a similar fate, Ranuccio had taken to hunting in the forests that still surged like seas around outlying farms and past tillage and orchards.

But, looking for something different by which to rule his depopulated life, he had also been drawn to the lures of Siena, Arezzo, and even, two or three times, to the diadem of central Italy, Florence. And, though he had little language in which to cast his understanding, Ranuccio nonetheless found himself sympathetic to the sweet sound of discourse, to reason's steady footfall from thought to thought, from proposition to proof, from thesis to antithesis, from the raw clever act of characterizing the world to the more serene bliss of categorizing it. Pico della Mirandola, a convert of Savonarola's, had laid it out so clearly: *A dog must always behave like a dog, and an angel could not but behave angelically.*

The world was wilderness on one side, full of twisting oak trees dropping their penile acorns, of wolves with ruddy jaws. Even the vines of ivy would reach their small dry-clawed hands up the inside of your calf and thigh if you lingered too long. And on the other side—the side Florence ruled over—it was rolled and leveled paradise, with cypresses and laurels trained to march in arithmetical arrangements, and gravel walks raked so purely that even the robins knew not to hunt for worms there, lest the symmetry be spoiled. Classical statues preened on cornerstone plinths, proposing by the perfection of their forms a range of states of being so sublime that Ranuccio had never had the temerity to ask for a glossary of their qualities.

But Florence, and the legislated and unspoken *regulae* that governed its civic life, both appealed to Ranuccio and made him mute before his superstitious grandmother. Love and grief had bound them, and mutual hunger allowed them to sit down and share what the skill of the hunter and the skill of the cook could contrive between them to put on the table, but conversation had not been their habit.

He had never told her, for instance, about the time he had come across a unicorn in a glade. He knew the lore about unicorns—that they only ever approached maidens, and in no conceivable way had Ranuccio ever been a maiden. But lore was only lore, a system of thinking decayed from some more ancient, blurry hypothesis, deteriorating toward a superstitious tic or ridiculous custom.

He had been up to see Fra Tomasso, his confessor, a crippled Franciscan who had retired to an oratory carved out of a cave. The friar lived there with a beaky merlin that perched most days inside the awesome dried skull of a Cyclops. It seemed that Ranuccio was the friar's sole disciple, and only an occasional one at that.

Fra Tomasso had bled him for health, and heard his confession (fornication, avarice, contempt for the name of the Lord, that sort of incidental sin), and fed him a scupperful of oil that purged his bowels in a sudden and unpleasant way. So, on the way down from the oratory, feeling hollowed and pardoned and ready to sin again, he had been pleased to come across a small but steep, slightly sulfurous waterfall he'd not seen before.

Ranuccio had shed his clothes and plunged into the pool beneath the waterfall with a cheery abandon, the more delicious for being so rare. When he emerged, cleaned outside now as well as, in every way that could be managed, within, he had staggered into the grove to find his clothes, and naked as Adam in Eden, he had startled the unicorn, who turned its head.

The unicorn, by virtue of its characteristic utensil, was presumed always to be male, but Ranuccio found himself unwilling to look and see. What did it matter? In any event there was a radiance, that radiance that stories occasionally remember to tell, and Ranuccio was blinded by the sense of being visited by light itself. Perhaps, in the creature's presence, Ranuccio's own maleness was unmade, or his maidenness called forth. Or some other mystical transaction, too confounding in its airy whiteness to name.

He knelt before the beast, and it seemed to Ranuccio that the unicorn hesitated. The hunter felt a stiff heat throb from its flanks, as if its suspicion could take on a thermal aspect. But Ranuccio put his hands down on his own thighs, turning his thumbs outward to reveal his open palms. He lowered his eyes. He heard the ground tremble, as hoof after hoof was set delicately down—in perfect synchronization, mountains a continent away were crumbling one by one. The creature brought its bath of light forward, and the great horn came near. Ranuccio could see ripples of gray-white line, fine as spiderweb, tracing through the ivorylike shaft, as if proof that the horn grew through minute accretion like anything else in this natural world. Then the unicorn set its horn into his lap. At once, Ranuccio's eyes spilled with bruising tears and his cock trembled and released its scatter of milky pearl. Ranuccio was as fully emptied, as fully hollow, as it was possible for a grown human male to be, and the unicorn turned its head and looked upon the shattered possibility of a man, and made its request.

The creature wanted to complete its life, to sing the song that gave its life meaning. It ought to have died naturally, and its song issued out of it in true time. But the world was changing. What had once been a dragon in a net was now just a bird born wrong, changed accidentally in its egg. Chicken livers could not tell the future precisely enough to prevent the death in war of a parent and an uncle. The unicorn had outlived its age. It was dog and angel both—damn damn Pico to hell—and there was no place for that much mystery in the world anymore.

How could he deny the unicorn its death? Was it commonplace mercy or superior cowardice? But he could, and he did: he might be naked as Adam, but he couldn't be as pure. Adam and Eve named the world between them, but Ranuccio wanted no knowledge unshared by his species. He would turn aside from the sacred Temptation and, in the consequence of it, risk the removal of the need for a Savior to redeem his other mundane sins.

How he communicated this to the creature, he didn't know. Did the creature pull back its horn? Did the hunter swoon? He was dressed, and singing a long ridiculous song about a Knight Templar, almost home by dusk, when he came back to his senses and remembered what had happened in the glade by the waterfall.

Ranuccio never spoke of it to a soul. He didn't confess it to Fra Tomasso in later conversations.

What the exchange had done for him—to him—became evident only in time. He was a hunter, a castaway in the shrinking forests of late medieval Italy, and, single-minded and uneducated, he'd been bred and raised to hunt and kill for food. And now he couldn't perform the duty without a certain cost to his spirit. He did kill, of course—it was that or die of starvation. He used arrows and traps, snares and cudgels, he netted when he needed. Once he even experimented with a short rifle, though the gunpowder stank and the noise seemed to rip the very trees out of the ground.

But he didn't kill without dread and shame, realizing that the lower creatures, the deer and fowl and boar, the rabbits, the wild pigs, all resisted, all preferred their lives to their deaths. The unicorn had offered its life, had petitioned for its death, and he'd failed, as a professional hunter, to oblige. He might learn, in the afterlife, whether his failure was a virtue or a fault, but in the meantime he suffered with not knowing.

And wondering, all along, in the crusty margins between dreaming and waking, if the unicorn was still waiting, or if it had found a more capable murderer.

He hadn't been able to murder the child, either, but he found a young buck and ably brought him down. The deer's hind legs crushed in unnatural position beneath him, Ranuccio straddled the powerful neck and pulled the head back, and readied himself for the reckoning that the creature would do with his eyes.

The deer didn't do as he ought. He didn't fight or thrash, he didn't stiffen at the threat of the knife's wild bite. It was as if he too had met the unicorn in the woods, and had learned about this moment.

It was as if—in a wild fantasy, he grappled to understand—it was as if the buck were as good as the girl's mother, that reportedly beautiful María Inés, so intent on the life of her abandoned child that she would die a second time to help the hunter build an alibi, to buy the child time, and safety. The mere sex of the creature didn't alter the mercy or the value of the sacrifice

"Thank you," he murmured, and slit the deer's throat.

"The heart of the woods," he said to Lucrezia, when, the next morning, he handed her the wooden casket she had requested.

I am a rock and my brothers are rocks

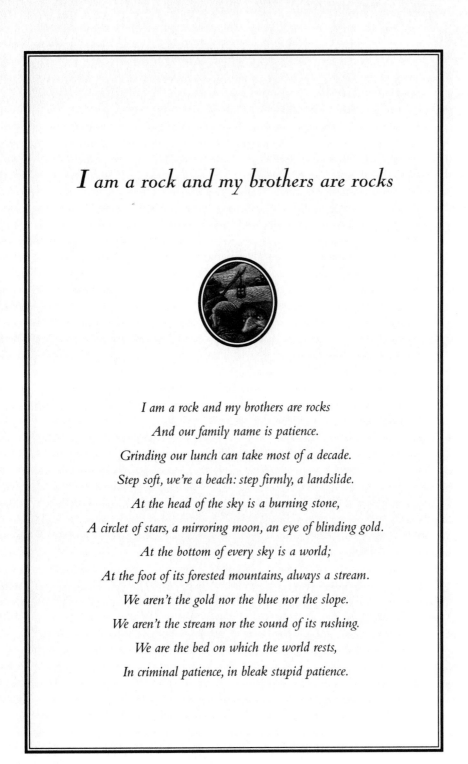

I am a rock and my brothers are rocks
And our family name is patience.
Grinding our lunch can take most of a decade.
Step soft, we're a beach: step firmly, a landslide.
At the head of the sky is a burning stone,
A circlet of stars, a mirroring moon, an eye of blinding gold.
At the bottom of every sky is a world;
At the foot of its forested mountains, always a stream.
We aren't the gold nor the blue nor the slope.
We aren't the stream nor the sound of its rushing.
We are the bed on which the world rests,
In criminal patience, in bleak stupid patience.

Seven

Was less than we were used
to being. We had once been the number one more than seven, we
clots in the earth's arteries. But the noisy one left and maybe for need
of him we were stricken with attention. When we were only seven,
there was something wrong.

It was a matter of balance. There is a smug assurance among pairs,
a possibility of completion that other creatures lack. We knew enough
of the world of beasts and men to see how males burrow and females
furrow, but the comfort of pairing isn't critically dependent on that
exercise.

We lived without the caw and twitch of sex, or to date we had.
Unaware of parents but for the mothering hills and the smothering
sky, we made do with what we knew: each other. We had no names.
We couldn't count until one of us left, and then we learned to count
to seven, and to figure out odd from even. With a departed compan-

ion, there was a looseness to our group. There was a way in which we were incomplete, and, perhaps, more alert because of that hunger.

The human mind—we have come to observe—tricks out distinctions in principles of opposition. A man more foul will likely be less benign. A woman with a greedy belly may also be mean with her widow's mite. The way a man slakes his thirst and a woman slakes her thirst are not identical, for they thirst for different things.

Perhaps that is why humans rely on the mirror, to get beyond the simple me-you, handsome-hideous, menacing-merciful. In a mirror, humans see that the other one is also them: the two are the same, one one. The menace accompanies the mercy. The transcendent cohabits with the corrupt. What stirring lives humans have managed to live, knowing this of themselves! And so we had made a mirror, and in our foolishness lost it, and the one who set out to reclaim it had never returned. Back into our unexamined selves we slunk, until she arrived at our door.

To say we were pairs is to propose, to the human mind, a system of marriages among brothers, as if 3 and 4 were one unit together in all things, as if 3 and 4 gave to each other something denied to 5 or 2. This isn't the case. To say we were pairs isn't to propose an intimacy or a singularity among our pairings. It's merely to say that we functioned, loosely, as teams of two, and it hardly mattered whether it was 1 or 7 on the other side of the table or the other end of the long saw or the other edge of the pillow. Indeed, until recently, we wouldn't have known to identify 1 from 7, or 4 from 6, or a pillow from a saw. In our efficiency we were blind.

But one of us left, and we eventually noticed that he was gone.

There wasn't enough of us to go around. It wasn't 7 who was abandoned, nor any other one of us. It was the all of us, and then we learned to count to seven, and saw that we ought to have been able to count to the next number up, the seven plus one. But we couldn't, for that one was gone. In his absence, we remembered once again our incompleteness.

We were shorn, softly and without pain, of our assurance. We noticed what was wrong. We began to notice one another.

The appetite for noticing having been awakened, we were ready to notice the girl who fell, faint from hunger and cold, at our threshold.

She might not have known it for a threshold at first. We have our clandestine ways. It might have looked to her like a log decomposing in the forest, or a ledge of gray granite outcrop. It's never easy to see through the eyes of humans and guess what they think they are seeing.

But we saw her, in our bumbling unsatisfied way. We took her in. We dragged her over the threshold, aware, some of us for the first time, of the fringed pattern of muscled digits at the ends of our arms that, for lack of a better word, might as well be called hands. We used our hands—hands. Hah—and we carried her into the smokelight, the better to look upon her form.

We didn't call her Bianca de Nevada, we didn't say, "Wake up, Bianca de Nevada." We didn't know that was what she was called. We hardly knew, I think, that people had names.

But we cast our glances sidelong, to see if she was our missing one.

She seemed not to be, unless he had changed a good deal.

She had hair of graven black lines, fine lines, each distinct but with like inclination; they spread upon the pillow in a soft fan that moved as her head moved. The brows on her face were pale as the underside of a dragon's gullet. Indeed, there was something of the look of a corpse about her, though we've come to realize this is true of all humans. They begin to die with their first infant's wail. But it was truer of her, because of the tone of her skin.

Her limbs were long enough to have uncoiled from their embryonic spasm. Her lower trunk was clad in a skirt the color of dried moss, and her torso in a tunic of meadowlark brown. Her hands—far more clever than ours, more completely cloven into separate fingers—lay back on the pillow, curled slightly like the legs of a crawfish, and the tenderness of her palms was enough to make us weep, though we couldn't say why, and I daresay to this day none of us would try to explain.

We didn't discuss her or touch her, but we drew to her chin a blanket of webweed, for we're accustomed to the damp and the dark, but we know human beings only learn what we know when they have died and been consigned to the soil.

For her comfort we kept away the mealworms and sliceworms and the dung beetles. One of us—none could say who, for we didn't yet distinguish ourselves one from the other—sat near her shoulder and brushed decay away.

We had nothing better to do but sit and keep watch over her until she had finished her rest. It was likely that she slept three, perhaps four years, before she stirred.

When her eyelids did flutter, we became shy, as if caught in a common sin, though without the individual soul to save or lose, we were as incapable of sin as a scorpion.

She breathed in and out several times, and sat up. Her hair, we were interested to note, had become longer while she slept, and as she blinked her eyes, she caught her hair in the crook of her arm and shielded her bosom with it. (Her tunic had fallen away into separate threads and couldn't behave as a tunic any longer.)

"Good Savior," she said, "preserve me from this dream."

We blinked; as none of us considered ourselves the Good Savior we didn't think it proper to reply.

"Who are you?" she asked.

This was a remark more likely dedicated to our family, but the one who was gone—the one that, plus seven, had made us whole—was the one among us who was oldest, and most capable of language. We worked our throats to find words within, with little success.

"I'm Bianca de Nevada," she told us. "I'm the daughter of Vicente and María de Nevada of Montefiore, on the edge of Toscana heading toward Umbria. I've never seen your sort before. Who are you?"

The question occasionally invents the answer. We heard her words, and saw her pallor, and perceived that *Bianca* meant *white*. So names were characteristics, then, and we chose from among the characteristics of stone to invent ourselves, out of charity.

"Stone can't see," said one of us, blinking. "So call me Blindeye."

"My limbs are like stone, so I'm Lame," said another. "Or maybe Gimpy." "Stone can't taste, so I'm Tasteless."

"No more can stone smell, so I might be No-Nose, but if I could smell, I would smell Bitter. So call me Bitter and have done with it."

"I didn't quite hear the question; stone is hard of hearing. So you can call me Deaf-to-the-World, thank you for asking."

"I'm Heartless, for I can't feel," said the red-bearded one, with a reluctant sigh.

The seventh didn't answer for a moment. When we looked at him, he said, "Stone can't speak, so I'm Mute, Mute; always was Mute, always will be Mute. MuteMuteMute. Why do you even bother to ask? Why do you bother me so?" MuteMuteMute, it seemed, would have liked very much to talk, and was therefore irritable at being reminded of his debility.

But in the naming of ourselves for the first time, we felt the absence of our missing brother more strongly than ever. "And then," one of us answered, "there is the departed one of us, who has more sense and more senses than the rest."

"And his name?" asked Bianca.

"Next," someone said, and we others thought about it, then nodded.

This is how we were born. She sat amidst us, more or less naked as a human baby, looking, but it was we older brothers—older than trees, older than wind, older than choice—who were born in her presence. Blindeye, Heartless, Gimpy, Deaf-to-the-World, MuteMuteMute, Bitter, and Tasteless: incomplete sections of each other, beginning our lumbering life of individuality—

—beginning our lumbering lives.

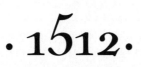

The dwarves

STIRRING, AWARE of small pains. The chamber had a musty aspect, as of a catacomb or an ossuary. She couldn't tell where the light originated. There were no apparent windows, there was no suggestion of sunlight, even behind panels of wood or draping folds of carpet. Yet she could see—she blinked—and the room swam into a cooler, more decisive focus.

She sensed the arbitrary, the conditional. Only when she tried to tell herself what it was did it settle down, the way telling a dream makes a dream gain its legs and lose its mystery. *The space was nothing like a room* . . . and as the word *room* is spoken, even to deny a likeness, the nonroom-like space becomes more like a room, regardless.

There was a space that became more like a room as she considered it. The long stone on which she sat seemed, on reflection, to straighten its angles, as if tending to think itself a bed; and then, belatedly, it grew or acquired bedposts of a sort, which became more nicely carved the more Bianca thought about it.

Her clothes had fallen and rotted off her, nothing less than that—and she was naked beneath the slightly clammy sheet. Was it linen?—yes, a fine linen, and look at that embroidery stitching itself as she watched, making the complicated turn around the corner, and the small white rosettes blooming at intervals!

How peculiar to be naked, she with her lifelong shyness about her form. It was distracting. It therefore took her some time to register the conversation she seemed to be having with other matters of business in the room—bits of furniture, were they, or seven boulders arranged randomly?

No, boulders don't speak, except in dreams.

The muscles of her neck ached and she urgently needed to urinate, not uncommon in a dream. So dreaming or not, she began to stretch and to draw the sheet around her, as modestly as she could. The sheet fed straps forward over her shoulders that bit where they ought, forming a yoke and bib and gown that allowed her to move with modesty. Then she stood and found a porcelain vessel for peeing into, and squatted above it.

One never pees in a dream, one only needs to. So what did it mean, that she could?

Only when she had finished, and pushed her hair back from her forehead—the hair that fell now almost to her waist—did the opinionated rocks begin to shift. Had the rocks been speaking to her? She had a sense that they had: what an odd dream this was being. She couldn't see them well at all. It was as if they drank the light in the room and emitted it as darkness, a kind of cloaking smudginess. She felt she was looking through a glass clouded with soot. She couldn't make her eyes work correctly, rub them as she might. The creatures were neither naked nor clothed, so far as she could tell, only rather roughly cast. They had a look of—how to put it—character. She thought of the way an outcropping on a ridge will resemble, suddenly, a crouching dog, or an angel's flexing wing, and once you have noticed it you can never pass by it unaware again.

How the edge of this boulder resembled the jutting brow of a scowling man.

A very small scowling man, but a man nonetheless, not a child. Nothing childlike at all.

And this one had a flared hump to one side that looked like a misshapen shoulder, drawn back; one could finish the thought of the boulder and imagine the swelling some inches down as a hand on a hip.

And this other, on her other side. A sense of its straining.

It was uncomfortable; she was surrounded by granite forms imitating creatures. It made her feel preyed upon.

She stood again, height being all she had against them. A painful tenderness in her groin, from where she had urinated. She groaned without caution.

She wanted to leave them, to train her eyes more carefully upon the walls of this chamber, and notice them into clarity: a wall of polished planks, of ruddy brick, of rusticated stones?—something to identify. Anything. Nothing would clarify unless she worked at it. She moved forward again, to leave the standing circle around her, and noticed—how had she missed it before?—that her fingernails had gone long and witchlike, ivory scythes splintered at the ends, capable of ripping skin. Her toenails curled like tusks, and nestled into one another like the overlapping segments of a flattish, chambered shell.

She felt she'd died and been buried, and was being restored to life, to a new life, as an animal. She was one step shy of being human now. Her breasts, though modestly sheathed in her gown of bedding, moved of their own new weight, and brushed against the cloth bib. The tender tips of her breasts blistered with a curious sort of pain, and she shook, from her elbows to her spine. The convulsion drew the cloth against her breasts again. She exhaled with a spasm of her cheeks and tongue, releasing a wordless sound of surprise.

Braised, tormented—the whole world leaning upon her in the form of a bedsheet fingering her skin—she stepped back, as if her sleep were still waiting for her on the bed, like body warmth left in the mattress for a few moments after you arise. As if she could subside back into sleep safely, and wake up some other time, some other way.

Then the convulsion, which had had a teasing aspect as well as a frightening one, took a deeper bite of her body, lower down, and the soft pain of her groin sharpened. As if in her sleep she'd been impregnated by a wolf, and a young wolf cub was scrabbling at her interior to bite its own exit passage. She sank to her knees, her arms crooked behind and her elbows pressing down into the mattress. She flung her head backward and clenched her fists. Her knees hit the floor and lifted and hit the floor again. Like a bellows her thighs worked back and forth.

"*Mamma,*" she said, "*Mamma.* Gesù Cristo. *Mamma, Mamma.*" Then her words gave way to mere syllables, lengthening inchoate sounds.

She voided her interior. The blood rolled and splashed, and bits of matter tore embery fingers against her insides. Whatever Primavera had predicted, it wasn't anything like this. She waited for the blood to take a face, for its airy bubbles to sit and wink like eyes, or for a form to slither out of her on its sluice of organic juices and devour her. She closed her eyes to protect herself from seeing whatever it would be, and she rocked more exhaustedly, from side to side. Her legs were slick, her buttocks and her heels slick, and she fell, almost fainting, as if she couldn't endure such loss of blood without a loss of breath or even life. She found herself rolled against one of the boulders, and then another. They were moving, they were closing in on her, like the stones of her tomb come to do their job, and her blood lapped against their roots, and splashed their sides. She swooned.

When she came to consciousness—the same, or another sort, she couldn't tell—the room had taken its own measure and settled down some.

There was no direct source of light, no oil lamps or hearth fires, no sunlight bleeding along the edges of a shuttered window. No windows at all. But the space had volume and there was even some color, of a sandy, ochre-tinged sort.

She pulled herself to her feet and looked about. Along the edges of what she could perceive ran ranks of stone boxes, all large enough to contain human remains. Sarcophagi, she guessed, with carvings on the front and sides, and statues of smaller-than-life-size figures reclining on the lids

It might have been horrifying, but it wasn't. It was nice not to feel alone. The long front panels illustrated scenes of war, naked Romans battling with naked Etruscans. The bas-relief was so heightened it almost looked as if the figures were going to detach from the stone. Greek letters, less regular than the human proportions, spelled captions she couldn't read.

The portrait sculptures up top were carved in an identical position. All the figures reared up on one elbow, pivoting on a hip, as if watching her. But their facial features had been eroded by age, and it wasn't easy to tell if they were male or female. They held shallow cups for celebration, and coins or wine were deposited within. She found it easy to accept a raised stone dish from a cheery effigy and drink a swallow of wine. Though open to the air of the tomb for a thousand years or two, the wine had aged well and was delicious.

Here were knives with handles of bone. Here, on the floor, bits of Roman glass. Here, an anomaly: a figure of Proserpina, her composure calm and unthreatening. She held one hand on her breast, as if feeling her own pulse, and her other hand was held out, offering a stone apple to the dead. It's not so bad, she seemed to say; half a life in the sun, half a life in the earth: I've learned to manage quite well. Call me Persephone and feed me a persimmon; call me Proserpina and hand me an apple. Whatever I have I share.

Her smile was sweet and eroded. Around her stood double-handled vases in black glaze, no doubt containing the ashes of the dead. It was a calm cinerarium. The only unpleasantness was a faint smell of *pietra fetida*—that stone with a faint reek of sulfur.

She couldn't tell what the floor was like, as she couldn't see much of it, except where her blood had splashed and dried gummily.

Standing amid the sarcophagi lurked the random uncarved boulders. She hunted about until she found a bucket that stood beneath a pump. Working the pump for what seemed hours, hoping that the hollow retching sound below indicated suction and water, she was rewarded at last with a gush of dusty water that quickly turned pure and cold, almost icy. She filled the bucket nearly to the brim and carried it to the side of the bed, and she began to scrub at the floor, to erase evidence of her blood flow.

She dabbed where she had to, where the blood reached, and as her eyes fell upon the first of the boulders, she remembered she had seen them vaguely featured with human characteristics. Now, though they remained still, she had an even stronger sense of presence. She mopped the blood gingerly, as if cleaning wounds, first from one and then another, and when she was done the bucket of water had gone red. She couldn't find a drain in which to slop it, and there was no door to the chamber—just walls and a floor. No windows, no door, no further world.

She sat back on her heels and looked the nearest boulder in the eye sockets, and said, "Well, forgive me my trespasses, then."

"Ah, we forgive you who trespass against us," said the boulder.

"I do beg your mercy," she said.

"Don't tire yourself. Mercy isn't something we concern ourselves with." The boulder was blushing to life, filling in its outlines with a rough musculature. A clothed, bearded obstinacy became slowly apparent—more or less like a man, though rather less than more. Not merely because of its stature, but also because it retained in its fixed expression something of the rock. It had eyes that didn't move in its skull, but its skull could swivel on its torso (there seemed no neck), and the head moved back and forth, surveying things, almost as if it were waking up just as she had.

"Gesù," she said. "Preserve me from this dream. Who are you?"

The boulders spoke—the others first—naming their incapacities, naming their attributes as stone. Blind, deaf, mute, and lame; lacking in smell, lacking in the ability to savor. The one nearest her, the one who seemed most like a figure, said, "I am Heartless, for I cannot feel." With the severe expression of an owl he turned his head and glared at her.

"Heartless," she said, nodding, as if able at least to understand this much.

"And our departed partner is named Next," said Heartless.

She didn't know what he meant. She was busy trying to understand that he was really speaking. She wasn't sure she could see his lips move, but perhaps the beard and untrimmed mustaches concealed motion.

The other stone senses shifted, like heavy creatures in swiftly flowing water: ponderously, thoughtfully, so as not to lose their balance. She couldn't be sure of their sexes—male or female, or whether they had sexes at all. But Heartless seemed the most finished in form, perhaps because he stood the nearest, and he was clearly male, anyway, from his overly bristling eyebrows to the pouching groin.

"I'm bewildered," she said. "Talking to a stone. How can this be?"

Heartless shrugged.

"How long have I been asleep here?" she said.

"It's not long."

"I've become a mature person. But I only remember falling in the forest."

"You fell at our door."

"Luck—?"

"Design."

"Why?"

"You could be safe here."

"How did you know I would fall at your threshold though? As I recall it, nothing was chasing me. I had fled a hunter, I'd been told not to return to my home. The night was a terror, the woods scrabbling their twig fingers—but how in all the world could I fall right where you planned?"

"We planned to be where you fell. It isn't the same thing."

"But how did you know?"

Again, he shrugged.

"How much time have I slept here? There are chores to do," she said, straightening up. "If not chores at the farm, then surely, chores here."

"You approve of our arrangements?" he said, brightly.

"Not as gloomy as I'd have imagined. But how long have I been here? I am older—my arms feel like paddles, my breasts turn at their own speed, my legs are monstrously long. Look at these nails. It'll take days to file them down."

"You've been here long enough to grow, I suppose," he said, without interest.

"I'm here four years, or five, certainly. Or six?"

"I don't know."

"And what have you been doing in all those years?"

"Waiting. Waiting for you to wake up."

"Standing here around me? For years? What did you do all that time?"

"To the extent we are capable," he said, with a slight grin, "we were thinking."

"What do you think, then?" she demanded of him.

He considered. "Slow thoughts."

The others came forward a little. They were like small children with decrepit faces. Their heads were large, noses bulbous and raw, beards tattered, or patchy, or bushy as broom. There was a family resemblance, of a sort, but only a little variety in the stitching on a sleeve, the color of a cloak. One had a full set of very black teeth inset with gold bands, an arresting sight.

"What do you want of me?" she said.

Heartless made a sign, dotting the air with a series of poking motions, as if writing something with his finger. "Once we wanted to change into something more human than we are. Now we only want our brother back. Without him, we shift, we adjust. We need to know where he is."

"I have nothing to do with your brother," she said.

"Perhaps you do," he answered. "He went to your father to propose a bargain, and when your father left, our brother went with him. We guess that your guardian, la Donna Borgia, can tell us where he is."

She had forgotten about her father, about Lucrezia. She had forgotten about the world beyond the room. It hurt her head to think of it.

"How does la Borgia know where your brother is? You're speaking nonsense."

"I'm speaking truth," he answered. "Your guardian now stands before our looking glass. We want it back. We want to look in it and see our brother. We don't want to change any more. We change before your eyes." It was true. The lips were more red, the fingers more divided; the beard looked less like carved granite and more like human hair. "We want to be whole and alone, and she has divided us into segments, as if we were lost individuals, the way humans are. We aren't humans."

"You are dwarves," she said, asking more than stating. He turned his head.

"We want our looking glass."

A hole in the world

TIME BEGAN to pass in a more customary fashion, which is to say that Bianca grew to be able to see better. The dwarves left her alone. At first she would sleep and wake fitfully, but in time more regularly. The befurred darkness overhead looked less like the inside of a marsupial pouch and more like a ceiling, with carved rafters, and a chandelier made of four stag skulls, with full racks intertwining, and candles set in their forking branches.

Though Proserpina remained to smile vacantly ahead, the accoutrements of the tomb seemed to be disappearing. Were the dwarves smartening things up while she was asleep? Providing a more habitable space for her? Or was she organizing it herself, out of interior boredom and memory.

In time, the walls of the chamber became paneled halfway up with a wormholed chestnut sadly in need of oiling. Above the chair rail the walls were sheathed in a sort of green stone with a pale black striation, and nooks and shelves and crannies were cut in them any which way. There were long deep shelves, suitable for salvers or shields to be slotted in, and cubbies large enough for nothing more than a mug, a ring, a pair of gloves. But the shelves were too high for the dwarves, for they were all empty.

The floor was littered with rags, ladles, cooking pots, boots, axes, gems, urns, swords, pelts, skeletons of small animals, bundles of dried vegetables, hooded cloaks, blankets sour with mildew, locked books, calcified turds, platters, coils of rope, candles, censers, colorfully glazed storage pots sealed with wax, belt buckles, pearls, lilies in bloom from their tubers, eggs, keys on an iron ring, several cats, bedding, and corked vials carved from ivory.

There was still no door, no window, and she couldn't say whether the dwarves disappeared or reappeared in the middle of the air, or if they just went and stood behind the bits of furniture for hours on end. It was almost as if they had some way of cloaking their access to the exit. As Bianca's thinking grew sharper, she thought: Maybe they project themselves forward or backward, so that some semblance of them lingers in the air after the essence has already removed itself. At any rate, there was always a murkiness in their aspect.

At the beginning the dwarves seemed to have interchangeable at-tributes. She couldn't keep them straight. The one with a red beard and a monk's tonsure at breakfast seemed, at lunch, to have a red beard but a full head of curly white hair, and the monk's tonsure was now being sported by the dwarf with the black teeth. Their voices were hard to track because only one of them ever seemed to speak at a time. Perhaps it was that they all had the same voice except the one who had said, crisply, that he was MuteMuteMute. But after a while it began to seem as if things were solidifying. As an exercise to prove herself canny, Bianca tried to catalog the dwarves' attributes, and the harder she tried, the more the attributes seemed to stay put.

Heartless was the one who most often took the voice. He seemed to have a certain patience for Bianca. It wasn't the patience of a dog, or of the vacant gooseboy, or of Primavera even; it was a patience with no expectation of a reward. Bianca grew to like the times when Heartless was there and the others, in their mysterious way, gone. He sat near her and ran fingers through his red beard, clearing it of pebbles, grit, sand.

She'd found a pot and underneath it, with some effort, she had located a fire. Though she couldn't see a flue, the smoke from a healthy fire slithered elsewhere, somehow, and occasionally the pot was helpfully filled with cold water. So she could boil vegetables, and leaves and scraps of meat. If she looked to the right or the left, and concentrated, she could find a table, and more often than not it was heaped with whatever she needed—a candle snuffer, a stole for warmth, a cut of lamb and a heap of onions, a tankard of warm milk.

Though she tried, she couldn't find a key to fit in some door that she might locate one day.

But she found her memories, bit by bit, working backward. She remembered Ranuccio, the hunter, and his abduction of her from the kitchen. She remembered him without remorse or contempt. Indeed, as he was the last person she saw before her long, dreamless sleep, she remembered him well, as if she had known him well. The long chin, the neat beard, the feel of his hand around her wrist. Four, five, six years later, she could still feel the heat and the pressure of his palm and his fingers against her.

She remembered Primavera next. Primavera. It was as if Primavera were a huge egg of a woman, a moon, bowling along in the corridors of the house. Bianca felt a wealth of fondness toward the old woman, who seemed to have been present at the birth of the universe and grown old long before the first drops of the Flood burst from God's vengeful clouds.

Of the others, she was less sure. She remembered Fra Ludovico a little, his blustery ways, his off-key singing. How he disguised his bravery as foolishness.

And then there was her father. She'd never forgotten him, ever, but he was so far behind her now. She'd been, what, six, seven when he left? And now she must be seventeen. Vicente de Nevada, who had left her to—to what? To follow some woman? To find his fortunes? To be rid of the burden? If she knew herself better, she'd know whether she could forgive him or not.

What was she, really? What had she become? What did it mean to be a girl, or a new woman, imprisoned on the crest of a lonely hill, imprisoned in a room without a window or door? She found herself dubious about basic personal matters—whether, for instance, she preferred peaches to figs, or the music of harps to the music of lutes. How could she be such a cipher? How could there be so little of her to know? And here she was, older and mature, but now as good as dead, with no one but ambulatory stones to talk to.

There had been other children at Montefiore, surely? In trying to picture them, she wasn't sure if she was inventing them as effectively as, an hour ago, she'd come up with a fresh camisole.

She remembered a lad with an expression of permanent surprise on his face; that grass was green when he went out of doors seemed to come as a pleasant shock every time. He waded about the world with a gabbling hedge of orange beaks and downy flowers—the geese. She remembered geese. So he must be the gooseboy. Sweet dim thing.

She remembered the maids of the kitchen, who might have been her friends, but for their rural ways. Though Bianca had slopped pigs and gathered olives and helped boil the tallow and hang out the laundry, she hadn't been a candidate for their friendship.

So she had been lonely. Yes, now she could see it. Lonely, in part because she hadn't been a rural farmhand. She had been the daughter of the house.

Montefiore.

She remembered it with a heady pleasure. The chapel without its roof, the steep walls on the house's cliff side, the way the house otherwise sagged comfortably down toward the approaching slope, its red roofs like plums drying in the sun. If she was the daughter of the house, the house was her real parent. The only one that had lasted. "I want to see Montefiore," she said to the principal dwarf, Heartless.

"You are bitten with the usual human rage of wanting," replied the dwarf, munching on a bone that looked unsettlingly like a human digit.

"Nonetheless," she said. "I am human, or used to be, and I don't see any shame in it. I want to see the place I come from."

"Don't we give you all that you need?"

"I have clothes, I have a book of devotions to read, and a small Spanish guitar to play. I have food of exactly the quality and variety I can imagine but no finer, nothing to delight me by its novelty. If I am to be restricted to the apprehension of anything I've known in my previous life, then let it at least include memory. I want to see Montefiore again."

"Aren't you happy here?" asked the dwarf, a bit morosely. And then more slyly, "Were you ever happy there?"

"I was something there," she said. "Aware of something sad, but real. Living on the forward edge of any ordinary day. Things happened. I don't know how to answer your question about happiness. Happiness doesn't signify. Can you give me what I ask?"

She didn't understand the equation by which her needs were met; at times she believed she was making the dwarves up herself. But Heartless, whose red beard seemed more and more likely to sit on his face and not wander off to someone else's, finished his meal. He pushed the bone to one side and belched, and got down off his stool. He walked to the middle of the room and said, "Were you to get what you want, poor thing, you wouldn't want it. Isn't the wanting richer?"

"I don't know what is richer," she said. "It's not a question that interests me."

"Then pick me up and help me, and you deal with your concerns as you must."

She didn't want to touch him. She hadn't touched any of them since the day she washed her menstrual blood from their stone feet. She was afraid he'd change in her arms. But he stood there with rude dignity, glaring, and she had no choice. She stood and approached him, and reached down and picked him up under the arms. She grunted with the effort. He was a boulder, after all.

"Turn my face toward the wall," he said.

She did, with some trouble, and when she had cradled his seat in her braced arms, she leaned closer to the wall, which today seemed a hairy web of roots and skittering stones, and soil falling in soft dry fans upon the granite floor.

Heartless reached out and twisted aside two protruding tree roots with as little fuss as if they were made of softened wax. He poked them into gentle swags. In the space between them, framed like a window, he put out his left hand and smoothed the dirt. Then, having removed a stone or two and eaten them, he leaned forward and breathed on the rude circle he had implied with his hands.

The air turned silvery, a vertical plaque of fog. Again Heartless pushed forward his hands and smoothed it. He patted it down till the air was still and gray as a slice of ice cut from a frozen lake. He breathed again. With an expression suggesting he regretted her appetite for the past, he gestured at Bianca de Nevada.

"Go ahead then. Look, if you must."

The beast in the wall

ICENTE PRACTICED remember-
ing the tricks that weather could play on the eyes.

—How fog could shroud the features of a person, making them
seem, at a distance, little more than the suggestion of a human.

—How the sky could glow with pale colored ribbons after a
rainstorm.

—One night the moon had bloomed over the plains with the
color of the juice of a blood orange.

—One day, the moon had swaggered up to the sun and punched
it in the eye, and the world had gone midnight at midday. Birds had
lost their bearing and smashed against the walls of the kitchen garden,
and Primavera had made a stew of them.

In the absence of any real weather in the dungeon, Vicente designed days, months, whole seasons in his mind. But how odd, wasn't
it, that the crispest memories were of aberrations. The snow in April,

that one year, when icicles formed on the clematis blossoms. The year it thundered at midnight, Christmas Eve, aborting the service. Was that 1500, when all of Europe was readying to be overrun by hellish vermin, in preparation for the doom of time? But whatever had been borne that frightful year had skittered away without much damage, smothered by the smooth round of normal days. And it was ordinary days—the lazy passing of sun over the orchards, hour by hour—

It didn't do to consider how much he missed them. He just imagined them, and let them drift away.

Since he couldn't be getting younger, he must be aging. As his muscle tone went, so, perhaps, his mind. He therefore wasn't as surprised as he might have been to notice one day that a portion of the wall seemed to be bowing. Perhaps it was a sort of erosion. He had been in here an awfully long time, after all.

For a while the wall just seemed to swell, like a buboes, though mercifully free of that certain rankness. Finally (after hours, or days, or weeks? Who could say?) the growth detached, and an accretion of boulder stood on its own single footing. Vicente, when he could pull himself off his mat, found he could walk around it. The place from which it had been evacuated seemed a deeper pocket than such a stone would require.

He sat and looked at it, on and off. Indefinitely. It seemed at times to have the character of a creature, though he knew if he began befriending random boulders, his final mental collapse was near. The stone had no face, which was the confounding part. Four legs clumped closely together, more or less the same shape, each lumpy with a bit of knee, slightly splayed at floor level to suggest a padded foot. The legs terminated above in a domed and sloping brow.

There was no mouth, or none he could be sure of. An orifice puckered at one side, off center, though it might as easily be an anus as a mouth, or an ear. Or just a beauty mark of sorts. The stone didn't radiate menace, though in a way Vicente would have welcomed even menace, to vary his days.

Then one evening (he still could tell day from night, mostly, thanks to the high window), the thing suddenly shook itself violently, like something belabored with a whip, and straightened up. Its lumpy brow elevated slightly, with a bestial sort of intelligence. Though there were no discernible sensory organs, Vicente had the impression he was being observed.

He began to speak in Spanish—most of his thoughts had reverted to the tongue of his mother. As well as he could remember, he told the thing how he had come to be here. The act of speaking brought words back to his tongue and thoughts to his head. Fra Ludovico. Fra Ludovico, for instance, of all ridiculous men! He'd been a figure of some ridicule, but how nice to find him around in the memory, capable of being mentioned.

The creature stretched its legs and shrugged its headless shoulders. A fruity, indecent odor emerged from somewhere, but it didn't last long and at least it smelled *warm*. And that was something.

Vicente said, "I've come to this miserable scrag-end of the world to find the food that fed the beginning of our race. I've come to find the fruit of the Tree of Knowledge."

The creature betrayed no surprise at this, though perhaps it didn't understand Spanish. Or perhaps it had no way to demonstrate surprise except by curling its sort-of-toes, which it did from time to time expressively.

Vicente was undaunted by the creature's taciturn nature. He found that he was standing and swinging his arms with excitement as he recalled the excitement of seeing Montefiore for the first time. His lord and tyrant, that scandalous Cesare Borgia, had seen to it that Vicente was accompanied to the new home with a small party of mercenaries sporting the Borgia pennant and equipped with an iron-spiked battering ram. "In any event, there was no opposition to my taking possession of Montefiore," said Vicente. "I came upon a place in mild disrepair, with sullen and uncommunicative *contadini* and house servants more or less attached to the property. They resented us at first. But they were won over. They took us in, and as time passed . . ."

He paused and looked at the stone beast, and several things happened at once.

"My Bianca, my sweetest Bianca. María Inés was dead, but she left me Bianca."

As Vicente spoke her name, the beast straightened up for a moment, alert and, it even seemed, respectful. If it is courteous to bow before royalty, it is courteous to honor the humble who deserve it. The behavior of the stone beast—its rough brow elevated—gave Vicente de Nevada his first experience of acknowledgment in years. A response to something he said.

"Bianca de Nevada," said Vicente. "My daughter."

He had come here, those years earlier, as a way to protect her. He was to have secured the limb of a tree, history's most ancient tree, out of duty toward her. He had forgotten. He had let his imprisonment overwhelm his memory and his duty, not to *il Valentino* but to his daughter.

"I need to leave," he said to the beast. "I need to claim that talisman and return. I can't tell if I've been gone for a year or a decade, but I've been *gone too long*. Let us finish this job, then, and away to Italy."

The stone beast lowered its brow and turned (by which action Vicente decided the lower beveled side was the front, and the higher side approximated a cranial hump rising behind). It began to crunch its way into the hole from which it had been disgorged. A sound of scrunching and grinding. Small dry streams of sand and pulverized gravel spat out. The beast didn't merely reclaim its stone womb, though. It kept going, apparently. To judge by the noise, the creature was burrowing through rock. In its wake was a tunnel.

In his prime Vicente couldn't have fit through such a narrow passage. But he had wasted into a reptilian slip of a thing. Having nothing to claim as his possession, he began to make his escape from the dungeon cell of Teophilos.

The stone beast carved out a sharply angled turn. It started to burrow upward. The detritus slipped down and backward and hit Vicente in the face. With every passing moment of effort, Vicente felt a bit

more awake. He was aware of his breathing. Of the trembling ineffi-
ciency of his muscles. Of the sand in his lungs. He was aware that his
flesh hung on his arms like rotting cotton cloth, and that his clothes
were encumbering as a winding sheet. But his mind felt sharper and
sharper. He began to feel affection for the stone beast, and to think the
simple thoughts that he had once had for his hunting dogs. Good dog,
he thought. Good boy. You have a nose I don't have, and eyes that can
see through stone. Apparently. Good boy. And on we go.

When the beast had made another soft turn and begun to rise
again, scrabbling, eating, bullying the rock aside—Vicente couldn't
imagine how it was done—it occurred to him that they were following a path within the thick walls of the monastery itself. They were
twisting around the soft curves of the building's grand and massive
salient. They were following the straight line of the wall of an interior
chamber. They might emerge any minute in a wine cellar, a laundry
room, a chamber for storing herbs and root vegetables, an apothecary.

The stone beast paused at last and made a final exertion, and then
pushed through. Vicente followed into a well of light that burned like
pitch against his eyes.

It was probably a mercy that he cried in pain, for his tears mois-
tened, cleansing his eyes of grit. The outlines of lighted things shivered. In time, he could sit up and look about himself, and clutch his
knees in astonishment. He had forgotten how convincing the world
could look, how sure of itself, its outlines and edges, its gradations, re-
cessions, protrusions, its startling and vulgar colors.

They had come into a room of prayer, with four high windows
in a cupola overhead, shafting hot broiled light yellowly down from
the sides of a high thin dome. Cristo Pantocrator was figured in gold
leaf upon a wall, staring with massive cold love and patience. The
Paraclete was opposite, serrated tips of fire crowning its head, seven
olive branches in one claw and seven laurel bows in the other. Between the two, on an altar, stood a tabernacle. The corners were pil-
lars of solid Persian lapis lazuli. The lintels and struts were knobbed
with dusty jewels. Each wall was a piece of glass about as large as a

man's chest. Inside, resting on a golden armature specially carved to support the thing in a natural arc, sprayed the bough of the tree of Eden, with silver leaves, and three well-formed apples in their first blush of ripeness.

Vicente felt little by way of awe. Whether the artifact was an object of profound theological implication or an exquisite work of art didn't matter. The whole room, with its motes of dust dancing slowly in the shafts of possessive light, seemed miracle enough. Gesù Cristo Himself, waving from beyond the glass, couldn't have made Vicente feel more staggered, joyous, alive.

The stone beast put out its two forward limbs. Easily it balanced on its hind ones, and reared up. It raised its digitless arms and laid them with a soft clipping sound against one of the glass facades. It knows, thought Vicente, why I've come here. It's been dispatched, or it has dispatched itself, to be my guide. Was it a calcified angel of some sort, or a friendly stone dog? No matter. It did the duty of friendship. It raked its limbs gently across the glass. The tips of its limbs, where there ought to be paws, or hands, puckered and settled. One limb gently swept the glass out of the air, into a ball, as neatly as a film of morning hoarfrost can be scooped up and rounded.

Then the creature fell back. The bough stood ready for taking. It wasn't the beast's job to take it. It was Vicente's, and he knew it.

Tremblingly he reached in and detached the bough from its stand. He held it with no more reverence than he had held Bianca, when she had been a spray of eternity in his arms. Perfection of bone, breath, and blossom.

Vicente set the artifact on the floor while he looked around for a sack or a casket in which to carry it. He didn't need to bother. With its strange limbs the beast secreted the thing somewhere in the folds of its stone form. It disappeared, harbored in stone.

They turned and left the treasury. From a distance Vicente could hear the soft keening of monks at prayer. Possibly they were on duty, guarding the doors. He wished them well and was sorry for their loss.

Back into the flank of the wall they crawled. The stone beast had

to go first, being able to intuit the way somehow, and Vicente to follow. Since Vicente couldn't rebuild the wall behind him, their mode
of escape would be obvious. Who knew how long it would be before
an alarm was raised and a party dispatched to reclaim the stolen relic?
Perhaps quite a while, Vicente thought, and hoped, and, yes, prayed.
Perhaps the monks looked in on their most precious possession only
on the highest of high holy days, or on the ascension of a new bishop
or prelate.

Or perhaps they checked on it on the hour; it was impossible to
know.

The stone beast burrowed. Vicente followed. They traced a long
tunneled route through stone as cold as ice. In time they emerged on
a beach of broken shale. All about them burned stars, making a span-
gled mess in the sweet black sky.

Al-iksir

THE SLIGHTEST poem of my dear Pietro Bembo, smuggled into my chambers when the dreadful Duca de Ferrara is away, and I tremble before unfolding the page. It might be anything. It might say anything. It might contain the secret that will make me more alive. I open the page. It's a poem, it's a thing of beauty, it's a testament of love, it is everything a woman could want. It isn't enough.

I can hear the legend they make of my life already. I can hear the scoundrels practicing their slanders and half truths about my vices. Donna Lucrezia, they say, in voices falsely honeyed: a patroness of the arts, a whore of Babylon, a murderess and a communicant, a mother and a mistress, a daughter and a Diana. They exaggerate my romances. They miss the point. Gossip serves some purpose. May their purposes fail in the end.

Sometimes I dream of the water. I saw the sea in Naples, of

course, and I am no stranger to views of our cold alexandrine Adriatic, of the more limpidly turquoise Tyrrhenian Sea. But I've not sailed
out beyond the sight of land, out between the slipping thumbs of
waves and the shapely varnished disc of the heavens. I've never been
beyond reach of father or brother or husband or lover. I should like
not to turn my back on my life, but I would be grateful for an escape
from the tyranny of family.

I was in Ferrara when I heard that Cesare had died in Navarre.
Died as a common soldier, fighting naked in a senseless campaign, one
morning before dawn. He still thought he might regain some
foothold of power from his wife, or threaten the family de Nevada
until they came up with an army or funds to hire one. I took to my
chamber. For a month I relived our childhoods. By day I honored our
family devotion through my penances of grief and guilt. By night I
remembered our crimes of love in dreams that came without cost or
consequence, the only regret being to awake from them.

I loved my brother. He had held my hand during the investiture
of our father into the See of Rome. I admired his ambition and his
cruelty. I collaborated with him in campaigns against the world,
against our father, against our respective spouses. He could look at me
and make me smoke with need just by angling a glance in my direction from beneath a single raised eyebrow. My insides felt as if singed
and sanctified with frankincense from Araby.

What more does one ask of life, really, but to stagger from moment
to moment with a reason to wake and wait for the next reason to
wake? This Cesare had given me, and this, in dying, he took from me.

His death occurred perhaps a year after I had sent that child out
to the forest. In that vicious year nothing had gone right—perhaps as
a punishment to me, perhaps just as proof of how callous the world
could be. Cesare's career being ended, horribly, I had my third husband, Alfonso d'Este, Duca de Ferrara, as an occasional visitor to my
bed, and Ariosto to sing me his epic romances, and to tease me with
sonnets, Pietro Bembo. But it was with the death of Cesare that my

world began to end too. For what could my husband, my lovers manage to mean to me?

With what ferocity did I push my court into diversions, though. Masques and balls, operas and recitations, feats of valor and feats of humiliation, lectures on alchemy, lectures on theology, lectures on the art of lecturing. And from each distraction I learned two things. There was always some small nugget to please or perplex me, accompanied by the larger and tired knowledge that nuggets of pleasure couldn't alter fate nor massage the broken heart into working properly again.

Niccolò Machiavelli would come and talk to me about Cesare. We drank wine in tall red goblets. We remembered Cesare's ambitions, his strengths, his loves. I think Machiavelli loved Cesare as much as he admired him, though I think he rightly feared him more than anything else. We talked about Florence, about the Republic; we remembered Savonarola and the bonfire, and how sad that the Medici themselves hadn't been included among the baubles to be scorched.

Machiavelli would leave. Darling Bembo would come, the love, and try to disarm my grief with the attention of his hand, his sex, his nibbling lips. The coy code names we had, the pretense at pretenses. As if my husband knew nothing, or, if knowing, as if he might care at all.

But I had a mind as well as a heart, and a curiosity as well as an ambition. And I paid attention. Ferrara has its university—perhaps not on a par with Bologna or Paris, Württemburg or Oxford, but it attracts eager students. Once, eager to try a student again, I cloaked myself beyond recognition and slipped into the galleries. It happened that an alchemist was speaking in the scholarly language of Latin, and it had been too long since I'd heard the Latin of Rome, of my childhood. I listened with grave joy as a slip of a thing, a lad, asked questions about the Elixir of Life.

"*Elixir,*" said the sage, "is derived from a term of the Moor—*al-iksir,* though they steal that root word from the Greek *xieron,* meaning a dry and powdery substance. A tincture." I listened with keener interest. The Borgia family has always had a fondness for what can be accomplished by the judicious application of a particular tincture in a particular glass of wine.

The young lad persisted and asked questions about quicksilver. One of the three elements on which the universe is based, said the lecturer. In days long gone by, wealthy Spanish families used it to coat a shallow basin, large enough for bathing in.

Not just in Spain, I wanted to say. Perhaps remembering stories of his grandfather, Pope Alexander VI had such a basin created in the gardens at Tremante. A sumptuous afternoon was to be had, as the sun heated the water. One could shuck one's heavy clothes and step in, as if descending into a mirror. The many times I sported myself therein, heedless of opinion. Cesare with me once or twice, more often than not my father looking on . . .

A foolish notion, continued the lecturer, as quicksilver has many dangerous effects upon our species. It can provoke drooling, and lassitude, and lapsing into a mental state of sharp terror, in which one can believe that conspiracies against one are being whispered in every quarter.

A Borgia doesn't need to bathe in a quicksilver pool to believe this, for it is always true, and always has been.

"The more common term is mercury," continued the alchemist, "and the mineral is derived from cinnabar. The celestial body that we call Mercury is red as the poison of quicksilver. The lost chapter of *The Secret of Secrets* by Rhazes, the Persian alchemist, concerned itself with the bodies of the world—the metals, stones, and salts—and the volatile liquids, or spirits. Though Rhazes couldn't complete the transmutation of base metals into gold, as the Emir of Khorassan had required, and was fatally thumped on the head with his own *Secret of Secrets,* there is much we learned about how the world is arranged, in its secret inclinations."

I listened, for secret inclinations are of abiding interest to a woman. In sometimes being able to determine the secret inclinations of others, woman has her signal advantage over man. I left with instructions to my attendant to summon the curious student.

In due course he presented himself at court and, without tedious delay, in my bed. He wasn't personally possessed of any Secret of Secrets, to my mind, and my attempt at spiritual corruption was an uncharacteristic failure. I couldn't induce in the young man anything approaching physical ecstasy. Oddly beardless, perhaps he was deficient in the manly properties. But he did chatter engagingly about the nature of quicksilver, and I learned from him much that would prove useful. He styled himself Paracelsus, though in his adoring letter of thanks and apology he signed his name *Theo. Bombast von Hohenheim.*

I gave what I could, in those years, and waited out my days. My father was gone, my dear brother was gone, and who was there to promote? My husband would always be an Este, not a Borgia. My young Rodrigo was being raised apart from me, as I in my day was raised apart from my mother. I had one miscarriage after another, and nothing worthwhile to occupy my time. I even considered becoming devout, in some benighted homage to Cesare's flares of faith.

Then at the age of thirteen Rodrigo died. We'd lived apart for eight years, and he died apart from me. I had imagined, eventually, he would grow old enough to deserve my company, strong enough of character not to be corrupted by me. I was anticipating that day with joy. It wasn't to be.

So more and more often I took to repairing to Montefiore. It pleased me for its obscurity. There, without courtiers to entertain or ignore, I pretended at being the widow of a farmer, and nothing more. I sat at the window and watched the laborers at their jobs. I berated the ancient Primavera, who no longer saucily answered back. I invented false confessions for Fra Ludovico. ("Father, there were three beautiful brothers, each untutored in love, and their own father dead from the famine, so how were they to learn with no whore to teach them? Out of the mercy for which I am so well known, I took them to my bed, Father, at the same time, and in the following way . . .") I enjoyed trying to talk him into an occasion of sin beneath his robes.

I was in the *salone* one afternoon, considering the range of alembics, the crucibles of ground minerals, and herbs I had Primavera gather by the roadside. A dog began to bark in the field beyond, and there was something urgent in its barking. Sometimes a *cinghiale* will lurch from the woods and stray too near the farm, and I always had the gooseboy on my mind, for he was slow of wit and liable to wander into the jaws of a wild boar without noticing. I stood and looked out the window to see the commotion.

Primavera was spinning in the sun, and squinting, for her eyes were no longer strong. The gooseboy was slack-jawed—as usual, no surprise. Fra Ludovico had fallen to his knees as if beholding an apparition. He needed Latin for the moment "*Ecce homo.*" But it wasn't Cristo Himself stopping for lunch at Montefiore, but Vicente de Nevada, trudging up the sloping road, accompanied by something that looked from this distance like a dog without a head.

I admit that my days had not been filled with surprise of late, and what is life without surprise? I had never expected to see Don Vicente again. I had not expected that someone would need to tell him that, despite his sacrifices, his daughter was dead.

I stepped to the mirror and passed a hand over my hair, and then tore from my scalp a circlet of pearls, to appear more common. I bound my stomacher with quick hard pulls of the cords.

I hurried down the flight of steps from the door of the *salone* to the terrace below the loggia. I stood with my hands on both my cheeks, to appear as I truly felt: terrified and overjoyed.

Vicente

HE SAW Donna Lucrezia appear, in a black cloud of silks paneled with gold brocade, like a thunderstorm slotted with stripes of lightning. He had to catch his breath, for the years in a dank dungeon had done their mischief in his lungs, and there were certain exercises he'd never undertake again. The last few miles, the soft approach up and down the succession of hills, slowly rising toward Montefiore's red roofs, had seemed to take longer than the weeks and weeks between Ouranopolis and Venice. But there was the famous Borgia, more beautiful than ever. More beautiful than any fishwife of the Adriatic or courtesan of the Doge. More beautiful than anyone but his Bianca.

The stone beast hung back, skulking in his shadow. On the shores of Agion Oros, once the sun had opened its Cyclops eye again, the beast had seemed less marmoreal. Its limbs took on the snapping energy of a puppy's, and its aspect was marginally more animal. So Vicente began to think of the creature as an improperly made dog, one with a faceless knob that passed for a head. The companion had certainly helped him obtain passage in every instance, as no one wanted to be bitten by a stone dog that had no mouth.

Lucrezia Borgia met him at the bottom step. She held her hands out at last. Her fingers touching his were like lilies set against burned twigs.

"Welcome to Montefiore," she said. Not *Welcome home,* he noticed, but here were Fra Ludovico and Primavera to do that.

He didn't turn to them yet. He could hardly get his breath. He hoped before he would need to ask, a shutter would fly open, a voice would ring out. Her hands would lift in the air in the gesture of surrender to the impossibility he knew he was manifesting: that, after all this time, he had come back.

But the day kept its secrets. The house teased him. His retainers and his unexpected houseguest waited for him to speak. With difficulty he discharged a clutch of phlegm and found his words. "Donna Lucrezia. My house is yours." He couldn't continue with the formal language, though. He couldn't afford to spend his breath in pleasantries. "My daughter. Where is my daughter?"

"Oh, there's much to tell you," she answered, "but we won't speak out here. You need to change those hideous rags. Come in, my friend. I'll decant some—"

"Primavera?" he said. "What is the state of affairs here?"

Primavera kept silent. He pressed her to explain, but she spilled tears down the netted wrinkles of her cheeks, and shook her head.

"Primavera," he demanded. His voice was a croak, a whisper.

Fra Ludovico said, "She can't answer your questions, Don Vicente. She doesn't have the faculties."

"Has she lost her mind?"

"She has lost her tongue, in some accident or feat of vengeance. It was ripped from her mouth. She could never write, as you might remember, so there's no way to learn what happened to her."

With some surprise, Lucrezia said to the priest, "You've become coherent with the return of your employer. I haven't heard you make so much sense in years. *Your* tongue will have to come out next."

"I have no idea if what I say is true, of course," continued Fra Ludovico hastily. "For all I know, Primavera slept with the famous octopus again and in a dangerous moment of passion swallowed her own tongue."

"What nonsense is going on here? Where is Bianca?"

"Vicente." Lucrezia laid her hand on his sleeve. "I'll tell you what I know, but not here, not in front of them. You don't understand about Fra Ludovico. In your absence he's gone mad and he gabbles like a lunatic."

"Where is she?" Vicente turned around and around, and the stone dog followed him in stone circles.

"Here's gabbing like a lunatic for you, my lady," said the priest. "No one keeps news of a child from her parent. Don Vicente, listen: by force of will or by the will of force, Bianca made her escape from this prison. We don't know where she is or what has become of her. I pray for her departed soul daily." He made to comfort Vicente, but the weakened man twisted and sat down on the ground, his legs giving up.

"You've been a comfort, clearly," said Lucrezia icily. "Escort him to the piano nobile, you two. I'll prepare a restorative for him."

When he had come to his senses some, he dried his face and looked about. The stone dog was sitting on its hind limbs alertly. Lucrezia reigned from behind a table of inlaid marble. Three candles, nearly invisible in the strong daylight, shifted their slender flames.

"I'd hoped to tell you news you could rejoice in," she began.

He didn't speak. But he turned and looked at Lucrezia. Though his lungs were enfeebled after his years in prison, his eyes seemed fine. He had learned that he hadn't tired of looking at things. Even now his eyes were greedy. The beautiful Borgia woman lifted her slender neck to be looked at. Her chin had the tight articulation of a well-made lady's silk slipper. He could imagine burying his damp eyes into that proffered hollow. But his years of celibacy stayed his mind from considering any pleasure more fervent than consolation.

His visions of Bianca—memories of her in this room—were of a child who didn't yet come up to his lowest rib. If he had seen his girl as a young woman on the road five miles out, he passed her without knowing. Would he know her again if he found her?

He said at last, "Let's finish the business first. I've brought Cesare the token he hired me to find."

She rolled her eyes. "Cesare isn't in a position to care, so you can save your breath. I'm not the desperate man grasping at straws that he was. I have no interest in sham and trickery."

"You supported him in his command of me to this task, Donna Lucrezia."

"It was his strategy to follow every hope, however fantastic or mundane. It gave him peace. And what calmed him calmed us all. As you remember. But whatever deceit you've concocted to abuse us with, it isn't worth my time nor your breath, which I see must be husbanded."

"Nonetheless. I've accomplished the task with which I was charged."

"Then you've done my family a great service. Thank you."

"In exchange for my undertaking Cesare's assignment, he was to keep my home and my family safe. He's broken his agreement. I'll have my words with him, and see how he can help to find my daughter."

"You'll have to find him first. In the afterlife."

He gaped. "Murder?"

"Of course. That's the only way Borgias agree to die."

He lowered his eyes to the stone dog. "I've been away so long," he muttered, "too long, for sure. I don't even know what year it is, nor who rules the states of Italy."

Mincingly she said, "There is a della Rovere in the Vatican. As Julius II. He pretends to do *good*. He is of no interest to the Borgia enterprises. Florence has its Gonfalonier for life, and the Doge of Venice is a certain Leonardo Loredan."

"That much I know," said Vicente. He paused to cough. "I've had an audience."

She raised a plucked eyebrow.

"I stopped to beg access to the Doge's treasury—for permission to lodge safely there the artifact I stole," he said.

"Please, Don Vicente. You're not well. You don't need to spend your breath on such lies. For one thing, a gentleman farmer wouldn't dare to approach the Doge of Venice."

"I dared approach you, once upon a time."

"For another, it's a crude ploy to pretend you found something Prince Dschem doubtlessly invented in a desperate moment."

"I did indeed. I found the branch of the Tree of Knowledge, and with such a credential I bartered for an audience with the Doge. Duchessa, I had had many years to think about the negotiations between your family and mine. I found that I didn't trust your brother to take possession of the entire artifact. I needed something to bargain with in the event he threatened me or my family. And wasn't I wise? He who took a good deal of my life from me, and in the interim lost track of my daughter's whereabouts—what right had he to this thing of unequaled magnificence?"

"So the Doge has the supposed relic of Eden."

He said, "I left one apple from the branch. I retained two of them for bargaining with."

"Is that so? Let me see it."

"I'll remind you, respectfully, that I went on Cesare's bidding."

"I am his sister and his widow and his heir. Let me see it."

"You don't even believe it exists."

"Convert me."

From his traveling sack he withdrew the few items of clothes he had acquired on his return journey. Within them, settled as lightly and safely as a walnut meat in a shell, reposed the sacred bough. He took it and lifted it with both hands. The stem shone as brightly silver as if a servant had only just finished buffing it, and the silver leaves shimmered delicately in an invisible wind from another climate. The two apples remaining smelled of rosy sweetness, though from where the third had been plucked, a blemish of black tarnish knobbed.

Lucrezia Borgia lowered herself to her knees and made the Sign of the Cross. "Upon the wood of this same tree was our Lord crucified," she said.

"The tree is silver," said Vicente.

"That is its aspect to our sight. It's not silver though; how could a silver tree support apples in an eternal state of perfect ripeness? This is no artifact, but proof adequate for the revival of a failing faith."

"One has to have faith first in order for it to be revived," he said. "I am through with this thing, whatever it is. I want no more to do with it. How did Cesare die?"

"I wish his body were here," she said. "He is buried in Navarre, they tell me. He was looking for the de Nevada family to raise up an army on his behalf."

"There is no de Nevada family in Navarre, or none that would recognize this wandering cousin," said Vicente coldly.

"You wrote to Fra Ludovico—?"

"I wrote lies for the purpose of protecting my daughter. Apparently it wasn't enough. Now you must tell me, Donna Borgia. I don't have any interest in sacred matters. I want to know how my daughter died."

"She went off into the woods on her own and she never returned," said Lucrezia. "Primavera's grandson found her body at the foot of a cliff. He buried her in an unmarked grave in the forest."

"I will see him now. Ranuccio, is that it? Do I remember? Ranuccio. Where is he?"

"You may not see him," said Lucrezia. "He disappeared from the region shortly thereafter. I believe he was caught poaching a pig from the barns of Don Mercutio down the valley, and rumor has it he was done in as a pig might be done in." After a pause. "I mean, on a spit."

Vicente said, "Why was my daughter wandering alone in the woods? She was a timid sort."

"She changed," said Lucrezia. "She became brazen and feckless. I couldn't stop her though I did my best. I hope you appreciate my efforts. Primavera was no use at all, you know, and Fra Ludovico has become a simpleton. His spiritual warnings made no difference. As best I could, with the obligations of my marriage and my life at the court of Ferrara, I have stood in your stead as a parent, Vicente." She raised herself to her feet, and held the bough in her arm as if cradling an infant. "I've done what you asked of me, what you begged of me. But I couldn't wander into her soul and make her love me or respect me. In the end she was a willful child, like most. Her ending was likely inevitable."

Vicente de Nevada stood too. He had to crush an inclination to beg pardon and leave the room, as the room was his, the house was his, even the sad history of what had happened to his daughter, whatever it was, belonged to him, not to Lucrezia Borgia. But unless she walked out of the room first, he would be ceding her the right to the house, and this he was unwilling to do.

"Tell me about your dog," she said, smiling at him. She put down the sacred bough and picked up a small pearl-handled knife.

"The dog doesn't figure in this story of grief. It has no name," he said.

"It?" she said. "Not he or she? Poor thing. Come here, poor deformed thing."

The creature came forward warily.

Lucrezia turned and neatly sliced from one of the apples a clean wedge. The juice beaded up on the knife. The moon-white flesh was flushed with pink and pale green and yellow. She held the knife down with the apple slice on it, and for this supreme honor the beast found reason and means to develop a mouth. A hole in its top opened, more or less mouthlike, and a helpful tongue leaped out and gathered the apple.

"I adore feeding the hungry, just as the Scriptures tell us." Her words were tender but their delivery flat: she displayed an alchemist's skeptical curiosity over a trial of elements.

The creature sat back and looked up at Lucrezia. It occurred to

Vicente that it now had eyes, and lids that could blink. It blinked its stony lids. One dry tear broke from each duct, and rolled to the terrazzo floor, there to shatter into a clot of dust and gravel. An improbable smell of rue.

"It would seem you are telling the truth," she said. "This really is the Apple of knowledge. It will give tongue even to the rock."

The beast turned to Vicente and put its head between Vicente's knees. With its new tongue it licked Vicente's hands.

Then the thing straightened up, like a little monkey, its forelimbs pivoting outward. On its hind legs it took a step or two. Lucrezia said, "Honor to God, the thing is walking." She backed up a step, and picked up the knife again. "Vicente."

The beast paid her no attention. With one of its forelimbs it reached forward and the stubby hoof was cloven in three. It helped itself to the rest of the apple that Lucrezia Borgia had offered it. "Vicente," she said, "what license."

Vicente made no move. Confident as a three-year-old and about as tall, the stone beast walked on its hind legs, up to the hearth. Today's fire was laid but unlit. The beast knocked the brush aside and shuffled through yesterday's ashes to the back wall of the fireplace. It leaned its head and—and its shoulders; there was no denying they were now shoulders—into the wall. It disappeared into the stone as neatly as a corpse is swallowed by a flooded quarry.

Vicente was stirred by the audacity of the stone dog. Its disappearance after all these weeks was a bracing shock. Whatever had rescued him from the dungeon in Agion Oros had exacted its price and gone away. Had it been traveling beside him, invisible, incognito, in the Greek fishing vessel? Its stone weight interfering with the boat's maneuverability? No proof of that. Who knows how long the stone had been with him, and in how many guises. Now it was gone.

He was bereaved further, this time for a stone.

The world seemed a punishing sleeve of bright changing lights and dark moods. Flawed and regrettable, the presence of it nonetheless clawed at one, claiming one's attention. "Get out," he said to the

Duchessa de Ferrara, hardly believing his temerity. "Get out of my house at once."

If Lucrezia Borgia was shaken, she didn't show it. She put her white knuckles against the desktop and leaned across to him. "In my own time and in my own way, and not before. I owe you nothing."

"You owe me my daughter's life," he said. "Will you pay me with your own?" He pushed the table with his hip, ineffectually; his hands strangled air.

She was frightened, though, and fell back. The bough with one remaining apple slipped from her grasp and rolled along the hem of her garment. "If you kill me you'll never even learn where your daughter's body is buried. You won't know where to have Fra Ludovico sing her the last rites, which I could tell you even now."

"No one will sing you last rites. No one in Italy will weep when you die, and the name Lucrezia will fall out of a fashion for a thousand years." But her parry had worked. His hands, hungry for resistance to overcome, paused.

"You are a father without a child," she said. "I am a child without a father. Surely we can understand each other's grief? In days to come it will not seem so hard."

He looked at her as if the concept of *days to come* was impossible to decipher. Then his hands opened, palms outward. "There is no way to live without her," he said.

"You must make your confession to Fra Ludovico," she replied. "Custom says God can speak even through the flute of a madman when forgiveness is required. Don't presume to know what your life may become now until you have yourself absolved of your sins."

He spat at her display of piety. She made a wincing smile and said, "I am as practiced at accepting absolution as I am at sinning with ever greater relish the next time. If you're going to murder me, Don Vicente de Nevada, do it in a state of grace, anyway, for a more illustrious contrast of effects. Cesare always mentioned the satisfaction of it."

He looked sideways at her. She had dismissed him, and now faced the mirror. "I must see to my hair," she spoke, almost to herself, in the way of certain women. She scooped up the single fruit on its silvery bough and held it alongside her face. It was such a feminine gesture, it brought back to him María Inés, and his child, Bianca, who would never become a woman. He turned to shutter his eyes, and followed the empty passage out into the empty world.

Mirror mirror

OUT OF our need we patron-
ize our artists, we flirt with our poets, we petition our architects: Give
us your lusty colorful world. Signal to us a state of being more richly
steeped in purpose and satisfaction than our own.

Thanks to our artists, we pretend well, living under canopies of
painted clouds and painted gods, in halls of marble floors across which
the sung Masses paint hope in deep *impasti* of echo. We make of the
hollow world a fuller, messier, prettier place, but all our inventions
can't create the one thing we require: to deserve any fond attention
we might accidentally receive, to receive any fond attention we don't
in the course of things deserve. We are never enough to ourselves because we can never be enough to another. Any one of us walks into
any room and reminds its occupant that we are not the one they most
want to see. We are never the one. We are never enough.

The holy find this some mincing proof of God. Damn them.

There was de Nevada, mourning the death of his daughter, and why shouldn't he? But he came into the room and brought back the treasure we never believed he could achieve—that I doubted the existence of—and he also brought back to me the brusque male fact of my brother, and how dead he is. How I can never walk into the room again and have him mean something to me, even in his drunken lechery with other women; I can never even suffer the pain of knowing I've not quite caught his attention. There is no longer a Cesare Borgia with attention to catch. Don Vicente's return brings it all up to me again; the phlegmatic humor rises in me and slashes hotly in my windpipe.

I lay the remaining apple on its silver branch and turn to the mirror. The light has shifted somewhat and I almost feel visited—beside myself. It's no doubt the effect of seeing that stone creature dissolve into the stonework of the fireplace, like a louse burrowing into the skin. It makes me feel that any wall or floor could shift its reliable shape and blurt forth into a creature again, as if the house were possessed of a stone ghoul. Uncomfortable. One would never be alone again, even in one's boudoir.

"Mirror, mirror," I spoke aloud, to steady my nerves, "who is the fairest of us all?"

I thought of my father, the great Pope Alexander VI, and how he had played at being the prelate of the Church of Rome. How he had had testicles of the sons of his enemies removed and gilded and returned to their owners in caskets beautifully inscribed with erotic carvings, to mock them. Yet he had also had baskets of overflow from our banquets brought out to those suffering from plague and famine on the banks of the Tiber just below Rome. What was fair in the use of power? Cesare's friend, Niccolò Machiavelli, would have sharp praise for the man who used power to his best advantage. But Machiavelli didn't consider the moral fairness in a ruler to be worthy of mention.

And who asks women to be fair, anyway, unless they do ask themselves?

I had sent Bianca away to be murdered, those long years ago. It seemed hard to remember. But my Cesare had cast his attention her way—he who had so little time left—and indeed, that was the last time we met in this life. A cock to every hen who staggered into his house, whether she was his equal or no. I couldn't have that happen. Not for his sake; not for hers. Was murder the right alternative? Ah well, too late to decide otherwise now.

I looked upon myself the way I did when I was an adolescent. When life beckoned from the horizon. I could only imagine growing more beautiful, more powerful, more responsive to life's beneficence and squalor. Back then, the figure who would look back at me in the looking glass was potent with mystery, more arresting than I could imagine actually seeming to anyone.

Now, the venerable apple nodded perfectly against my cheek. Beside its immortal perfection I looked wan, a fishwife, a sister to old Primavera. I could see the thin struts of my shoulders making a yoke under my skin, and my neck arose from a shallow well. My eyes had fallen prey to a snare of webbed lines, too fine to be visible to anyone across the room—but what do we ever want but for someone to come nearer? And then all our imperfections are magnified.

I put my head to one side, criticizing my aging beauty. "Who is fairer?" I begged the mirror to lie and say "No one; you are beautiful as a legend." I knew it wouldn't lie. But I didn't expect it to speak, either.

It spoke in the language of mirrors, not of words. A mist crept over the skin of the glass. Mistaking it for my hot breath upon it, I leaned forward to smear the fog away with my hand, to see some further truth, something consoling, that I hadn't yet thought or imagined.

But when my hand reached out, I felt for an instant something other than the cold touch of glass. I cawed a sound of alarm. Before I fell to the floor, twitching with disbelief, I saw the child again. Bianca de Nevada. In my delusion she was no longer dead. She had a grave and magnificent expression. I can't explain it. Puzzled curiosity. A raging patience. An articulate simplicity. A womanliness.

Or perhaps it was that she seemed like one who didn't worry about what it meant never to be enough. The absence of such a care on her brow filled her with an unearthly beauty that I could neither achieve nor abide.

The return of the prodigal

THE CIRCLE of mist gave onto a room Bianca remembered, though for a moment she thought it was empty. By leaning near she could see beyond the margin—it was more like looking through a window than into a painting, for as her angle changed, more came into view. That was when she saw the woman on the floor.

Bianca couldn't tell if she was weeping or—could it be?—thrashing in laughter. She rolled over and over, and her limbs seemed unfamiliar with each other. A white worm of spittle drooped from her lower lip. On the floor nearby lay a branch of an apple tree with a single fruit attached.

The woman there on the floor is convulsing, thought Bianca, and her heart moved cautiously. She reached out her hand, forgetting for a moment that she was entombed in a room without exits. Her hand met a barrier of hard air and couldn't penetrate it.

As she regarded it further, she recognized the floor of the *salone* of Montefiore, its shiny waxed bricks laid in herringbone. The woman who suffers is someone I know. It's the woman at whose word my father left me; the woman who looked in upon my childhood with slight but steady interest.

It took Bianca a while longer to remember the name of Lucrezia Borgia. Borgia! With the reclamation of that single word, a tide of memories surged forward, and each small wavelet made her older and fiercer, but also more amazed and incredulous.

How she could think, these years later, of bits of childhood things that she hadn't realized she was taking in. She had the whole of Italy in her mind—murkily, but there it was, a long pennant of a land, with so much to know, so much to appreciate. The shallow hills of rusty scrub in the south, and white villages around tourmaline harbors; and sweep after sweep of wheat and rape and olive, and gnarled nap of grapevine halfway up the slope of every river valley. The blue distances of the lower Apennines, the wind-twisted cypresses and the fierce patriotic pines; the sheep in a panic in the fold, the fox on the prowl in the hen yard. Everywhere, the ruins of Roman temples, like ancient discarded teeth of the long dead giants of the past. The polished glory of the states today, of Florence preening, of Milan preening, of Venice curled up knee-deep in the waves, of Rome too vain to preen. Siena, Lucca, and then Savoy, and the lakes of the Dolomites, splashes of blue and gold whenever you looked, except in snowstorms, when they went white and silver instead.

She saw all this, she saw the land with an encompassing catalogic clarity, though she had scarcely ever been off the hill at Montefiore, at least not in her living memory. She saw the dozen duomi like so many pepper pots on a table linen painted ITALIA. She saw the separate characters of the seas, and knew that the northern Adriatic swelled with different and more insidious force than the southern Tyrrhenian. She saw the remains of the Etruscans and the Athenians and the Phoenicians and the Egyptians and the Cretans and the Visigoths and the Franks, like so many spices scattered into a meat pie. She saw the roads spoking from Rome a vast asymmetrical wheel. She saw Mithrais in his lair, and Jupiter broadly speaking to Neptune, thundercloud to wine-dark wave She watched Romulus and Remus suckle from the wolf and then, when their appetites grew more human, eat her. She saw the Bishops and the pagan priests and the soothsayers and seers, all much the same man, and she saw much the same woman nearby, watching and helping and performing her little anonymous sabo-tages. (She looked like Primavera, small and gnarled, an onion left in the root cellar too long, and gone a little soft.) She saw Christ wait in Sicily to be recognized. She saw Saint Peter crucified in Rome, and Savonarola roasted in Florence. She saw the rivers tie themselves in knots of blue, the clouds spell the names of popes in the sky, the rocks pick themselves up and rearrange themselves, and she saw Vesuvius and Aetna lose their tempers.

But it was Lucrezia Borgia that she cared about, Lucrezia Borgia who was as enmeshed in all this particularity as she herself was. The woman was now sitting on the floor with her legs stretched straight out in front of her. Then she opened her legs slightly and threw back her head and closed her eyes. Her pelvis lifted from the floor and she shuddered.

Bianca had often seen Fra Ludovico at prayer, and knew that his mutterings could grow so intense that he often forgot he wasn't alone. (Well, he wasn't; God was around somewhere.) Now, since Lu-crezia Borgia couldn't know she was being observed, Bianca felt sor-did. She dropped her gaze and looked away. When she looked back—yes, as she'd feared; the window was gone. A matted bit of old cloth hung in its place, a tattered moth-eaten tapestry with a picture of a unicorn picked out in dirty white wool, and a hunter peering from a thicket.

She became impatient; the world of Montefiore had sprung up like a tang in her mouth, like a hexed appetite, and she would have more of it. "Heartless," she called, "where are you?"

She looked about. The creatures were there, doing something. Making a meal of some sort. Uselessly. "Can't you scrape a carrot, even?" she said. "Give me that." Bianca had scraped few enough carrots in her childhood, but her hands were human hands and could invent a way to do it more efficiently than the dwarves.

They looked at her with baleful gloom, as if scraping carrots efficiently was their chief ambition in life.

She thought of several niggling things to say to the seven of them, but as she was sorting out which one, she realized with a start that she was clear that they *were* seven. She could count them now. "*Martedì, mercoledì, giovedì, venerdì,*" she said to the four on one side, "*sabato, domenica, lunedì,*" she said to the others. "What are you doing here all at once?" They jostled like small children, eager and untroubled by sentiment, watching a cook wring the neck of a chicken.

"What are you doing?" said MuteMuteMute.

"I'll make you a meal," she said. "Why not? I need things, though, things to cook with." She realized that though she'd eaten—occasionally—the sight of that apple in Lucrezia Borgia's lap had made her hungry as hell. Hungry not to eat, but to feed someone.

Suddenly she became happy. "Things to cook with?" MuteMuteMute and Tasteless brought her a large earthenware jug that she recognized as a ghirarium, a storage jug for dormice. She lifted the lid and saw that skeletons of dormice were splayed on the ramps molded against the inside walls. "You'll have to do better than this, men," she said.

They became lively with the game of it. A bloody haunch of venison from a drawer, a splash of melted butter in the heel of a shoe. Eighteen ropes of garlic. A damp heap of hairy borage leaves. Four dried peas. A handful of pine needles and acorns, which she set aside as a garnish. Two giant potatoes, each one as large as the head of—was it Gimpy?—who carried them, one under each arm. A pot of fish eyes like buttons, all still damp and intelligent. Laboriously she lined the fish eyes up along a shelf, like the serving dishes for a party of sea horses, and the eyes followed her as she moved around the table. She'd serve them to Blindeye and see if they helped.

The room came into crisper focus as she worked, and a smell like real food began to fill the space. The dwarves took to tussling on the floor and singing mean songs about one another, and asking repeatedly when the meal would be ready. "When it's ready," she answered, stirring.

"Bowls," she said at last. "We need bowls."

They stopped their capering and looked at her.

"Well, wash your hands and get your bowls," she said.

They looked; they all had, more or less, hands.

"There's a pump in the corner; use it," she told them. She pointed. By now she knew, yes, there it would be, and there it was.

They washed and splashed and plugged the pipe with their fingers to spray one another. They found bowls somewhere and brought them to the table. Bianca could locate no spoons, but soup could be drunk from a deep bowl. She used the first bowl as a ladle for the others. When she had supplied each of them with a meal, she found a small stool and sat down with them.

"Let us thank God for our blessings," she said.

"What blessings are those?" asked Bitter.

"Ourselves, one another, food, and bowls, and God," she answered. "Come now, fellows." She made the holy hand gesture and dropped her eyes, and began to mumble in Latin. The dwarves watched her closely and did as she did, though they had no Latin to speak of, and mumbled nonsense instead.

When they were halfway through with their meal, a bubble of stone began to form in the floor near Bianca's feet. She watched with curiosity as it swelled in a manner oddly organic "The floor's calving," she remarked, and so it seemed; before her, in a minute or two, stood another dwarf, who looked less human than the others. He stood on two feet, tentatively, though his arms seemed not entirely convinced they were arms. He wore a tunic of sorts to cover his nakedness.

The dwarves looked at him as if surprised, as if unfamiliar with him. Yet he seemed to be something less than an invader. He seemed to know where he was. He looked at Bianca and nodded, as if there was something about her presence that was satisfying.

He spoke. The language was gutteral, the accents dark and shapely. The seven dwarves flinched. Deaf-to-the-World said, "It's growling at us."

"It wants some of our supper," said Tasteless. "It's a fool; the supper's awful. Who calls this food?"

"Besides, there's not enough to go around," said MuteMuteMute, which was hardly true; the pot was still nearly full. But the newcomer dwarf seemed to need a bone upon which to gnaw, or a scatter of pebbles on the floor, like seed thrown to the fowl.

The newcomer spoke again, more urgently. The resident dwarves leaned forward, as if trying to understand, but their patience was slim, and one after another they went back to their soup.

The newcomer came forward and pounded on the table. The dwarves smiled at him as one might smile at a child saying something innocent and stupid. But the soup seemed powerfully good, all of a sudden. They sucked at the marrow from the bones, they splashed the broth, they poked whole onions with their spoons so that onion sleeve gave birth to smaller slimmer onion baby, and onion baby regurgitated onion sleeve again, and so on.

"Behave," said Bianca.

The newcomer growled like a dog. He made his throaty remarks again and again, more and more desperately. The seven dwarves began to make fun of him, to imitate his succulent murmurings, and mime his anguished expressions. "Oh, it wants to be loved," said Bitter. "What a hopeless thing it is."

The visitor straightened up as if a new thought had occurred to him, and he brought out of an inner pouch a nice enough apple, from which one thick slice had been taken.

"Oh, something sweet for after the soup," said Bianca. "And I've been thinking about apples. Well, you're kind enough to offer this, whoever you are."

She found a knife when she put her hand out for one, and she gripped its ivory handle firmly. When offered it, she took the apple, and she saw that the slice that had been taken out was roughly an eighth. She divided the remaining fruit—rare wonderful fruit!—into seven other segments. She offered a slice, one after the next, to the seven dwarves.

Each dwarf accepted the fruit. Each one took a piece in his dirty hand, and regarded it the way Fra Ludovico considered the Holy Host. Each one partook of the offering, for good or ill.

Bianca sat back, bemused, affectionate, interested. The chair was suddenly comfortable; it had cushions, and a small stool for her feet, carved in the Roman style.

The dwarves made little display of their satisfaction or their regret at the sweet, though they didn't clamor for more nor immediately push away from the table. Gimpy folded his arms across his stout chest and achieved a look of reflection. Heartless stroked his beard—he was the red beard!—and began fishing through his pockets as if for a pipe. MuteMuteMute smiled and began to hum a melody Bianca almost thought she remembered: a sprightly, cogwork melody with no apparent beginning or end. Deaf-to-the-World took up the knife and began to play with a splinter from the edge of the table, teasing it into a form of some sort. Tasteless sprayed a glorious smile in everyone's direction and began to snore. Bitter scowled at his brother's laxness and pounded one stubby finger on the table, as if rehearsing arguments internally so to be ready to drive points home when the conversation began in earnest. And Blindeye turned his head and looked at Bianca as if he had never seen her before. When she caught his eye, she smiled, but he ducked his chin and lowered his eyes, suddenly mortified at his temerity.

The whole party seemed sprightlier, more vigorous. Bianca felt like dancing. But the newcomer would have none of it. "Brothers," he barked, and Bianca was surprised that such were the improved spirits in the room that she could understand the language now. "Brothers," he said again, snapping, "I've returned, and you have forgotten who I am to you?"

The dwarves snapped out of their several reveries and games, and turned to him. "You petition for our attention," said Heartless.

"I am your kin," said the newcomer. He straightened up, and either the dwarves had grown more like him during the meal, or he more like them, for they seemed familial now, in look as well as language. "Do you forget me?"

"Well, yes," said Heartless. "Actually."

"I am—" He paused, as if not quite having sorted it out for himself. "I am Nextday, you cretinous lumpheads."

They may never have heard the name before, and indeed Nextday seemed surprised by it himself, but somehow the concept made sense to them. The dwarves looked at Nextday with more careful, judging expressions.

"I was one of you, before I left," said Nextday, "and you've forgotten I was ever here. So I come back to claim my moment with you. Let us go to our work, now we are fed, and see what of the world can be seen."

She could sense the change. The dwarves were full of purpose. They pushed back their chairs and went to cupboards and found cloaks and boots, and put them on. The whole room snapped into being. A wardrobe bolted into a corner, a bench popped along the wall; the floor brought forth a woven carpet, rather a nice one too, in golds and greens. The vague piles of mess retreated into darker corners, as if cowed by firmer intentions.

"Come," said Nextday, "there is a lot to do yet, before night has fallen."

"Take me with you!" said Bianca.

She knew she could go, now, because for the first time there was a door, a wooden-slatted door with stout iron hinges and a bolt and a lock besides. The door had a small hinged window of real glass, and the strangest yellow soup stewed on either side of the glass in an acidic, shrill sort of way. It took Bianca's breath quite away when she realized it was nothing but sunlight.

She followed the dwarves out the door.

Beware beware

FOR A while they stood blinking.
Bianca couldn't tell what season it was, if any; the gentle rise on which
the door gave was unkempt and confused. Wild rose blossoms, given
over to the blowsiest excess, reclined on hoops bowed with ridges of
snow. Spring ferns uncurled their tender heads in a runaway patch of
autumnal gourds. The air had a glazed, unnatural quality, as if steeped
in the air of something violently alcoholic. Undertones both of dry
rot and damp decay. Bianca felt herself swim in her clothes, and eager
to be out of them.

The dwarves seemed to have forgotten her. Nextday stood on a
rock so he could be seen, and addressed his brethren. In the air his language was harder to follow. They were speaking about the mirror.

"What mirror is this?" said Bianca, pushing forward, reminding
them that she was there.

Nextday said, "It isn't your concern, nor should it be."

"But I may be able to help."

"You aren't able to find your way through a draped doorway into the next room, or you'd have left our home long ago," snarled Bitter. But Nextday continued for her benefit in a vernacular she could more easily follow. "I'll remind us all what we are after, and let the world have at us if it must. We're the ones who made the mirror; we're to be the ones to reclaim it, if it's to do no harm."

Bianca had a thrilling sense of possibility similar to the sense a mirror gave: of otherness and familiarity at once.

"Tell me about the mirror," she said.

Nextday considered her request. He said, "I've been learning much in these days. To speak of something, I find, can help clarify it in one's own mind. Therefore I'll tell you what I know, and perhaps I'll learn something in how I put my knowledge forward."

"Or perhaps I'll reply with something you don't yet know," said Bianca helpfully.

"Thrills unbounded," observed Bitter in a low voice.

"I hope she speaks better than she cooks," said Tasteless. "I didn't care for that stew at all, did you?"

"Be quiet," said Heartless. "She can hear as well as speak."

"Stay on the matter," said Bianca, unflustered. "The mirror."

"We are a race more stalwart, more stubborn, than yours," said Nextday. "We've spent arcs of years thinking a single thought. But in our vast and tedious life, we've come to realize that what divides us from the quixotic human race is the quality of quickness. Cut to the quick, they say; the quick and the dead, they say: They mean life, liveliness, when they say *the quick.* And we see that if we're to benefit at all from our neighbors here—the human herd—we must quicken.

"So, being adept at all things having to do with the earth—the soil, the mines, the precious stones and metals, the juice of lava—we found it easy to ferret out the secrets of the Venetians. We blew a quantity of glass and shaped it into a shallow bowl, and painted the inner skin with a coat made of tin and quicksilver. We made for ourselves a mirror that could look like an eye into a room, so we could watch how humans look at themselves, and learn by their example how to look at ourselves."

"A clever trick," said Bianca, "and possibly a mean one."

"Minerals have no morals, and we are little more than ambulatory stacks of minerals. We weren't stymied by reservations. But we suffered a setback. To ready the mirror, we left it out in the air so its shape could fix, and it could adjust to the code of the world in which humans live, and not to our code. Then to cure it we submerged it in a bath of water. But it sank, and we couldn't see it. It had become invisible to us."

"Lago Verde," said Bianca.

"We watched it being reclaimed. From a distance we saw that it worked, well enough. But quicksilver is strong enough stuff when found in nature, and stronger still when dwarves work with it. It corrupts the mind, and confounds the separate humors. It can make humans suspicious of cabals in every crowd, of treason at every turn. It causes tremors and drooling. It's a dangerous substance to humans."

"Can't you just steal it back? To protect the humans who found it, if nothing else?" said Bianca.

Nextday said, "Humans can steal all kinds of things; perhaps that is what makes them change and shift and thrive so. Dwarves can't steal."

"But you told me that minerals have no morals," she said. "If you can't steal, perhaps you are made of more than minerals."

"Cleverness is unbecoming in a corpse," sneered MuteMuteMute.

"And you stole the secret of glassmaking from the Venetians," she pointed out.

"Is this a court of judicial law? Are we on trial?" said Lame. "Goodness, I'd have worn something more attractive."

"If it's a question of donation, let me just give you the mirror," said the girl. "It's as simple as that, surely? If my father is dead then the house is mine, and I'll have nothing in the house that doesn't rightly belong to me."

Nextday looked at her with a quiet sort of consolation. He didn't offer an opinion about whether her father was dead or not. He only remarked, "The house isn't quite yours. And we don't steal."

"What do you do, then?" she said. "Where do you go? What is your task?"

Nextday said, "I am going to take my kin to Arezzo, to see the fresco in the choir. Someone has painted a dwarf on the wall there, a creature of dignity and intelligence, calmly interacting with the family of man. Perhaps he is both a dwarf and a human being; this is something of which we have not heard. We are too long underground. Now we've awakened, now we've eaten—"

"If you can call that food. Pfaaah," muttered Tasteless.

"—now we are above, and more solid in new forms than we expected." Nextday looked about at the small men in tunics and leggings, hoods and boots. "We must pass in the world and see how we fare. Perhaps, though it had hardly begun, the time for the mirror is done, and now it's time to look with our own eyes."

He blinked sadly at Bianca. "Can we leave you safely here?"

"Of course," she said.

"You are not to run off," he told her. "Donna Borgia would see that you were killed again."

"I haven't not died yet," she said, laughing.

"No," he said. "All but that, but not that, no."

With that he began to lead his brothers away. Heartless came up and pressed his hand to hers, but then hurried after his kind.

Such was the increased corporeality of the tribe that she could see them leaving, and waving at her, and hear them when they were gone, tramping softly in the impossible season. When their boots no longer thudded upon the rock or skittered stones on the pebbley path, she could hear them hissing musically through their lips, like infants walking down the lane to greet the goat in his pen or the fowl pecking for breakfast along the verges.

She sat down and looked around her. The exterior of the dwarves' home had the aspect of a hummock at first, little more than a mound of grass on the side of a hill, but as she looked it shrugged off its green roof and grew scales of pantiles. The sloping sides of the dwelling straightened themselves up and became timbered, and the windows made an effort to line themselves up on something of a parallel, to be more pleasing. The hill dropped some bulk behind, and what remained looked more like a cottage, more or less freestanding, with a chimney of stone and chipped brick, and a smell from within of mushrooms, sage, and Parma cheese.

"Not such an ugly grave," she said to herself, "not an ossuary, not a churchyard; no, quite respectable."

Respectable, but lonely, after a while. The sun went behind a cloud and the more wintry aspects of the garden seemed to dominate.

Then, when she was just about to give up and go inside, she heard a noise in the brambles, and she called out, "Who is there?" She turned to see a figure make its way across the clearing.

The figure in the clearing

wasn't looking to find you," said
the figure. "Are you a goose?"

"I know you," said Bianca.

"All my geese know me," he said proudly.

"I'm not a goose," she said. "But I know you just the same."

He bit the corner of a fingernail.

"You're the gooseboy," she told him.

"I know," he replied. "I'm looking for the lost goose."

"I am lost, in a sense," she said, and she began to laugh, "and in a
sense I am a goose—but not the one you're looking for."

"Can you help me find her?" he said. "The house is full of
hunger, and they will have a goose upon the table."

"Do you remember me?" she said.

"Not if you weren't with the other geese."

"I was, sometimes."

He looked at her sideways. "I've never met a spirit of the woods before," he said. "Primavera used to say that the wood spirits are as old as Roman times and I must beware hags and graybeards. You don't look much like a hag."

"Nor a graybeard." She was teasing him, but that she had always done. "Do you really not know who I am?"

"Neither goose nor dryad. Some saint with loosened garments?" He saw that her tunic was unlaced. She put her hands to her breasts and covered them.

"Not a saint," she said and sighed. "I never lived enough to have the chance to become a saint. Saints have to endure trials, and I was too innocent even for a trial."

"How do you know me?"

"You are the gooseboy from Montefiore." But she didn't know his name. Had she ever known his name? He was too simple to need a name, just the gooseboy, or, addressed directly, *Boy.*

As she had grown and changed, so had he. A young man now, he was somewhat stooped of shoulder, as if practicing to be a codger. One leg seemed shorter than the other, or withered; anyway, it kept itself slightly arched behind, looking a bit like a high-spirited colt's rear leg. Without much success his cheeks and lips were trying to grow a beard. His chin was stronger than it had been, though his eyes were still jittery with caution.

"I am your friend," she said.

"If I've learned anything from the kitchen tales that Primavera used to tell, it's that the likes of me are to beware of friends like you," he answered. "Maidens of unusual friendliness, that sort of thing."

"Don't be a fool," she said. He flinched and retreated.

"I am only looking for my lost goose, nothing more."

"I'm sorry. I didn't mean that. I merely mean this: don't you recognize me? I am your friend from long ago. Bianca, who played with you in the road below the house."

His eyes looked more hooded than ever. "Bianca died years ago. Are you her spirit?"

"I didn't die," she said. "I just—went away."

"What do you want with me?"

She shrugged. "To help you find your goose, I suppose. What else does a friend want, but the same thing?"

"If you aren't going to ensnare me into your wicked bed," he said, sounding faintly disappointed, "you may as well help me find my goose. Have you seen her? It's the one with the long neck."

"Don't they all have long necks?"

"Well—yes, now that you mention it."

"Where are the other geese, while you look for the lost goose?"

"With themselves, of course."

"Safe?"

"As safe as geese can get. Which isn't very safe, I admit; after all, I keep them together and free of the fox only so they might end up roasting on the spit."

She said, "I'll help you find her. Where are you looking?"

"Here and there." He indicated to the left, to the right, broadly and without fuss. She looked around, and began to take in the world again.

Beyond the clearing, there was no correction to the world. The trees had a certain snap to them, a self-assurance, that was offensive at first. They didn't shrug themselves into more respectable shapes, more graceful curves; those limbs that were ragged with disease or hollowed by the boring of insects stayed ragged, insouciant. As she ventured a few steps farther, the rocks and stones jabbed her tender soles, and a fly pestered her about the ears. The air grew colder again by degrees and wouldn't warm as she might have preferred it to. It was, in short, the real world.

She took his hand and they walked together, he with his lopsided lope, she gingerly, to protect her feet. It was bizarre and even cruel, in a way, to see the world insist on being itself, with so little regard for them. Coming upon an ungainly promontory, they had to scramble around it, as it neither retreated nor developed convenient footholds for their use. Balsam pitch smeared against her gown, rubbing a gummy mark in it. Her breasts were cold and the tips of her breasts stiffened uncomfortably. She ought to have willed herself some decent clothes, but she hadn't remembered the world to be so unaccommodating.

"I don't know your name," she said.

"I am the gooseboy," he told her fondly, as if to have heard that she could forget was proof enough that they had once known one another.

"But your other name," she said. "I've a name. Bianca. Bianca de Nevada." It felt odd in her mouth. "Didn't you have another name?"

"Michelotto," he said. "Nothing more."

"Michelotto." She found herself smiling. "I think we were friends once."

"I think so too." He said it out of a passion to please, not from conviction.

They skirted a stand of slender trees with slender trunks like the legs of fawns, and bodices of white leaf.

"How many geese have you?" she asked.

"Seven," he said, "or eight."

"Seven when one is missing, eight when one is found?"

"Seven or eight."

"Well, there they are, then." They had come to a gentle dip from which a spring burbled; a vernal pool shimmered with the reflection of a gaggle of geese. White curvets upon green water. "Four, five, six—seven."

"Seven!" he said. "That's the right number, I think. So she's come back."

"She came back while you were looking the other way."

"That's often the way you find someone who is lost," he said. He smiled at her as if he were competent, just for a moment, and his gaze looked clear and friendly. In all her childhood she hadn't thought of him as much more than a goose himself, and the realization caused her grief.

"Come back with me," he said. "They will be happy to see you."

"Who is there?" she asked.

"Donna Borgia, for one." He paused as if trying to remember the others.

Her fear was profound, though she didn't know why. She pulled back and said, "You are trying to lure me back!"

"I am looking for my goose, nothing more," he said. "You must believe me."

"Play with your geese, gooseboy," she said, and pushed him on the shoulder. He stumbled and fell to one knee, and while he maneuvered and huffed to find his balance, she fled.

It wasn't hard to find the dwarves' cottage. While she was gone, while she had ventured into the world, it had solidified more. A rich moss adhered to one wall. The door was now lime-washed and opened in two segments, like the door of a byre. A concavity shaped like a shell at the top, perhaps a shrine, was set in the side wall. She went to look. Within stood no Virgin with open hands, no carpenter with a Child on his shoulders, as she might have expected to see. Instead, a crudely carved stone tree with a coil of serpent wrapped around its base. A single apple, outsize, weighed down one branch. The serpent ignored the apple. Though its head was turned toward Bianca, its fangs were weathered into stumps.

Interviews

VICENTE FOUND Fra Ludovico in the little yard behind his cell, where he was keeping watch over a kettle. He was boiling up berries and bark, which Vicente remembered was the basis of some unsavory potion famous for the stupor it induced. The foul smell was comforting in its familiarity.

"Are you the mad priest or the quiet sage today? Be the coherent one, if you can; I have to hear someone making some sense."

Fra Ludovico seemed less interested in conversing with Vicente than in governing the flame and making sure sediment didn't scorch on the bottom of the pot and ruin the batch. But he said, "Sit, sit, my friend," and Vicente squatted, upwind of the drift of vapors.

"I left you in charge," he began.

"You didn't leave *me* in *charge,*" said Fra Ludovico. "In charge of la Borgia? I can't even get up on a donkey anymore without a ladder, a hoist, and a week of fasting. The notion of asking me to govern a

Borgia! But I did my part nonetheless, you know."

"Yes. You played the part of a blithering fool. What for?"

"A canny disguise. So I might be considered harmless, and not need to be disposed of. So I might protect my position and protect your daughter."

"But you didn't protect her."

"I did what I could. If you're going to blame me for the way things happen in human affairs, you're wasting your breath. Have a drink instead. It isn't ready but it'll burn your tongue and stop your nonsense."

Vicente asked Fra Ludovico for more information about the disappearance of Bianca. He wanted a more certain sense of when the disaster had happened. The old priest—for by now he was old—shook his head and tried to remember. "It was close to the time that Primavera's grandson disappeared," he said at last. "And she will know exactly when that was. She will know," he added, "though she won't say, of course. She can't."

"But how many years ago? Your cheek has gone hoary, and I can't escape the sad eyes of Primavera. I gather I've been away about a decade, but when in that span of years did Bianca disappear? And what prompted it?"

"I measure time by the seasons of the Church," began Fra Ludovico, "and every year begins anew, with Advent; it's the same year, over and over, indistinguishable one from another—"

"I'll turn you out on your fat old behind, you pious fool—"

"About six years, more or less."

This was clearer but hardly a comfort. "But why? What happened? How had she changed?"

"She changed only as every child changes, no more, no less. I appreciate your sorrow but you must understand: Had I seen signs that she intended to flee I would have intercepted her. She was still docile enough, still a timid child in her way. Well, you'd never let her meander—"

Vicente gave him a look. "I'll say what I will," said the priest. "I blame you no more than I blame myself, Don Vicente; facts are as they are. You rarely took her as far as the village."

"She was a *child*."

"And she grew up while you were gone. Or began to, anyway."

"Was she threatened here? Soldiers sniffing around?"

"We enjoyed the customary blight of daily life. We delighted in tedium."

Vicente could sit no longer. He strode back and forth, stroking his beard. "Have you blessed what you can of her spirit? In the event she has died? Have you performed the offices of the dead?"

"She was blameless," said Fra Ludovico. "About that you can rest assured. I'm no theologian, Don Vicente, but I can't bring myself to worry for the state of her soul in the afterlife. She was too pure a child to need serious pardoning." He stirred more vigorously. "Besides, I used to note that you didn't take much stock in my feeble efforts."

"Who are you to deny a child spiritual benefit because her father is a doubter?" Vicente overturned the pot, scalding the priest's bare toes. Fra Ludovico yipped in pain and irritation. "Are you a pope, to determine who deserves forgiveness for their sins? You have no right to deny my child sanctity. You have no way to see into her heart."

"You've been changed by your adventures, I see. I suppose I might as well get used to it. Now look. I have my convictions. Maybe they are born of a little too much liqueur in the colder days, but they are convictions just the same. And I don't sense that Bianca has departed this life."

"What are you saying?"

"Nothing more than what I've already said. No hunting dogs have found her body in the woods. Villagers, whose gossip and conjecture often signifies, have been as mystified as we at Montefiore are. Primavera insisted on augury after augury, trying to learn the truth, and she could read no sign of Bianca's demise in any entrails. That was when the old sow could still speak, of course, though her tongue became detached shortly thereafter."

"For blasphemy?"

"If she'd been subject to that punishment for blasphemy, she'd have been mute since she was three." He continued. "Maybe Bianca escaped over the hills to Ravenna. Maybe she found a little convent somewhere and offered herself to Christ. In any case, I've more to do than say the Mass of the Dead for a healthy young girl who lights out on her own."

Vicente hugged his own elbows. "You didn't go after her."

"Maybe she went after you," said Fra Ludovico, scowling at the

hickory bark and sanguine berry slopped on the ground. "She was growing up, you know; she couldn't help it. You can't fix a child in time."

"If I find her corpse, or hear word of her death, you will bless her spirit?"

"I bless her spirit daily. I'll bless yours too, if you take to wandering the woods and fields looking for evidence. And I'll not say the Mass of the Dead until I know one or the other of you have died."

Vicente had to smile despite himself—weakly, affectionately. "You're as superstitious as Primavera, in your own way," he said.

"Now that's blasphemy."

Vicente wandered through the airy chapel and out into the stable yard. The gooseboy was settling his flock behind their brambly hedge, and fixing what passed for a gate with a twist of moldy rope.

"You never known which goose you will lose and which goose you will find," he was muttering to himself.

"Fidelio," said Vicente, "Fidelio, is it? Or Paolo? I can't remember."

"Michelotto. Everyone seems to want to know today."

"In your wanderings, lad, have you come across anyone who could tell me the whereabouts of Bianca? Your friend from those years back—you must remember her? With the skin so fair, and the black black hair—"

The gooseboy twisted his face as if trying to remember. He opened his mouth to speak, but another voice cut through the air first, calling him away from Vicente. Lucrezia Borgia stood at a window, her beautiful hair falling to one side, an ivory comb in her hand. "Michelotto," she called, "Michelotto, my boy. It's time to brush my hair. Come and give your poor mother some attention."

The gooseboy shrugged at Vicente and raised his eyebrows, and went to do as he was told.

Vicente made his way at last to the kitchen. He found Primavera squatting upon a stool in the middle of the floor, sifting through a bowl of lentils. When she came upon an occasional stone, it went skipping out the door into the lettuces.

He didn't know what he was after, nor could he bear to plague the old *nonna* with questions when she had no way to answer. But he sat down on a bench along the wall, and she put aside her work and looked at him with eyes gone nearly glassy with milky film. She reached out and held his hands. She squeezed them again and again, as if there was a signal in the pattern of her grasp, but he could read it no better than he could read the comments of clouds scrawled against the sky.

An ivory comb, my dear

THE PREMONITION in the mirror was accurate. The girl was alive. Any day she might come forward to stake her claim on the future, and tell the truth about what had happened.

"You're certain it was she?" said Lucrezia.

Michelotto had his hands on her head, playing with her hair, plaiting it. She slapped his wrist and said, "You odd thing, listen to me! How could you know it was she?"

By the time the answer to Vicente's question about the whereabouts of Bianca had surfaced in the gooseboy's brain, he was no longer speaking to Vicente but to his mother. She got the benefit of the information instead. Michelotto, though, couldn't remember how the conversation had come up, nor what proof he had to offer her that Bianca still lived. "There was a house," he finally said, "not as far away as all that, but one I never saw before."

"Could you find it again?"

"If it wanted to be found, I suppose."

She was gripped with a desire to smash his skull with a heft of marble. He lived to mock her all her days, but he was the one person she couldn't be seen to kill. He was too thoroughly a Borgia. Would she had managed it when he was a toddler, would she had been able to throw him off the aqueduct at Spoleto! But Michelotto was her son and nephew both. In the years following the death of her father, her brother, and her son Rodrigo, and with the collapse of the romance of her marriage, she had come to cling to Michelotto, despite all his fancifulness. And she had begun to feel fondly for him. Because she could expect nothing of the Punishment—not even that he bear the family name—she had found a way to love him without stint or mercy.

This didn't keep her from wanting, on a regular basis, to brain him.

"We will walk," she said, "this very day, we will walk for a while, and you will suggest a path to take. This way, that way? Whichever way you think best. Just give me a moment"—she was thinking quickly—"that I might ready myself. Put up my hair." She held the ivory comb in one hand and considered the various recipes at her disposal. "Go downstairs now, Michelotto, and speak to no one. Wait for me on the steps and I'll be with you in a trice."

Michelotto did as he was told. He sat on the bottom step of the outside staircase and played with a kitten as, nearby, Vicente cut himself a staff. Michelotto watched the wheezing man begin, with effort, to scale down the steepest slope behind Montefiore. He couldn't guess why Vicente would be risking the integrity of his limbs in such an exercise. He didn't bother to guess.

Vicente thought: perhaps Bianca had gone sleepwalking and fell from a window, and her corpse has laid buried in undergrowth at the foot of the bluff? Or perhaps she was pushed by hands accustomed to murder? In any case, one had to start looking somewhere.

The comb was a lovely Spanish piece that had belonged to some courtesan of her father's—perhaps her own mother, for that matter. It was carved with an expressive burst of orange blossoms. The rack of pins curved inward for better purchase. It wasn't difficult to coat the tines with a lethal substance that dried quickly and would liquefy again when it came in contact with blood. Now: how to disguise herself. She thought at last of the vestibule of the chapel, where Fra Ludovico hung old garments for use while gardening. She found a cloak and draped it close upon her face, pushing her own hair back so its luxuriance and color wouldn't give her away. Then she smeared her face with soot from the inside of the fireplace, and surveyed herself in the mirror over the mantel. She looked agreeably like Primavera's older sister.

The sun was bowling down the sky, and the yard clear of laborers but for Michelotto, who took a bad start when he saw the old hag coming down the steps. "Shhh, my boy, it's a masquerade game!" she cawed, trying out an appropriate voice. "As when we wear metal casques at carnival, nothing more."

"You terrify me. I don't like a masquerade."

"Oh, I'll let you wander home alone then, when you have shown me what I need to see."

She wasn't sure the light would last, nor that Michelotto would be able to find a path at all, daylight or not. But he had the idea to bring a goose along, and give it instructions. The goose seemed disinclined to assist in the exercise. But after a good swift kick in her downy behind, she focused her attentions and began to waddle down the road.

Lucrezia found something liberating in the disguise she'd taken on, and she enjoyed hobbling and sighing as if she were really a healthily farting old dame instead of a lithe and beautiful thirty-two. Michelotto kept a good distance from her.

Across the bridge and along a ways, and before long the goose left the track.

"Is this the way?" asked Lucrezia.

"She thinks it is," said Michelotto.

"What do you remember of where you were?"

"I can't say for sure that we were here. Or that we weren't."

"You sweet cunning idiot. I'll have Primavera bake you your own private tart if you lead me correctly."

"An apple tart?"

She glared at him. "A goose tart, of course. Are we still true?"

"Are we?" he asked her.

The goose paused. The gloom was thickening in the underbrush, and a wind twitched the canopy of leaves high above. "There's the pool in which we found the goose," said Michelotto at last, unhappily, honestly, for he wasn't quite capable of guile. "Look, she heads for it. The house was just up that slope and around the copse of trees with white leaves."

"Very well," said Lucrezia. "Now you may take your ladygoose home. I will proceed alone."

"You'll get lost coming back," he said. "The dark is falling."

"I see in the dark," she answered. Her eyes swam with a silvery light; Michelotto couldn't tell if she had bewitched herself or if it was merely a trick of the dusk. "Now off with you, friend, and leave me to my work. I intend to pay a social call."

"I would like to see her again," he ventured.

"If you would like to see anything again," she answered, "I suggest you heed my advice. Good-bye."

He wouldn't leave and she wouldn't go on with him in tow. At last she stooped and found a small, sharp rock. With a steadiness of hand that surprised all three of them, she pitched the missile at the goose. It drove into the back of the goose's head and a small flower of blood bloomed on the white scalp. She honked her irritation and rage and with an explosive clatter of her powerful wings she lifted out of the pool. "Your goose is gone," said Lucrezia. "You are the gooseboy. So find her."

Tending geese was his life. He knew no obligation more pressing. So Michelotto lit out after the goose. She was smart enough, Lucrezia observed, to head back in the direction of Montefiore, so there was no need to worry about Michelotto's getting lost in the woods at night.

She followed the imprecise directions, and they proved precise enough. Before long she discovered a cottage in the woods, with a lit wick sitting in a stone basin of oil at the window. The cottage was improbable, and Lucrezia puzzled about it as she drew nearer. There were no fields, no byres for sheep or cows, no orchards nearby, no rutted track for the approach of a farm cart. The thing had grown up in the middle of the woods like a toadstool in the rain.

Yet there was glass in the window, real glass—small circlets and lozenges set in a grid of lead, and a splash of color here and there. A bit of shapely *ferro battuto* ornamenting the roofline in a festive scroll, that looked from here like the iron letters of a very foreign alphabet. A smell of roasting venison, with autumn gourds and onions, hung in the air. And then—she leaned forward to assess it—the sound of a lute being plucked in a desultory and unpracticed manner, as if someone had nothing else to do but try to make music while the meal finished cooking.

"A meal for a mendicant," called Lucrezia in a small voice, to try it out, and then lowered her voice and roughened it up. "A meal for a wandering monk, who will bless this house."

The music stopped. Lucrezia had reached the door, and she thumped on it. "There must be a good wife at home, preparing the evening meal. I beg for mercy." She drew the shawl down upon her face so that nothing but her chin might show.

The door opened. Bianca de Nevada, exactly as word had had it.

Lucrezia flinched and flushed. Simple rage—that Bianca de Nevada should somehow have escaped the death sentence issued years earlier? Or rage supplanted by pleasure, that the girl lived still, to be killed again. Another chance. The Borgia blood quickened.

And the cause? It would take an Ariosto to unravel the root of her guile. Any murder, even suicide—especially suicide, perhaps—is an attempt to stop the future from happening. Though Lucrezia Borgia knew herself to be as comfortable as a well-born woman could wish, with influence, romance, fame, and luxury, she couldn't stop the future without Cesare from unrolling. Every day, every hour, both she and the world further adjusted to soldiering on without him. On the day that Cesare, secretly and in pain, had made his last assignation with his sister, at the mountain retreat of Montefiore, he had grown distracted by the beauty of Bianca de Nevada. He was leaving not just for Spain, but for ever, but he left Lucrezia an hour or two earlier than he needed, by noticing Bianca.

Lucrezia couldn't murder to bring Cesare back. She wasn't Zeus, to cause Phaëthon to stop driving the chariot of bright Helios: she couldn't halt the daily chariot of crushing light and rushing time. But she could murder to stop the innocent virago—the only seriously dangerous kind—from living and thriving when Cesare couldn't.

"Mercy," Lucrezia repeated.

"I've been alone such a long time," said the girl child, in a voice of surprise at itself, a voice that leaned toward womanliness, "and now the world repopulates itself in my direction."

"Forgive the world its intrusions, if you can," said Lucrezia, husking her own voice in a masculine manner as best she could. "The wandering hermit such as I makes effort to avoid the snares of the devil, so often hooked and crooked into the words and doings of humankind. But even I become hungry, and I must eat if I am to pray for our salvation. You tempt me with aromas of dinner. May I come in and share a meal with you?"

"This isn't my home, and I've no permission to welcome a guest," said Bianca. "But I won't turn you away hungry. I'll give you a bite, and you can bring news of the world to me. Can you tell me much of the doings of the day?"

"You need to know whether the wheat is sewn in the fields yet, or the sow has had her spring litter? Or are you more interested in the status of Pope Julius the II's campaign against Bologna? Or the latest fashions from the court of Louis XII of arrogant France?"

"I scarcely know what to ask," she said. "Can you tell me of Montefiore?"

"I don't know the place. I avoid towns and estates where I can, preferring to take my meal with the small farmholder and the vagabonds of the woods. But by the aroma of it, you eat more agreeably than most tenants. Where do you get your fulsome table, here in the middle of nowhere?"

Bianca de Nevada said, "Let me cut you from the heel of the joint, where the meat is cooked already, and spoon you some marrows and carrots and the like. I'll pass you a plate through the window." And so, in a minute, she did, and Lucrezia took the offering with a fine and sudden hunger. Primavera with all the grounds of Montefiore, and the hunters and poachers and snarers at her disposal, hardly could prepare a meal as sumptuous as this. But Lucrezia couldn't bother with food, however enticing.

"I can't pay you for your kindness," said Lucrezia. "What coin I collect is dedicated to relieving the suffering of the poor."

"My needs are supplied," said Bianca. "Your company is payment enough."

"Let me hunt in my cloak for a token of my gratitude then," said Lucrezia. "A monk is often thrust trinkets by blushing gentlewomen who confess the sins of their boudoirs to his holy ear. But we have no use of such finery, and they weigh down the hems of our garments as well as our souls. You have a face as beautiful as the evening; you will be ornamented as you deserve."

Bianca cast her eye down, unused to compliments from men, even monks. She didn't ask for the gift, and had not yet found words to decline it, when Lucrezia fastened her grip around the comb, and raised it high.

"May it bring you much happiness," she said and drove the ivory implement down into the back of the girl's lowered head. She felt the tines scrape and then dig into the scalp, as fully as that stone had driven into the skull of the goose. Bianca de Nevada gasped and her hands fluttered like two doves in the gloaming. She fell against the casement of the window, then slumped back inside the cottage, lost in shadows. Lucrezia flung the plate of food, uneaten, in the window over the girl's corpse, and made her way with haste back up the hill and toward Montefiore.

I am a girl who did little wrong

I am a girl who did little wrong.
I courted loneliness to be my lover.
I spoke in tongues to insensible rocks, pretending
Only I their natures could discover.
Each of us wishes more than the world can offer.
The hermit his coffin, the prince his princely coffer.
To thirst for solitude while the carnival rages
Is the curse of fools or the saintly goal of sages.
Neither a simpleton nor a saint, I suffer
The attentions of my coldly unvarying lover.

She wakes once more

THE DWARVES were around her, snuffling like colts.

"We leave you alone," they said, more or less in one voice, "and provide you a window upon the wicked world, and your vanity betrays you. There is nothing but grief out there! Haven't you learned this yet?"

She sat up and felt the back of her head, where blood had matted.

"Have you been to Arezzo and back?" she said. They shook their heads.

"The farther we got from you, the less sure we seemed of ourselves," said Heartless sadly. "Your kind imagination of us—as individuals, with names, of all things—has begun to seem a kind of nourishment. Without your regard, our initiative was sapped."

"You must get that mirror back and regard yourselves," she told them. "Oh, my head hurts so."

"It would have hurt you worse until it couldn't hurt you further, had we not come back." Heartless held out the ivory comb. Several of its tines had broken off, and among those that remained was a residue of blood and dried matter and threads of her raven black hair. "A serried rank of small poisoned *stiletti,*" he said.

Still, it was a beautiful thing, even with broken tines.

She steadied herself with a hand to her temple, and then said, "You are too kind, and too . . . too . . ." She wanted to say *little,* but that would have been repaying their kindness with rude honesty; she thought *too incomplete,* but that also seemed uncharitable. And *too attentive* was wrong. Without their attention, she would be dead.

She didn't finish her sentence. They helped her to her feet. Across the room—and didn't the venison smell wonderful! Where had that come from?—she saw the silvery fog in the wall, the oval through which she had once seen Montefiore. She walked over to it and put up her hand to her head, and held the ivory comb gingerly in place, taking care not to scrape her scalp with it.

She didn't know if it was herself she was seeing. The reflection was imprecise, varnished with mist; but there was a woman's face therein, and as its lips moved, so Bianca moved hers, as if under a spell. "Mirror, mirror," she said. "What is to become of us?"

"What is to become of you, if you don't take care?" complained Gimpy.

"We won't be here forever to guide your every step," snapped Deaf-to-the-World.

"As if we have nothing better to do," added MuteMuteMute.

"We have nothing better to do, damn the fact," observed Bitter, "but that still doesn't mean we want to do it."

"We will be here forever," said Heartless. "That's the truth of it. But you, dear Bianca . . ."

He didn't finish his sentence, just stood looking at her fondly.

"You must take the mirror back," said Bianca. "What are you waiting for? You want to be human enough, you have to learn to steal. What was the first act of disobedience but a theft? Let me come with you, I'll lead you as a band of rogues. The robber queen! I like the notion."

"It isn't safe for you yet," said Nextday.

"You're less than men," she said. "How do you know what's safe for me?"

They had protected her and she had shamed them. Bitter made a rude gesture before the others could stop him. "We'll go as far as the bridge anyway," said Nextday decisively. "We'll look to see what we can."

"I ask your pardon for my crude remarks," she said, but they paid no attention to her.

A bodice, my darling

So THE mirror revealed that the girl had survived, and the comb clasped to her temple lent a further beauty against her black hair.

Lucrezia discharged her lady-in-waiting and took to the dressing room herself. With abandon she rooted through trunks and leathern satchels and the *armadio* in the corner until she located what she was seeking. There had been a masquerade at New Year's, in January of 1503, when the guests and revelers all cavorted behind masques shaped crudely like human genitals. She had found the affair sumptuously corrupt, and had kept several of the masks for their comic or aphrodisiacal effect. She dug up the most objectionable and, making sure the door to the hallway was shut and bolted, she affixed the creation to her head by means of a pair of leather straps.

It looked crude and terrifying, and she was satisfied. If her turn as a holy fool had not worked, let her make more of a mockery of things.

She could hardly sleep that night, in anticipation, and she arose long before dawn. Even Vicente, who slept poorly, could be heard through the door still moaning in his dreams. She took a torch from the stable. A horse stamped and whinnied—then nothing but silence. She left the house behind in green moonlight.

How long had Cesare been dead?—three years, four, and her father only a year or more than that? Since then she had turned into a monster—look at her, a fiend sneaking through the fields beyond Montefiore with a lecherous disguise hidden under the skirt of her tunic. She felt the very blood in her heels pound, and she had to run along the road, the papier-mâché genitals hidden under her apron slapping her again and again in the groin, mocking her failure as a mother, her loss as a sister.

This time it was early morning when she came to the cottage. As before, an enticing aroma suffused the mysterious clearing, something of eggs and cheese, onions and herbs, and the nutty snap of breakfast ale. How could there be eggs and cheese here, without the cackle of hens or the barracking opinions of a goat?

Extinguishing her torch in a ditch, she paused behind a stand of hawthorne. It had blushed into fuller leaf since her last visit and gave her enough protection to listen for the sound of voices. And, to be sure, she was wise to wait, for she heard a clamor of unfinished male voices. Then, ridiculously, the bottom half of the severed door opened, and out came creatures that she hesitated to call dwarves, though what else could they be?

Lucrezia Borgia had dwarves in her court at Ferrara. Dwarves were a mischievous and important presence in royal society, serving as confidantes, jesters, aides-de-camp, and chaperones. Generally they possessed expressions of profound gravity, whatever their social station or native intelligence; there was something dignified about how their solid, full-size heads sat without remorse or apology upon bodies that had to work harder than most to manage an outsize world. The tendency of dwarf legs to bow, of dwarf hands to be clumsy at small work—managing broth in a soup spoon, the hilarity!—oh, oh, that was a common enough cause of low humor. But even the cheeri-est and most self-deprecating dwarf, capering like an imp, couldn't shuck off a self-possession, which left audiences somewhat uneasy, even while holding their sides from the pain of laughter.

These small men who departed from the cottage in the woods were a different breed of dwarf, from a different race, perhaps, though what little she could see of their faces suggested they were swarthy, bearded, compact, like dwarves. It was something else; it was that the shortened torsos and small legs were proportioned differently—nei-ther better nor worse, just differently. These dwarves—six, seven, eight, she lost count—seemed more like children still forming their milk teeth. Their rib cages were not barrels but slender butter churns. They talked with one another in a language she couldn't make out—it seemed to be a Romish language, full of slanting vowels and sur-prising stops and starts. But the small men were gone soon, traipsing away from her, and the clearing took on a fresher bloom, as if they swept away with them the last miasma of night.

She removed her apron and affixed her indecent headdress. Then she hurried to the door and pounded upon the closed upper half. Her legs were swathed in leggings, like the tight, flattering crimson apparel that Florentine youths wore, making codpieces a boast, an es-cutcheon, rounding buttocks to seem as fervent and inviting as a courtesan's cleavage. She could stand like a man—hadn't she admired enough men in her time, and learned their pendulums by heart?—and she had an airy tunic to disguise her breasts, which anyway were bound flat in lengths of cotton.

The girl called, "You've forgotten something, how kind to knock, but I'm just here with my meal—" and came to the door, expecting a returning dwarf. She must have seen the male legs, for her sentence stopped, but then she was drawn by courage or curiosity to swing open the top half of the door, and she stood face-to-face with the ob-scene reveler.

Lucrezia Borgia marveled at how musical a girl's scream could sound. She tossed her head like a horse as it nickers, and the thread-haired scrotum and the half-erect member (cheesecloth wrapped around a length of toweling) flopped menacingly down over her nose.

The girl couldn't speak, and couldn't breathe. Lucrezia advanced upon her into the room, and put her hand as roughly upon the girl's waist as she could manage. She pushed Bianca against a post in the middle of the room, and flipped the girl's long apron up, as if intending to forage between the girl's legs. But instead she caught the corners of the apron and pulled them back around the post, and she ducked behind and tied the corners together, so the girl was caught, at least momentarily, tied like Saint Sebastian at the pillar, and in nearly as lusciously fainting a state.

Lucrezia wheeled about again. Her eyes in this cottage worked poorly; was it the mask, or did the light bleed improperly from the lamps? She found she could make out little of the furnishings. There was nothing with which to attack the girl—no poker from the fireplace, no conveniently clawed kitchen implement. Only a few carved stone tables, or were they sarcophagi?—and a statue of someone very like Proserpina in a sitting position, munificently holding out an apple.

The woman turned back and looked at Bianca. The tightened apron around the girl's rib cage had pushed up her small breasts and made them prominent. With a roar Lucrezia pushed her masqued face against the girl, rubbing, and the girl sagged against the post, which now looked like a stalagmite in some cave.

Lucrezia didn't want to leave with the job incomplete this time, but she thought she heard a sound. A sound, surely? The tramp of small feet? Were those creatures coming back? She wouldn't be caught here by a tribe of midgets. Or was that the roar of time in her ears, had she been here longer than she ought? The girl's pale skin was whiter than before—was it cadaverous! Perhaps. Lucrezia fled, praying it might be so.

Two bites from the apple

BUT THE mirror wouldn't let her alone. Try as she might, shroud it in black lace from Seville, blow out the candles in the room, close her eyes—the mirror still gripped her. At last she could take no more, and she positioned herself in front of its harsh eye, and demanded the truth of it.

She no longer knew, nor even cared to question, whether the shapes revealed therein were phantasms of her mind or whether there was a magic at work. She wiped the spittle from her chin—she was chewing her own lips from rage and frustration—and saw the dwarves reviving the young woman once again. They loosened the makeshift bodice formed by the tied apron. They settled her upon the floor and rubbed her wrists with oil of lemon flowers. She could smell the tang of coastal fruit through the looking glass, and she gashed her wrist against the side of the ornate frame, wanting to beat the offending scene out of the bowed mirror. But the mirror would have none of it;

it showed her Bianca de Nevada until it was through. It showed how young she became, when refreshed by the dwarves; how the color stole back into her cheeks, and her anthracite hair bloomed more luxurious than ever, and her limbs, flexing for circulation, the more perfect and admirable than ever. And her life more hers than ever.

Lucrezia watched as the dwarves presented the girl with a small leather sack drawn closed with a cord. The girl opened it and a splash of water flowered in her lap. She withdrew a handful of coins, which she set aside, in a bowl held up by a reclining statue. Lucrezia felt a scalding of gorge in her gullet.

So she fell back, at last, to the tradition perfected by her ancestors. What a library of recipes they'd amassed—poisons that had killed cardinals and princes, dukes and their wives, inconvenient lovers overstaying their welcome.

When Cesare had abducted Caterina Sforza at Forlì, he'd wrested from her the secrets of her signal achievement, a *veleno attermine,* which promised perfect sleep. But Lucrezia Borgia would improve upon this unfailingly reliable decoction. She'd assure her own ascendancy while dooming the durable child to death at last. She'd use the last apple brought from Agion Oros, use it for her redemption and Bianca's downfall at the same time. The same fruit that killed Bianca would give Lucrezia mastery unfathomable. Perhaps even the wisdom to adjust the mistakes of time, to correct the past.

She had seen what a bite of the apple had done to the stone-faced beast. A mere slice of it had given the creature a mouth, an upright posture, the talent to pass through stone. What might it do for a person more magnificently human than most?

The mirror, maddening one minute, was helpful the next. Lucrezia began to realize that it alerted her when the dwarves were ready to leave. They would begin to appear in garb more clearly like human garments. They constructed a clumsy box with wheels and shafts, and practiced hauling it about. They were on a campaign of some sort. What were they up to? No mind, never mind; enough that they were gone.

She couldn't guess the colloquy the dwarves engaged in: whether to behave as their kind didn't behave, to leave behind the morally neutral state of their natures and commit a more human act. Lucrezia didn't associate the stone dog to whom she'd offered the apple and the dwarves who had gone on to eat the rest of it. She was an unwitting Eve. But now they were on their own. They would take the mirror, without permission, and damn the cost. They wanted to keep Bianca safe.

She wouldn't be a crone this time, nor play the role of a waggish courtier. She would face the child in finery. She had Primavera wring the juice from ten lemons and work it into her fair hair. If Bianca, stars glowing in the highlights of her midnight hair, would preen as Hecate, Lucrezia would pounce as Aurora. She sat on the top step of the flight above the loggia, turning her tresses in the strengthening sun. Summer would be here before long; she would reign as the goddess of dawn. The peacocks screamed at the competition; she threw her head back and answered them.

The time came at last. She plucked the apple from the silver stem—the second of the reported three, the third said by Vicente to be hidden in the treasury of the Doge.

The apple sat in a bronze dish like something pagan. Had Lucrezia a more fanciful mind she would have supposed it to be humming at a level just below the threshold of the human ear to comprehend. But fancy was for servants and infants, and poison was the real work at hand. She set about with the tools of her trade to recreate, in the darkest way she could, *al-iksir.*

Roots of mandrake, a knife with a handle made from human pelvis carved into obscene figures, a mortar and pestle for the mashing of savorless mushrooms, a drop of Fra Ludovico's communion wine for perversion, an alembic, a small fire underneath it in which she fed scraps of human hair, bits of the girl's old childhood garments, a letter from María Inés to Vicente, feathers of geese, and a live mouse she'd caught by overturning a water bucket. (The mouse escaped with a singed tail.) But the crucial ingredient of choice was quicksilver, crushed and refined in a crucible, then reduced into a more docile and transparent state through the private alchemy for which her family was known.

She varnished one half of the apple with the poison—the half toward which the last remaining silver leaf pointed, like a trembling needle. The tight, unwithering red skin of the holy fruit took the application sympathetically; indeed, only by the closest peering could she see the faint line the marked the edge of the brushwork.

One side, holy improvement; the other, an instant death.

The world was so easy to face with a tool like this in her hand.

She dressed carefully, finely, in the richest gown she happened to have on hand, and tied ropes of pearls about her waist and looped other strands of pearls through her hair. Then she flung open Vicente's wardrobe and pulled from a hook a crimson cloak that had belonged to María Inés de Castedo y Nevada. Lucrezia didn't know if Bianca would recognize the garment, but it felt superb to dress herself in it. The fit was perfect.

She swept through the *salone,* startling Primavera, who was just getting around to opening the wooden panels at the windows. The old woman crossed herself and followed as fast as her legs allowed.

Lucrezia flung open the door onto the loggia. Fra Ludovico was carting armloads of brilliant yellow *ginestra* to the roofless chapel. "Looks like our Duchessa is off to market," he said, but at a second glance he added, "and she intends to *buy* the market. Where on earth are you going?" Her look was so venomous and straitened that without delay he flung down the blossoms in two intersecting lines, making a yellow cross on the ground. It didn't hold her back. She trod upon it and kept going.

Appearing at the corner of the house, Vicente was on his way to continue his search. Daily he was making ever wider circuits out from the house, and one day he knew he would not come back. Now he gasped and fell into a fit of catarrh, raising his staff against her. That very cloak. "Villain," he said, or tried to, his voice merely a throttle of phlegm in his throat.

"Bother," she answered, distractedly. "Who can tell me where Michelotto is?"

Vicente wouldn't and Fra Ludovico wouldn't and Primavera Vecchia couldn't even if she wanted to. Lucrezia found her son by herself, loitering in the sheepfold at the bottom of the slope. She proposed that he escort her into the woods for a walk. She was eager to see the rural springtime flowers. She would have company, and a young man's arm, as she didn't want to slip into a bog or tread upon a snake.

"You are too lovely to walk in the woods," he said cautiously.

"Then let the woods improve themselves as I pass by."

The cottage came into view. Michelotto seemed surprised to find it; perhaps he didn't remember having seen it before? Or who might live within? No matter. Lucrezia paused at the edge of the clearing and said, "Let's pause, have a bite to eat, you and I."

She withdrew from an inner pocket of the cloak a portion of cheese, a small loaf of bread, and the apple, which was wrapped in a coppery silk cloth for safekeeping.

"I don't care for bread or cheese," said Michelotto, "though the apple looks fine enough."

"The apple isn't for you," she said. "But isn't it appetizing?"

She held it up, and her own hunger for it began to gnaw at her. The air in the clearing fell still, and the bees about the doorway of the dwarves' cottage seemed to cease their noisy commerce with flowers.

"Please," he said. "I rarely ask you for anything."

"Eat the bread if you're hungry," she said again. "The apple is for another."

"Who?" he asked, and she realized that, just possibly, he didn't see the cottage before them. What a liability a slanted mind was.

At last, cursing mildly below his breath, he grabbed the bread and broke a segment off, and fitted a hunk of cheese upon it, and ate the two together, his eyes on the apple all the while. It took little enough time for his eyes to grow heavy, as she knew they must. Still, waiting, she was almost driven mad herself by the rosy scent of the apple.

Then Michelotto stretched, and yawned happily, and fell to the ground, heavy as lead. She waited a minute or two, and shook him roughly, but her labors over the bread had proved effective. He didn't stir. Had she a mind to, she could have sliced his heart out of his chest and held it up for review, and he would never have awakened until the sedation wore off. How helpful to have a talent for cooking.

She got up and walked to the door of the dwarves' cottage, and rapped upon it with impertinence.

"I am told not to open the door to anyone," came the voice of Bianca de Nevada from within.

"And a sensible precaution, in these times," said Lucrezia Borgia in her own voice. "I hear tell of men abusing the lonely maidens in their cow stalls and convent cells around here. But I'm a friend of your family's, and I'm in sorest need. You may remember me or you may not; you may think of me well or ill; it doesn't bother me. But my companion has fallen ill, and I want a scupper of water to revive him."

She could hear Bianca pause.

"There is water in every stream," she said.

"I don't have the time, and I don't want to leave him alone here. Rogues roam the countryside in these perilous times. Weren't you bothered by someone yourself, recently? For the love of mercy, Bianca, open the door and at least pass me a flask of water; I ask for nothing more than that."

Such small charity couldn't be denied a traveler in need, Lucrezia knew, and Bianca was forced to open the top half of the door.

"Oh," she cried as Lucrezia had known she must. "Not you, no," and she went to slam the panel shut. But Lucrezia nudged an elbow in and stopped her, and pointed wanly at her son, ensnaring the girl's attention through her instinct for good works.

"Michelotto, Michelotto. What has happened. I'll fetch water—"

She disappeared for a moment and brought back a small earthenware flagon.

Lucrezia accepted the water without comment and crossed to the body of the boy, which looked convincingly crumpled and lifeless. She knew that water would revive him shortly. She had only a handful of instants in which to finish her task. Gently she raised his head onto her lap and used a finger to work his mouth open. She dribbled a little water onto his tongue. Some of it trickled out the corners of his mouth, making him seem more like his slack-jawed self, even though comatose.

"Is he recovering?" asked Bianca. She hadn't come outside. She'd been well warned by those dwarves. But her hands twisted at the top of the locked lower portion of the door, worrying.

"He may, in time," said Lucrezia. "I'm glad I remembered you were here, Bianca de Nevada. I had heard about it, but hardly believed it."

"Who knew such a thing?" said Bianca warily.

"Your father."

Bianca drove the heels of both hands into the sockets of her eyes. Her spine shook and her garment slipped off one shoulder. "Don't speak to me of my father," she said, when she could talk. "He made it his career to leave me, when I needed him. He took his instruction from you and your brother, when he might have stood up to you. He might have taken me with him. You lie to me, you old woman."

Lucrezia Borgia couldn't be moved by the sentiment, nor could she forgive the insult. Old woman. *Old.* But she smiled with the wiles of a thousand years, and said, "A child will rail against the inevitable, and then, as an adult, will learn that the inevitable can be avoided. My dear, you are marooned in a magical grave, a tumulus of ancient embittered spirits, and you refuse to emerge, out of fear and horror of the world, and of me. But I am atoning for having borrowed your father from you. I've come to withdraw you from your grave, to restore you to life and to your father. Vicente de Nevada has come back to Montefiore. He's there now. He has sent me here to collect you. He has sent his proof."

She unfolded from the sepal-like corners of the cloth the magnificent apple. "Here is what he has found for us, the treasure he was
dispatched to collect all those years ago. Though we need it no longer,
it retains its holy magic. It will release you the rest of the way into
your life, and you can come with me. When Michelotto awakes we
will, the three of us, return to Montefiore, and reunite you with your
father."

Lucrezia had been speaking without design, by instinct, but she
could see by the widening of the girl's eyes that she had put into
words some silly belief the girl held. "I don't know why I should trust
you," Bianca said at last, but her chin yearned forward, out of her
tomb, and her voice was soft. She was still so young, so foolish. Petty
ignorance has its charm, to be sure.

"I'll show you I mean you no harm," said Lucrezia. "Your father
brought this holiest of sacred totems for Cesare, but it can do him no
good; he is dead, and his corpse rots in a graveyard in Navarre. But let
it do you good, and me besides. Look, I will show you it's safe; I will
eat some of it myself."

She held it up in the sun, and turned the leaf so it pointed toward
Bianca de Nevada. Then she slaked her own hunger with a single bite
from the unvarnished side of the holy fruit.

She couldn't say how she felt; she had seldom had words for happiness. Happiness was a cruel hoax, usually, eclipsing momentarily the
true sour nature of the world. Yet now she had a moment of rankest
hope, that perhaps beneath the shining aspect of the world there was
a dark richness, a vein of clarifying joy. She waited for the *giubilo im-
menso* to pass, for that is the nature of visions; they slam to a close and
then, my dears, that is that. Better not to have had them at all. But the
moment lingered until it wasn't a moment, or she was inside the moment in a way so full it had infinite riches to it, aspects of immortal-
ity her usual apprehension denied her . . .

Like the sun coming out unexpectedly on a prospect of lagoon,
lighting the surface of the water on fire with white, and someone like
Cesare coming forward on the quay.

Michelotto burbled behind her insensibly, and she knew that time was passing, she knew it must be, though she couldn't feel it. She smiled more genuinely than she expected to, and held out the apple to Bianca de Nevada.

"Oh, you try too," she said.

The girl held the fruit in both hands and trained her eyes upon Lucrezia. "You are known for your poison," she said, "but if God would will it, I would rather be removed from a world in which you can lie to me so." She bit from the side, the silver leaf trembling. Michelotto sat up suddenly and retched all over himself. Bianca dropped the apple and her eyes slid up into her skull.

The oval window

Whether it be the highest of holy days or the day a comet smites a granary, the farm chores always need to be done. Despite the shock of seeing Lucrezia Borgia in glamorous dudgeon, the household had gotten on with its day. Fra Ludcovico and Primavera were down in the fields, Fra Ludovico to perform a blessing over the spring planting, Primavera to supply some pastries and ale to the *contadini*. No longer interested in his estate, Vicente had taken a small bark onto the mirrored surface of Lago Verde, and he stirred at the muddy bottom of the water, trying to dislodge any corpse he might find.

Montefiore had stood undefended.

So the dwarves had come in, without invitation, and made their way with some effort up the flight of steps to the piano nobile and through the door. It wasn't their noses so much as their ears that turned their steps leftward beyond the entrance hall, because the glass made a sound of rippling, a kind of crystalline lapping. They could hear it sag. They weren't so far beyond their earlier selves that they had lost that capacity.

There it was. The mirror waited for them. They still had a choice.

Getting it down from the wall was harder, though, than it looked. Nextday decided at last to enter the wall and unhook it from behind, and let the other dwarves wait before the fireplace and catch it. But he couldn't enter the wall; it resisted, a convincing otherness, separate from him. He felt as if he couldn't breathe, for an instant, and the dread was full and interesting in itself; he rather liked it. But the job was neither to panic nor to observe how to avoid panic, but to get the mirror. So at last they pulled a table over from the center of the room and scrambled onto it.

In the end, they managed all right, and the mirror was removed from the place it had hung the past decade or two—a mere breath in their long life, but a painful breath, a held breath; and they felt coarser, richer, more devious, more themselves, to have it back among them.

Nextday found a length of fabric to blind the mirror's eye. They carried it out as miners will carry a fallen brother, among them; there was something corpselike about the slight bulge of the glass beneath the shroud. It was stored in the wheelbarrow, and Gimpy, the roundest among them, got in with it, to cushion it with the softness of his belly.

They began to sing, merrily for them, as they made their way from Montefiore. A rooster crowed, a dog or two barked tympanically; the winds contributed atonal *sostenuti*. It felt good to be unformed, ready, capable of possibility.

No one saw them come or go.

In time, they reached their lair, which to them had never looked like a cottage, nor hardly a cave, but was still home, with all the musty coprolitic warmth and personality of home. The glamour of the mirror, even behind its shroud, commanded their attention, and they were well into their fourth or fifth argument about how and where the splendor should be set, and in what ways to revel about its recovery, when they finally stumbled upon the body of Bianca, and took her for dead.

They began to weep and curse. Not for love of her, particularly, but because their transaction had been compromised. The mirror had come at too stiff a price, and while they had it, it wasn't free and clear. So Nextday tore the shroud off the mirror and they looked at themselves therein.

They were seven or eight or nine small men, bleeding obstinately toward some kind of humanity, stuck in a process of change that they could no longer vary. They might have used their mirror as an escape hatch, to ask it the single correct question, the only question a mirror ever cares about: not who did I use to be, nor who am I now, but who am I to become?—for the secret act of light that fires a mirror is this: a mirror's image is always forward of the truth by an instant or so. While a question is formulating—*Who is the fairest of us all,* say, or *How many crow's feet can I pretend not to have today?* or *Is this the face of a murderer?*—the mirror always knows the answer before the question is asked.

The dwarves had hobbled out of their stony natures partly by accident and somewhat by design, but they had hoped, at last, to be able to choose whether to consider the experiment a failed one, and, if so, to retreat into their lost selves, and subside, insensate, insensible even. But now they couldn't empty their pockets of memory, of irritation, of regret or conundrum, of paradox or paradise. They were trapped by the laws of their own devising.

Feeling the old moments silting away, Nextday took his all-but-human hands and put them upon the bowed glass of the mirror. He was able at least to remove the glass from the poisonous quicksilver behind it. However, he could no longer absorb the constituent parts of glass into his skin. He was left with a long oval of glass that could reflect nothing—a long anonymous shield, barren of deceit. The looking glass, clear enough now, without the looking aspect.

Putting the glass down, he huffed and ejected a knob of mucus, and his back bent over. He looked as if he would vomit with grief, but he didn't. He dropped his head lower and scratched in the ground for something, and his tail hung in dejection.

The others set about to construct a coffin for Bianca de Nevada, and partly from sorrow—for their sadness strengthened as they began to recognize their castaway status—and partly for punishment, they set the glass from the mirror into the lid of the coffin, so the girl's beautiful form could decompose as they watched, and as it rotted, their own indictment and incarceration would be more fully nailed upon them too.

I am a woman who killed for love

I am a woman who killed for love.
I am a woman who killed for lack of love.
The mirror declares that the twin accusations are equal.
I am the black dove who pecks at the coffin
Wanting to manage a more reliable insult,
To chew her eyes from their sockets, say, to wring
The hair from her head, to desecrate the silk
Of her unblemished skin in the way that birds do best.

Reflections

THERE WAS no apple left, for when she fell, the apple rolled into the door behind her. I didn't think to try to reclaim it until I was thirty or forty feet away, hustling that sluggish goose of a gooseboy up the slope. When I turned back, uncertain, I saw that the house had disappeared. There was simply a tumulus in a glade. Shadows of blue and granite. Traces of winter's snow lingered in long striations, like the thin fingers of ancient women who refuse to clasp their hands in prayer and decently die. There was no door, no smoking chimney, and all I could smell was leaf rot and mold, and the wet earth waking up again.

Michelotto, small miracle of contradictions, was chattier as we came closer to Montefiore, and began to ask about the cottage in the forest. I hadn't thought he noticed it, or remembered it at all if he did notice it, but he seemed clarified in mind. As if his episode in a coma had given his feeble mind a better rest than it was used to getting. "A girl lived there," he said. "And I spoke to her."

"Oh, yes," I said, "I'm sure there was. When you were little you used to speak to the geese, and you claimed they spoke to you too."

"They did," he said. "They told me many things that I didn't understand."

"Fascinating and marvelous. What secrets do geese know?"

"Who they like and who they dislike. Among the other geese, I mean."

"I see. A hierarchy among the gaggle. I'm sure that was spellbinding to listen to. Look sharp, you clot, you're trampling in the mud."

"They also mentioned who they liked among the humans. They didn't care much for you, for instance."

"Well, I cared for them, dearly, especially when braised with red wine and currants from Corinth."

"They said you will listen to no one but yourself."

"Well, you listen to the geese and the wind and the farting of frogs; you do the hard work for me."

"They said you would listen to them someday."

"Have they anything interesting to tell me?"

"I don't know," he said, but in a complicated tone, as if he might have meant *I don't know if they do,* but he might also have meant *I don't know whether you will find it interesting, but others would.*

"It was Bianca," he then said. "Bianca de Nevada, who used to live with us."

"Is that so." But I didn't care to speak about Bianca, nor to allow the memory to take hold in his usually incurious shell of a mind. So I took his hand, and I let my middle finger trail across the center of his palm, as faintly as I could manage given we were lighting out cross-country. He took a swig of breath, being startled in a new direction, and my efforts were fruitful. I turned to smile at him and said, "You have grown to such a man, my Michelotto. If we knew each other better I might be a better mother to you."

In this light vein I dragged him away from the subject of Bianca and turned several keys in that ill-regulated apparatus of a human being that had not been turned before. Raising a child is hard work, I've found; and this is why I've seldom kept myself to the task. But moment by moment, as a responsible parent is able, one must help the young fledgling to encounter more adult arenas of engagement.

The house was still empty. The pagan rites that attended the sowing of the fields were well under way and, I understood, would last into the night, when a bonfire of last year's rubbish would announce the satisfactory preparation of this year's crops. I pulled Michelotto into the house and tutted him for the barnyard smell. "You are old enough to perfume yourself with something more redolent than goose shit," I said. "Oh, it falls to me, I see, to teach you how to clean yourself up for a woman. Take off those filthy clothes and throw them out the window to be burned. Your days as a gooseboy are over, my dear."

I was busy watching him, though he seemed wary enough—and that was a good thing; it suggested he hadn't been initiated into the holy mysteries of sex by the sluts and bored soldiers' widows in the hamlet below.

I have always liked to watch a man remove his clothes. The faint modesty that all men evince—once or twice in one's career with them anyway—makes their bodies the more beautiful to behold, when at last the tunic is hauled over the shoulders and the loin wrapping is untucked and kicked away. I made to give him a semblance of privacy, and turned to fuss over the heating water. But there was the mirror in which I would glimpse his handsome form, because mirrors don't lie about men, only women.

It was then that I saw the mirror was gone. Michelotto's emergence from the clothes of his childhood had distracted me. I wailed from a rage I didn't understand. Maybe it was simply that I'd been denied the right to hear from the mirror that she was dead. It was all I would have wanted, to look at the mirror and see nothing but myself.

Michelotto worried himself over me, and came forward to calm me in my distress. I suppose I was keening, and it made him uncomfortable. He didn't know what he was doing. Anyway, there was no mirror to see.

Vigil

HE WAS out in the forest, higher up than usual, and the plains of Umbria stretched below in their pulsing washes of green and gold, brown and blue, beyond. He looked to the west, to see if he could find the roofs of Montefiore glinting in the noon sun, but the trees, on the slopes where he guessed his house should be, had come into the full leaf of late spring.

He came upon the casket first. Its top was clear as water. He looked down at it, and wiped away a scattering of spring pollen. The smeared powder gave the glass a greenish tinge, and for a minute he felt he was looking into a box of ice, or the clearest river water, for the figure inside seemed to float in a current. Then he realized this was merely a trick of the glass, the way that glass plays with and distorts light.

He wasn't surprised to see that the figure resembled his daughter Bianca, for in the months and years since his escape from Agion Oros, most of the people of the world reminded him of her one way or another, either by startling contrast or by painful similarity. He had never seen a corpse in a glass-topped coffin, and that was surprise enough for the day. That the corpse should imitate his daughter seemed only fitting; what other more crucial business had a corpse to attend to, when you come right down to it?

He hauled part of a fallen tree trunk to a convenient place and settled himself upon it. He had nothing better to do; he had been able to decide no other course for his life to take. He hadn't been able to return for any length of time to a Montefiore without Bianca, and the rest of the world lacked savor. So he came and went, an itinerant on a quest without shape. He didn't mind resting for a while, keeping an eye on the figure in a coffin.

He rested, and couldn't decide to move on. In the hours or days that followed he began, slowly, to realize that he wasn't alone. Seven small men and a rather large dog began to be seen about the coffin. He couldn't always tell when they came or went, but he had a sense that even when he couldn't see them, one of them was always present. They didn't talk to him, but from time to time they bowed and shuffled in his direction.

The dog came up and put its head in Vicente's lap. He scratched it behind the ears, courteously enough, but in time he shooed the mongrel away. He had never liked dogs much.

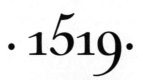

·1519·

Thaïs

T HE YEARS had shunted past, and life had never resumed in the way it ought to have done. When she was thirty-three, Lucrezia Borgia d'Este ordered an inventory of her ornaments. Rosaries, enameled buckles, hundreds of pearls, broaches of finely wrought silver, clasps and combs beyond figuring. And a single stem as if from an apple tree, made in what appeared to be the finest silver, though in three places where rubies as large as apples might once have hung, dots of black tarnish proved resistant to any means of removal.

In 1514 Lucrezia suffered terrible wounds with the birth of Alessandro, who entered the world with a huge head. It was a mercy that he died a year or so later. Anyway, he was survived by his new sister, Eleonora, and was replaced by another son a year later. Lucrezia paid a call on one of her favorite lovers, Francesco Gonzaga, to find him supine and withered, attended by several greyhounds and a pet dwarf upholstered in brocade. She showed him her new baby—named Francesco—but she wondered if she had named the baby precipitously, for Francesco Gonzaga was troubled by the French pox. Though he was being treated with mercury, taken internally, he seemed in danger of losing his handsome nose to rot. He wasn't interested in her new baby. She didn't visit the sick man again.

Another new pope was elevated, in time. This one cast his lot with the resurgent Medici. The campaigns in northern and central Italy swept back and forth with the usual shifting of allegiances, granting of concessions, revocations of treaty, accusations of betrayal. The winds from the north, the *tramontana* and the *scirocco,* had anyone the nose to detect it, carried the first whiffs of Protestant objection to papal vice and corruption. In 1517 Martin Luther nailed the ninety-five theses on the door of Wittenberg Castle Church. Strong stuff.

In Lucrezia's repose at the Belvedere on an island in the Po near the Castel Tedaldo, intimates and prospective lovers and her husband discussed these matters over the fine strong broth known as chocolate, the beans for which the Genoese navigator had discovered fifteen years earlier in the spice islands in the seas weeks west of Lisbon. The sun seemed as secure in the sky as ever. It wasn't, though.

Lucrezia became qualmish about everlasting life, which, as her energies began to fail her, was of increasing concern. How had her obsession with an ignorant farm girl brought her to such grief? How had she squandered the very apples of Eden—if such, indeed, they were—on an act of revenge and hatred? The convents and hospitals she had founded, the pious works tediously entered into and sometimes completed—these works of mercy seemed insufficient when posted against her crimes. Acedia chief among them.

Pregnant for the eleventh time in 1518, she spent her autumn nourishing the fetus with pastries, sugared fruits, honey by the spoonful, roasted nuts seasoned with salt from the Venetian suppliers at Cervia. She grew plumper than usual and feared that the next baby would have the same large head as Alessandro, or even larger, and that the force of its passage would split her asunder.

Within a matter of months she lost not only Francesco Gonzaga, as expected, but also her mother. Lucrezia had never been close to Vannozza Cattanei, and so the shock she experienced at the news of her mother's death was unexpected. She found herself lighting candles in chapels whose adornments she had commissioned but whose doors she had seldom darkened. She remembered leaving her mawkish mother when she was only eleven, and the mean-spirited glee she'd felt about it. She recalled succumbing to the lure of Vatican Rome, the mobs, the ceremonial parades, the glints of color, the pageantry of power—how drab all that seemed, considered now against the tears her mother had bothered to shed at Lucrezia's breezy departure.

As Lucrezia's confinement neared the end, she removed herself to Belriguardo, one of her *luoghi de delizie,* pavilions of delight. It wasn't a score of miles from Ferrara, but when she arrived and inspected the frescoed chambers, the cloistered gardens, the choice meals laid out to tempt her appetite, she turned away. She decided she would go to Montefiore instead, and settle in to give birth there, and pretend to be the widow of a farmer, with another kind of life.

She lay beneath sumptuous trappings of cobalt blue and gold, tossing and turning in her sheets of silvery silk. The physician would not allow her to travel. She was too near to term, she had had too many problems in the past. *I have had problems in the past, she replied in her own mind, and they all center around my appetite to know everything.*

Had she been a farmer's wife—had she been Vicente's wife!—instead of the daughter of a pope, she might have had humbler tastes. She dashed the wine upon the floor and asked for clear mountain water instead. She laughed at the sight of the hefty haunches of the chambermaid who had to wipe up the mess.

I saw one bite of the apple turn a headless dog into a squat man-cub, she remembered, a creature who took the apple when offered and left with it into the chimney wall. I nibbled one small bite myself—and it hasn't changed me dramatically. I have had no immunity from illness or sorrow, and I hear the doctors murmur in the antechamber. Maybe I needed more of the thing—with my wretched past, one small bite was too little. I need more.

Then she raised herself up on an elbow and recalled that one apple remained. It was in the protection of the Doge of Venice, someone who had professed, from a distance, an admiration for Lucrezia Borgia. That was sensible enough, for Venice was within striking distance of Ferrara, scarcely a day's travel if the roads were good, the brigands busy elsewhere, and the weather helpful.

She had always meant to return to Venice, and now she realized it wasn't Montefiore but Venice that called her. The final apple would heal her, would kill the child within her womb if such were needed. It would grant her some measure of fuller life than she, even with all her advantages of beauty and birthright, had ever managed.

She called upon the midwives, the surgeon, her confessor, and, an afterthought, her husband, and declared her intentions to take a retinue to Venice. The heat of the summer was almost upon them, she said, and the breezes off the Adriatic would calm her, would sing her new baby through the canal on easing tides.

"Yes," said Alfonso, looking down his strong hooked nose at her, eager to be elsewhere. He glanced at the confessor and made a motion: Confer the appropriate blessings and administer the sacrament of Extreme Unction. If she continues to fail, we'll petition the Pope to send a more senior prelate, as befits her station.

She tried to flail at them, to rip the dressings of her bedstead.

Alfonso patted the pillow and blessed her mildly and without conviction, and withdrew his hand before she could bite it.

Her labor pangs began shortly thereafter, and the death knells sounded on her horizon. They weren't immediate but they were imminent; they were nextday. She wouldn't give in, though, until she had risen from her bed and made her way through the watery highways of Venice, to greet the Doge at his palazzo and bargain or beg or steal that apple that rightly belonged to her.

Decades earlier, some hack of a poet seeking to make a reputation of his own by sullying hers had called her a Thaïs. He'd embellished beyond recognition her appetite for venom, lust, and vengeance. A Thaïs, a Roman harridan, a maenad, a murderess, a corrupt and unforgivable harpy. Once she had laughed in delight at the sound of her fierce reputation. But she wouldn't be unforgivable; she would see to that. She would find the final Apple and lunge at it, before it was too late. Learning all there was to know at last, she would find a good reason to forgive herself her random sins and well-cloaked crimes, and insure she would be forgiven in the afterlife as well.

She was thirty-nine.

Fire and ivy

STUCK AS we all are in the maw of time, the dwarves learned to age, and discovered a new variety of patience, one that required effort. Around the glass-lidded coffin they kept their vigil, even after the eyesight of Vicente de Nevada began to fail, and his memory to falter, and he returned to the hilltop bier with infrequency, and then not at all.

Springs came and went, interspersed with sequences of summer, autumn, and winter, in a regular pattern that, the dwarves decided, wasn't all that hard to follow. Their beards grew longer and grayer, and Gimpy showed up once with a pair of black scissors.

"Where did you get those?" asked Deaf-to-the-World.

"I bargained for them from a shoemaker," he replied. "I did hard labor for a week, tanning leather in a foul warehouse, and for my efforts I was repaid with this implement."

"What is it for?"

"Our beards are growing into the soil. Haven't you noticed?" Gimpy wandered about the clearing and snipped off the beards at waist height. Indeed, some of the dwarves had been rooting in the soil. The dog alone seemed impervious to hair growth, or maybe it was that he shed.

"What else are scissors good for?" asked Heartless.

"Oh, well," said MuteMuteMute, looking around. "I suppose we could cut back the ivy growing over the coffin."

No one could not think of a reason to protest, not even Bitter, so the dwarves, enjoying the mobility they hadn't realized they'd been lacking, gathered about the bier. Deaf-to-the-World, Tasteless, Heartless, Blindeye, and Bitter clutched handfuls of ivy and hauled it back. Gimpy and MuteMuteMute took turns snipping. Once they'd been accustomed to breathing through solid stone, and now they found gardening strenuous work. Well, they were aging too. Tasteless was losing his black-and-gold teeth, one by one, and Blindeye complained that white smears were beginning to cloud his vision.

When they had finished, they laid to one side a pile of dead ivy the size of a small house.

Midsummer day was approaching, 1519, and more of the world's timelessness was evaporating by the hour. MuteMuteMute fished from his pocket a tin box with a hot coal inside, and used the coal to light the older, browner parts of ivy. Within a short time the burning vines became a beacon on the hill, and they smoked all day, until by sunset they had attracted attention.

The gooseboy, Michelotto, came thrashing through the summer growth. He was still a gooseboy, though he was twenty-two now. His shoulders were less hunched. Perhaps due to having enjoyed a hearty if belated introduction to the joys of the flesh, his right leg no longer trailed. Indeed, he was a specimen of surprising beauty. He had Lucrezia's aquiline nose and shapely chin, and his eyes were a liquid gray, water in a pewter goblet.

"You make a fire to call me here?" he asked.

Away from the farms and villages, the dwarves were rarely addressed by a human. It took their ears a short time to remember how to decipher syllables.

"We make a fire to burn the ivy," said Heartless.

"Oh, but look," said Michelotto. "It doesn't seem to be burning."

Michelotto seemed to be right. Anyway, he was more human than they, so the dwarves paid attention. They could see that the fire was burning. The leaves of the ivy seemed green as ever, though perhaps it was merely that they hadn't burned long enough. Leave it to a human to fiddle over such minute distinctions as *burned* or *not burned* in a matter of so few moments.

Michelotto went down on his knees before the coffin and leaned across it. He breathed on the glass and rubbed it with his hand.

"Is the box full of someone?" he asked. "I can't rub away the mist."

Stoneheart said, "She waits in our time, while we have moved on into hers."

"It's a maiden then," said Michelotto, more or less approvingly. The dwarves nodded.

Michelotto's pressed his hands against the lid and felt as if for a spring lock release. "But the glass is very pure," he said. "I can't see what is inside, for something like breath clouds the inside of the glass. But the breath makes a silvery beaded backing, and the oval glass does the work of a mirror. Try as I might, all I can see is myself."

"That is ever the trouble with human beings," snapped Bitter. The other dwarves looked at him with surprise. "Well, what of yourself do you see?" he continued, "if you must go on about it so?"

"Not very much," said Michelotto, "and that's the sorry truth. There's not all that much of me to see." He smiled at himself, though, forgivingly, and with a touch of his mother's self-admiration.

"May I open the box and view the corpse," said Michelotto after a while. "Are these the remains of a saint, like Lucy of Narni? Perhaps a necessary holiness would be conferred upon me, and my mental slowness would be corrected. I'm surer of thought than I used to be, but even so, I could do with any blessing."

"She has the innocence of a saint," said Gimpy, "but she's only a young woman who has slipped sideways a few feet, into another realm."

"Still, I'd like to have her blessing, even if she is dead. Will the body stink after all this time?"

"Little offends us," said Tasteless, shrugging.

"Is it time?" asked Heartless. "Is it time already? We have been here only since morning, surely! I've hardly had a chance to contemplate."

He lifted his nose and sniffed and listened. Several tears tracked into his beard, which was now more white than red. "The old threat is hearing the knell of bells calling for a funeral Mass," he said. "The next danger may be kneeling here before us, for all I know. The only way to be kept from danger is to be kept dead, and all we decided to do was to try to keep her from the one who would destroy her then. Let life go ahead and destroy her now, in a new and novel way. We have no right to forbid it."

Michelotto took this as permission to continue, and with more dedicated efforts, he worked at the clasps and hasps that secured the lid to the coffin. The dwarves didn't help. They stood back. Deaf-to-the-World backed into the fiery mountain of ivy, and yelped.

Michelotto laughed—silly little men!—and wrestled the lid, at last, away.

He leaned over and looked at Bianca de Nevada, and his breath stung in his chest.

"She hasn't changed a day," he said. "And I remember her now, and the fate that befell her. She was my friend, my Bianca, my good true friend. How has she come to rest like a painted marble beauty in this box of wood and glass?"

"Your mother took every step she could manage to destroy her," said Blindeye. "Here she lies, though, rich as rain. Isn't she delicate."

Michelotto leaned over the box. The girl was unblemished and incorruptible. Her hair had grown in the box, and made for her a sort of black pool of netting, in which her pale face and her pale hands floated. The clothes in which she'd been put to rest may have rotted away; it was impossible to tell, for the hair covered her as respectably as a nun's habit. Her eyes were closed, but the face appeared un-sunken, unblanched. She looked as if she were asleep.

"May I kiss her?" he asked.

"No, no. No, Michelotto."

The gooseboy turned to argue with the dwarf, who had professed to be excused from responsibility, to find that it wasn't the dwarf speaking. It wasn't any of them. It was someone else, pressing through a clot of undergrowth.

The dwarves thought it was Vicente, for he was the only one, be-sides them, who had come to sit with the girl. It had been some years since he'd shown up, and they had presumed his bad lungs, bad legs, bad eyes, had gotten the better of him at last, and death had allowed him some peace that life had withheld from him. But Vicente could only have gotten older, that much they were sure of, and this was a younger man, one they had never seen.

Michelotto had seen him before, but he couldn't remember his name. They hadn't known each other well. But he remembered the stride. The face was older, the beard and the temples flecked with early silver. The eyes were like knotholes into a deep and complicated tree.

"I came upon her just as you did, but held back, hardly believing my eyes," he said. "Neither that she was there at all, nor that you opened the casket. But in any case, she's not there for you to kiss."

"Who are you to say?" asked Michelotto.

"The one who put her here," he answered. "Not knowing what I was doing."

"I had heard you were slaughtered like a pig," said Michelotto.

"I just disappeared. That's all."

Heartless drove his thick fingers into his beard and fished out, one after the other, a stack of florins. "These," he said to Ranuccio, "I be-lieve are yours."

"I didn't want them before and I don't want them now. Give them to the poor," said Ranuccio.

"Ah, I'm poor enough," said Heartless, and put them back in his beard. "You were the one who brought her to us. Did you know that?"

"I don't know where she's been, nor, hardly, where I've been. And I've never seen you in my life."

Ranuccio Vecchia had confessed his deed in the forest not to Fra Tomasso, but to his grandmother, Primavera, who hadn't been able to keep her tongue still, and for her gossip had lost it. To protect what was left of Primavera's life, he'd disappeared from the district. He housed himself, for his penance, under the tutelage of the abbot at Cirocenia, reading what could be found of the Alexandrine and Coptic monks and the desert fathers.

The abbot has released him at last, divining that it was time for him to request forgiveness of the girl's father. Ranuccio had been making his way to Montefiore across the spines of the hills, trying to avoid the temptation of villages and farms. The smoke on a promontory attracted his attention as he approached, though. It was in his path, so he decided to steal up and peer at what was happening.

"It is hardly possible that the Signorina de Nevada lies here in perfection," he admitted. "Perhaps I've died, and my soul makes its last perambulation about the world, to face its sins and to accept its punishment.

"I might have kissed her in the forest, but she was a child, and it would have been a kiss of Judas, leaving her to her fate," said Ranuccio. "And so, Michelotto, as far as I can determine, you have no right to interfere. A kiss now cannot kill her further." He knelt at the coffin's edge and put his hands beneath Bianca's shoulders, and pulled her up a few inches. Her head fell softly back and her mouth opened. The teeth were pearls and the breath, if breath it could be called, smelled thinly of apple blossoms. Ranuccio put his mouth to hers and apologized.

The heart of the matter

SHE WOULD have what she wanted, at last.

She passed without impediment into the mouth of the Grand Canal, and the gondolier silently worked the boat between the cliff faces of Venetian palazzi and *scuole,* churches and shopfronts. The dawn sky was a clever silver, not unlike the water, and it felt as if she were slipping away between sheets of purest silver silk. She leaned back in an ecstasy of release. The fullness of knowledge she had always craved was within reach.

Rome and Ferrara had often been at war with Venice, or at least worried about Venetian interests in the north of the peninsula, but who could not love that principality built on blocks of water, its buildings fringed with Moorish fretwork and stone lace? Its marble facades had a grandeur and dignity that no duomo in Italy could imitate, streaked as they were by the reflective play of sunlight or moonlight upon the canals.

It was odd, she thought, to arrive in a busy municipality like Venice and find it empty. It must be one of the innumerable saints' days. Or perhaps an invasion had come from the sea, and the armies and the merchants and the beggars and friars and painters had gone lurching toward the Lido to watch the battle. Uncharacteristically, the approach from the south had been left unguarded, and while dozens of gondolas tipped smilingly by, and hundreds of dark windows were unshuttered, no citizen gazed across the water at Lucrezia. No shy girl looked down from a cloistered aerie to spy the Duchessa de Ferrara. No awkward new-bearded soldier, distracted by her beauty, tripped upon his halberd and plunged into the canal, to the roaring laughter of his companions.

It was like lying between sheets of mirror, that was it: the water reflecting the high scoured-kettle gray of the sky, the sky rippling with ribbons of light tossed back by the shallow tidal canals.

She knew the city enough to recognize the gentle S curve of the Grand Canal. She recognized the Albergo del Leon Bianco, its asymmetric arched doorways at gondola level like so many separate mouths into which a corpse might slip. What did the Venetians do with their dead, when there was no place to bury them? She had known this once but couldn't recall the answer.

Slavs, Mamluks, Levantine and Spanish Jews, Africans, Greeks— the city of a thousand nationalities, its canals like a sieve allowing Asia and Africa to flow into Europe, and Europe to flow out—how could Venice be empty today? And silent. The crash of barter, that noise louder than war, was silent today, as if it were the Nativity. But no bells tolled, and the church steps were empty of the unwashed hoping for alms.

She passed under the Rialto bridge, which was as clear of crowds as if plague had wiped its bloody bottom on both approaches. The Grand Canal made its last turn south and sliced east again, toward the Bacino di San Marco and the Doge's palace. San Giorgio Maggiore, like a virtual headland of religious reassurance, mounted its domes in the light that seemed dustier than common sense might allow. The details were less firm, though the light was still strong.

And the gondola made its single ceaseless step beyond the Punta della Dogana, to where the water widened with the merge of the Giudecca Canal, and the greatest piazza in Europe spun wheelingly to her left, and the winged sentry opened its mouth and roared from the top of its pillar.

But we stop here, she said, or meant to say, though her words didn't reverberate in the air. We go to the Doge, to reclaim what is ours. Have you forgotten your instruction? We are not to head toward the open water. Are you mad?

Her mind began to race, though in a slow heavy way. With effort she brought herself to an elbow and managed to turn around. The gondolier must be woolgathering; he needed a sharp reminder.

She gasped, or tried to gasp, but her lungs gave forth no air, and no sound. She clutched the hem of her robe, as if to rend her garment and her skin if necessary, to expose her lungs to air. They must need it. She couldn't breathe without air. What nonsense was this? Her hand was caught in a rosary of grey-silver pearls.

You must deliver me to the Apple, she cried.

The gondolier paid her no mind. He kept plying the waters with his pike. In the stiffer breeze blowing in from the open sea to the southeast, the cloak that he wore against the morning chill pushed back from both sides, just as she had tried, but failed, to do with her own garment. His hood fell back.

The gondolier raised his rack of horns. The hide on his chest was sliced open, and through the aperture a small cavern was revealed, about the size of the cavity that his heart must have once required. He had no heart, though. Within his chest burned the final apple, a delicate condensation beginning to form upon it as the cold wind strengthened off the most endless sea.

Montefiore

OFTEN I have traveled the road to Montefiore in memory. Today I travel it in true time, true dust, true air. When the track lends me height enough, I can glimpse the villa's red roofs above the various ranks of poplars, cedars of Lebanon, pines, across the intervening valleys.

Ranuccio doesn't say much. A habit of silence still obtains from his days in the abbey. But he tries to break it, naming the things of the world for me as if I have lost language. Perhaps I have. By cataloging the road we introduce the world to each other. Newborns in a new world.

But when I ask after my father—or Cesare—or Lucrezia—or garrulous Primavera—or sweet dim Michelotto, and why we left him weeping in that circle of stones on the hill—or vain and frightened Fra Ludovico—Ranuccio has no answers. He will only squeeze my hand. He will not let go—he won't let go! Not unless I need to escape into the bushes to relieve and cleanse myself.

I won't let go of him, either, for reasons I don't yet understand. But there is time. Again, there is time. It rushes like a cloud of insects, billions of instants fluttering up from fissures in the ground, against my face; I brush them to see through them, beyond; but I try to see them as well, the instants. Each leaf, whether she be like her sister or not. Each creak of the brother timbers of the world. Each moment of rot and blossom, by turns and simultaneous, and the world in colossal panorama behind, ninety billion instants flying up like snow blown in my face.

We turn at the bottom of the final slope. The world seems emptier than it once did, as if the Four Horsemen have done their job too well, and I have lived on into an afterlife. But no afterlife could smell as sweet as goose shit, could ring with nonsense hammering as of someone most mundanely fixing a warped window casement just out of sight.

We begin to rise. I am hardly equal to the task, after my long rest. Ranuccio would carry me, but I refuse the offer. We pass a flooded field. We cross a stone bridge. We study a green lake for its secrets. I stop to rest on a rock wall I had forgotten—how dear even simple rocks can be. A bit of thornbank I remember from long ago, wilder now, overgrown, grips with all its might to its life.

I see a priest in a soutane, and a straw hat against the sun, making wide gestures in the roofless chapel, preaching, for all I can tell, to a gaggle of geese. I see a stout figure on a low stool in the kitchen garden, pulling up radicchio and flecking the dirt off it with a vigorous motion. I see a figure beside her helping—man, woman, I cannot tell—who puts one hand to a hip, and straightens up.

The hand goes up to the eyes, shading them, to study me as I approach out of the shouting light. Then both hands go up, the gesture, in all the dark places that we humans live, of surrender. He suffers what is inevitable. He surrenders to the impossible. He can't get breath at first, but then he does. He calls my name.

Note

I've taken certain liberties with the life stories of historical figures Cesare Borgia and Lucrezia Borgia. I've omitted details that didn't serve (the other Borgia siblings, for instance). The Borgia involvement with a de Nevada family is fictional. However, I have used selected scraps of history to lend credence to the narrative.

The glamour of the Borgias rests on the rumors of incest, poisonings, adultery, conspiracy, murder, striking physical beauty, vigorous sexual appetites, hedonism, nepotism, and papal fallibility of the most egregious sort. That the Borgia family is also credited occasionally with bouts of wise and just governance, with art patronage, with interest in the scientific developments of their day, makes less good copy.

Bayezid did send the spear of Longinus, or something purported to be such, to Rome, which suggests that artifacts with biblical credentials, whatever their provenance or their imputed spiritual pizzazz, had some political value.

Prince Dschem was believed to have been murdered through a slow-acting poison administered by Cesare before the Bull of the Borgias escaped from the custody of Charles VIII.

Paracelsus spent time at the university in Ferrara while Lucrezia was Duchessa there. It's unlikely she ever attended lectures, but she was said to have a lively mind about all manner of things and, like many highborn women of her day, took license to do as she liked whenever she could get away with it.

A bridge on an aqueduct spans the gorge beside the castle at Spoleto, where Lucrezia, at the age of nineteen and newly married for the second time, was *governatrice*.

During the High Renaissance, the medical use of mercury (to treat syphilis among other ailments) was accompanied by the growing awareness of a side effect of what we might now call paranoia. And grand Spanish families a few generations earlier did bathe in pools coated with mercury. I have imagined the transplanted Borgias might have brought that old custom to Rome with them.

The identification of Cesare Borgia as the model for Machiavelli's *The Prince* is well known. And Lucrezia Borgia's coloring of her hair with lemon juice was a venial sin at best. The most egregious examples of corruption in the Vatican aren't my invention, though some of them may well have been exaggerated, the result of a public relations campaign that plagued the Borgias while they were in power and besmirched them further when they lost it.

The Borgia family reputation hasn't been helped by Victor Hugo's sensational *Lucrèce Borgia,* the basis of the Donizetti opera. However, Montserrat Caballé comes closer than anyone else to redeeming Lucrezia Borgia's reputation as an amoral murderess simply by singing the aria "Com'e bello!" in a voice of silvery purity. (A recording of her 1965 performance is available on cassette or compact disc.) Recent biographies of Lucrezia and the Borgia family by Rachel Erlanger, Ivan Cloulas, and others will supply more information for readers interested in separating verifiable fact from fiction— either mine, or that promulgated by the Borgias' enemies.

May I be excused for embroidering upon the history of a dynasty whose career has already entered into legend? Cesare Borgia might have had my head for it, and Alexander VI recommended the eventual disposition of my soul, but I like to hope that Lucrezia Borgia, who commissioned Ariosto's *Orlando Furioso,* would have understood some of the licenses I've been bold enough to take.

And wherever they are, those Borgias, may they rest in peace.

Acknowledgments

With thanks:

to Jane Langton, Jill Paton Walsh, and John Rowe Townsend; roaming about Lucignano, Arezzo, Siena, and Cortona together gave me a golden week to remember;

to Mei-Mei Ellerman for opening Il Vallone to us;

to Mary Norris for her companionship in Spoleto;

to Ann, Sid, and Heather Seamans for company in Castiglione del Lago, and to Anna Tapay for hospitality at Villa Elianna;

to Paolo Chiocchetti for help in Florence;

to Andy Newman for tending to the most pertinent matters at home while I traveled, to the Concord Public Library and to Tuscany;

to the reliable crew at HarperCollins: Judith Regan, Cassie Jones, Jennifer Suitor, and Carl Raymond;

to William Reiss of John Hawkins and Associates;

to David Groff for literary counsel;

to Douglas Smith for the particular magic of the jacket art and interior decorations.